Perfectly Reckless

When love is determined, it will always find a way. From New York Times bestselling author Megan Hart comes PERFECTLY RECKLESS, a new novel about love, lust, loss and rediscovery between two people who should never have fallen in love…or out of it.

Praise for Megan Hart

"Hart's beautiful use of language and discerning eye toward human experience elevate the book to a poignant reflection on the deepest yearnings of the human heart and the seductive temptation of passion in its many forms."
-Kirkus Reviews on Tear You Apart

"Naked is a great story, steeped in emotion. Hart has a wonderful way with her characters....She conveys their thoughts and actions in a manner that brings them to life. And the erotic scenes provide a sizzling read."
-RT Book Reviews

"[Broken] is not a traditional romance but the story of a real and complex woman caught in a difficult situation with no easy answers. Well-developed secondary characters and a compelling plot add depth to this absorbing and enticing novel."
-Library Journal

"An exceptional story and honest characters make Dirty a must-read." -Romance Reviews Today

Also by Megan Hart

Tear You Apart
The Favor
The Darkest Embrace
Precious and Fragile Things
Exit Light
Ride With the Devil
Beneath the Veil
Reawakened Passions
Hot and Haunted
Collide
Dirty
Broken
Tempted
Stranger
Deeper
Naked
The Space Between Us
Pleasure and Purpose
Switch
Stranger
Vanilla

ISBN-10:1-940078-20-2
ISBN-13:978-1-940078-20-5

Perfectly Reckless

Copyright © 2015 by Megan Hart

All rights reserved. By purchasing this digital book, you have been granted the non-exclusive, non-transferable right to access and read the text of this e-book. No part of this text may be reproduced, transmitted, down-loaded, decompiled, reverse engineered, or stored in or introduced into any information storage and retrieval system, in any form or by any means, whether electronic or mechanical, now known or hereinafter invented, without the express written permission of the publisher.

This is a work of fiction. Names, characters, places and incidents are the product of the author's imagination and are fictitiously. Any resemblance to actual persons, living or dead, business establishments, events or locales is entirely coincidental.

Playlist

I could write without music, but I'm so glad I don't have to. Below is a partial playlist of the songs I listened to while writing Perfectly Reckless. Please support the artists by purchasing their music.

In Your Room — Halestorm
The Last Time — Taylor Swift featuring Gary Lightbody
Familiar Taste of Poison — Halestorm
Break In — Halestorm
Stay (I Missed You) — Lisa Loeb & Nine Stories
Use Somebody — Kings of Leon
Nicest Thing — Kate Nash
Swans — Unkle Bob
Cross That Line — Joshua Radin
If You Want Me — One Less Reason

All of this is fiction,
and all of this is true.

One

"It shouldn't matter when I fell in love with you. Or how. All that matters is that I did." Even as Maura spoke, she knew her words wouldn't matter. She could see it in the cut of Ian's gaze from hers, the way he covered his mouth with his palm, the fingers curving over his cheek toward his ear. She knew nothing she said would make a difference, but she said it all anyway. "I am crazy in love with you, Ian. I didn't look for it, but there it is. And I don't regret it. Not a single second."

Maura paused, leaning forward across the table, smiling and hoping to urge him to return it. "Well. This part's not so great. But all the rest…"

He didn't smile, but he did look at her. At least he gave her that. "Maybe you shouldn't set yourself up to get disappointed."

Maura flinched, helpless against that blunt sting. Frowning, she warmed her hands on the mug of coffee that Ian had pushed toward her earlier. Sweet and black, exactly how she liked it. Because he knew just how much sugar she wanted, Maura thought. Because he knew everything about her.

There were plenty of words to give him, but if Ian knew her so well, Maura also understood him inside and out. He wasn't going to listen to her, no matter how pretty she made the words, how compelling her argument. She let her silence speak for her instead, and it stretched on and on until finally, Ian met her gaze.

"I can't seem to give you what you want," Ian said.

At that typical male bullshit excuse, that final slice that severed the already fragile thread of her patience with him, Maura stood. "Have you ever even asked me what I want?"

He had no answer for that.

She watched him struggle to find one for a few seconds before she leaned toward him again, both hands flat on the table. "No. Of course you haven't. You just assume you know. It's not that you can't give me what I want, Ian. It's that you don't want to give me anything."

"I'm sorry."

She shook her head. "No. You're not. You're scared. There's a difference."

That made him angry. "You're the one who always told me it wasn't going to last. This is not an exit, remember that?"

She remembered, all right. "I was wrong. I was scared, too."

"And now you're not?"

"I'm terrified," she told him in a low voice. "But at least I'm willing to try. Can't you even give me that, Ian? Can't you even try?"

She'd always been able to read his expressions, but now whatever went on behind his eyes was masked with a blankness no less impenetrable because she knew he was forcing it. Ian turned his mug in his hands, around and around and around. This was not the man who'd once made her come in the backseat of his car without ever taking off her clothes. This was someone else. A stranger, and though her heart cracked, it didn't quite break.

"I think we shouldn't see each other again," he said.

No. That was not what she'd come here for today. Not the reason she'd lined her eyes and mouth and scented her skin and curled her hair. She'd known the conversation was going to be uncomfortable and probably fraught with emotion. She hadn't been certain of the outcome, not exactly, but not seeing him again could not be it. Never that.

"How can you say that?" She asked him. "After everything, that's your answer?"

He looked at her. "You need time, Maura."

"Time. I took my time. It's been months, Ian. I waited until everything was official before I called you. I did that so there wouldn't be any reason to hold us back." She shook her head, trying to keep her voice from shaking.

"All of this is going to take time before you're ready for a relationship again. You need time to figure out what you really want."

"I know what I really want. How long do you think it would take me?"

"At least eighteen months," Ian told her, and Maura's jaw dropped.

"You think I need a year and a half to figure out that I'm in love with you and have been for the past three years, and that I can't imagine the rest of my life without you in it? Ian," Maura said, "have you ever known me to be a woman who wasn't sure about what she wanted?"

He gave her a stubborn frown. "You're asking if I can make a go of this with you now, and the answer has to be no."

After all this time, the years, the grief, and now he was deciding he had to tell her no?

Maura straightened. Shoulders square. Chin high. Not accusing, not demanding. Not begging. "You're going to let me walk away."

"Yes."

She swallowed her anger. Made herself calm. "When we are together, everything shines."

"You'll find someone else."

"Of course I will. You think I can't walk out that door right now and find someone? A dozen someones?" It should've sounded arrogant, but it was the truth. "I don't want someone else. None of them will be you."

He tried to laugh, to make a joke. "C'mon. You'll have your pick."

Maura wasn't laughing. She moved around the table while he still sat. It gave her a little power, at least, standing over him this way. She made her face and voice cold because she wanted to be warm. "You don't get to pick who makes you shine."

And then she left him in his spotless kitchen, alone.

Two

The text came a few hours later, in the dark of night. Their favorite hour, when the numbers on the clock all aligned, 11:11. Make a wish, the message said.

Instead of typing in her reply, she called him. She could do that now, without hiding anything. She didn't have to make it a secret.

"It's always the same one," she said when he answered, before he even had a chance to say hello.

"I'm sorry," Ian said.

"Not sorry enough," Maura replied without malice. Tucked into the comfort of her bed — the one she no longer had to share, her pillows and sheets and comforter all brand new and never used by anyone else but her, she nestled into the warmth and stared up at the ceiling of her new bedroom. "If you were really sorry, you'd be here with me right now."

To her relief, because she hadn't been sure if she and Ian would ever laugh together again, he chuckled. "Oh, yeah?"

"I find it intolerable, as a matter of fact, that you aren't here. That I'll never kiss you again," she added, stomach twisting at the very thought of spending the rest of her life without him. "That you will never touch me again."

"You don't know that," Ian said in a low voice still perfectly clear through the phone.

Maura let out a single razor blade of a laugh. "You told me you thought it would be best if we didn't see each other again. That seems pretty clear to me, Ian."

"You never know what might happen."

Maura shifted under the weight of her comforter. "Don't fuck with me."

Silence. Then, "what?"

"I said," she told him very slowly, very clearly, "do. Not. Fuck. With. Me."

"I'm not fucking with you, Maura."

"Oh, yes, sweetheart. Yes, you are." The endearment tasted bitter, but she didn't regret allowing it to slip out. It was sincere. "Because that's what you do, and you're very, very good at it. It's an old game, isn't it?"

Pull her close, push her away. Give her just enough, then not enough at all. He'd been doing it for a long time, but she kept letting him, she thought, so who was the one at fault?

"I wanted to talk to you, that's all."

"Let me guess," Maura said coldly, "you've got a hard-on."

More silence told her she was right. She closed her eyes and saw his face. And then his beautiful, delicious cock. She should be angrier. She should tell him to fuck right off.

"Yes," he admitted finally.

She let out a long, slow sigh. "Fuck you, Ahab."

She hadn't called him that in a long time. It had been a private joke between them — the man chasing the white whale, elusive and always out of reach, the thing he wanted most that would also destroy him. Except he hadn't been the one destroyed, had he? No, that dubious honor had gone to her.

"I'm sorry," he said again.

"You said that already."

"Do you want me to hang up?" The soft hiss of his breath reminded her of how it felt when he murmured in her ear. Of the brush of his lips and teeth and tongue against her throat.

Her pulse throbbed in the spots he used to nibble and suck — the base of her throat, the place just below her ear. Her wrists. The backs of her knees. Her cunt. Against her will, her hips rocked, pushing her suddenly too-sensitive clit against the soft weight of her pajama bottoms. Every place he had touched her remembered and mourned the loss his mouth and hands…and Ian had touched her everywhere.

"No. Goddammit, Ian," she muttered. "You know I don't."

"You want me to touch you."

"Yes." The reply gusted out of her with a hitch of breath. An admission, nothing shameful about it. Simply the truth. "I want you to touch me."

"Where?"

Her hand traveled the path she wished his would take. "The back of my neck. Then over my shoulder. I want you to tease my nipples until they're hard."

Her flesh tightened beneath her touch as she spoke, and pleasure roughened her voice. "Put your mouth on them while your hands move lower."

His low groan sent a tingle of arousal through her. "You taste so good."

"Suck my nipples, Ian," she whispered as her hand moved over her belly and came to rest on her hip, fingers twitching. Her back arched at the sound of his muttered acquiescence. Her nipples jutted against her pajama top and she pulled it up to let the night air tease her. The bedroom was chilly, but that made the heat on her skin at his imagined touch all the more real. "Touch me."

"I'm touching you. I'm using my tongue on your nipples now."

A fucknoise slipped out of her. Maura licked her fingertips and used the wetness on her skin to simulate his tongue. "That feels so good."

"I want to make you feel good." The rasp in his voice made her imagine his prick in his fist, the slow pump of his grip. The slant of his mouth as he concentrated on fucking his hand.

"I want to kiss you." She'd meant what she said — the thought of never kissing him again was intolerable. The idea that she would never feel his breath on her face or taste him, or feel him inside her. More than intolerable. Insufferable. "I want your mouth on me. Bite my neck, Ian. Scrape your teeth against me. Leave a mark."

He huffed a breath. She knew that sound. She was pushing his buttons, turning him on and embarrassing him a little at how easily it happened.

"Sink your fingers into my hair at the base of my skull," Maura murmured. "Pull my hair…"

"Oh, shit," Ian muttered. "God, girl, I'm so hard right now."

Triumph and vindication warred with her leftover anger and disappointment. She was letting him play her, giving him something he'd told her he didn't want. Denying him now would prove a point, but what exactly would it be? That she could cut off her own nose to spite her face? She wanted him. She always wanted him. That hadn't changed.

"I love it when you call me your girl." That was her embarrassing turn-on. Any other man who'd ever tried to call her that had been shut down with a raise brow and pursed mouth, what Ian laughingly called "The Face." She'd been nobody's "girl," insisting on her womanhood. But for him she'd been many things she'd never been for any other man.

For him, she was a flower.

"I want to kiss my way down your neck, over your whole body. Over your belly, even if it makes you giggle."

She did giggle, thinking of it. "I'm ticklish, I can't help it."

"I love it when I kiss you there, and you wiggle around, and you sound all out of breath. And you beg me to stop." Ian laughed, too.

Maura snorted softly. "I don't beg."

"You will," he promised. "When I have my mouth so close to that sweet pussy, and you want me to kiss you there and I hold off. You'll beg."

She had never begged him for that, but then she'd never had to. He'd always willingly put his mouth all over her. The thought of this now, that he would tease her in that way, sent another slow rolling wave of arousal and heat all over her. "You think so?"

"Oh yeah." So cocky. So fucking smug. It set

her on fire. "I know so."

"Tell me what you'll do to make me beg. I won't. But you can try to make me. I want you to try," she teased. "Try real hard."

She could play him, too.

Ian's voice rasped against her ear. "First, I'll nibble my way down over your hip. I'll bite you a little harder there. Then lick, just a little."

Fuck, he was good. "I can feel you there."

"I'm going to kiss your knees."

She laughed, but it was breathy and harsh.

"Then up the insides of your thighs."

Maura groaned. Her knees fell apart, opening herself to him though he was so fucking far away and all she had of him was his voice. It was all she might ever have.

"What are you wearing?" Ian interrupted himself to ask.

"Pajamas."

"Take them off. I want you naked for me."

She was already wriggling out of them and kicking off the covers to expose her entire skin to the chilly dark. Her nipples peaked and her skin pebbled into gooseflesh that was also as much a result of Ian's whispered words as the cold. She ran her warm hands over her body, imagining again they were his.

"I want you naked for me," she told him. "I want you stroking yourself."

"Don't worry, girl, I am."

She let her fingers drift over her belly, her own touch not tickling but the memory of his mouth there making her shiver, anyway. A little lower, over her soft curls. The heat there. She was already wet.

"I'm not begging yet," she told him in a husky voice. Daring him, knowing he'd rise to the challenge. Pun intended.

"You will be."

"Tell me," she ordered. Her muscles tensed as she slipped a finger inside her to draw her slickness up and over her clit. She circled it lightly, then stopped, teasing herself. Letting the arousal build. She wanted his words to seduce her.

This wasn't the first time they'd ever gotten each other off on the phone. In the beginning it was all they'd had. The hush of voices and touch of their own hands. Later, after they'd become lovers in the flesh, Maura had sometimes yearned for the times like this, when the sound of her voice was enough to make him hard. When she could make him come with nothing more than her words. Here they were again, only now instead of only imagination to urge her on, she had the memory of his weight on top of her, the press of his teeth against her flesh, the slide of his body in and out of hers.

All she had were memories.

Bitterness slid down the back of her throat, the sting of unshed tears a parody of the times when she'd taken him in her mouth and tasted a different sort of salt. She licked her lips, thinking of his musky flavor. Craving it.

"I want to kiss the insides of your thighs, up and up, so close to that sweet pussy." Ian made a low, hungry noise. "I'll slide my hands under your ass, holding you still, because you're moving. Your hands dig into my hair, urging me closer, but I don't move."

As always, his dirty talk flipped her switch. He was so mild-mannered, so outwardly steady and stable and clean-cut, nobody would ever guess he had a mouth on him that could rival any sailor's. Maura's hips moved, pushing her clit against her fingers as she circled, circled. Then she stopped, listening.

For a moment, all she heard was the low rasp of his breath. Then, "I want to taste you."

"Oh, yes. Please. I want you to."

"Not yet." She heard the hint of smile in his voice. He didn't say that he was waiting for her to beg. But she knew that's what he meant, and she smiled too at the game. "First, I'll just let my breath cover you. Your fingers pull my hair harder, you want me to move closer, but I stay still. And then, just when you can't stand it any more —"

"Put your mouth on me." She gave him that, not begging, but still a clear proof of her desire. "Don't make me wait, Ian. Put your mouth on me. It feels so good when you kiss me there."

"Your clit's already swollen, ready for me when I use my tongue on it. I'll slide a finger inside you. Then two. Slide them in and out so slow you can't stand it."

She let out a low, stuttering groan as her fingers moved faster. She was swollen and slick and hot. She pushed her fingers inside herself again, curling to find the slightly rough bump of her G spot. She didn't always love that pressure, it could be too much, almost distracting, but right now it sent spiraling coils of pleasure through her.

"Are you wet for me?" Ian asked.

"Yes. So wet." Fucktalk, nothing much eloquent about it and all the hotter for that. "I'm so fucking wet for you. My cunt's a furnace for you, Ian."

He made another of those low noises, and Maura had to stifle a laugh. She liked it when Ian gave himself up to explicit language, but sometimes hers seemed to shock him as much as it turned him on. He'd never said it was too much, and in fact there'd been times when she'd been whispering to him while she jacked his cock or as she rode him that she swore the filthier she spoke, the harder he got. But she thought it embarrassed him a little that he liked it so much.

"Put your mouth on me," she said again. "Please."

It still wasn't begging, not quite, but it must've been close enough for him, because Ian gave another of those hoarse breaths that sent shivers of desire straight to her core. "I want to lick your clit, soft and slow. Steady circles while my fingers fuck inside you. My other hand's under your ass to press you close to my mouth. It feels good, doesn't it?"

The first time he'd ever gone down on her, Maura had finally understood why people talked about orgasm as "the little death." He wasn't the first guy to give her head, but the pleasure of his lips and tongue on her clit had been so effortless, so surprising, that she'd come twice before he'd even had to come up for air. She loved sucking cock, but receiving oral had always been so fraught with anxiety — how long would it take her to get off? Would he get bored, give up, what if he didn't like being down there…so often her orgasms from a man's mouth had been so hard-won they'd almost not been worth it. Not with Ian. His mouth was magic. Everything about him was magic for her.

"I like that noise you make," he told her.

She hadn't realized she'd made a noise. It had slipped out of her when she remembered the feeling of his face between her legs, the soft brush of his hair on her thighs. The press of his tongue flat on her clit and the way he used it, moving slow and steady just as he'd described. He always made a meal out of her. Appetizer, entree and dessert, he said. Her fingers were a sorry substitute for his tongue, but it was all she had.

"I love it when you use your mouth on me." Her fingertips grazed her erect clit. Back and forth. Barely brushing her heated flesh. She rocked her hips, teasing herself.

"Your hips move. You want me to go faster, but I don't. Slow, that's how I go. I lick you so nice and slow. Now I have three fingers inside you. Stretching a little."

"Oh. God." She mimicked his description with her own hand, the flick of her thumb acting as his tongue while she filled herself with three fingers. His were bigger, thicker, would stretch her more, but she was so caught up now in the mesmerizing whisper of his words, so hypnotized by the picture he painted for her, that it was almost like he were there. Not quite, it could never be as good imagining as the real thing. But close enough.

"You want me to keep going?"

"Yes, Ian."

He paused. She imagined him palming the head of his delicious cock, then stroking the shaft. He had this trick he did when jerking off, this method of fucking into his fist instead of moving his hand, and it always drove her crazy to watch him. She wished she could see him now, too late thinking of how she should've asked him to get on video chat with her. To ask now would break the mood. She had to be satisfied with what she had — something of which he'd accused her of being incapable. Now wasn't the time to point out to him otherwise. Not with her fingers deep inside herself and her clit so hard all it would take was a couple of tweaks before she'd tip into climax. She didn't want to come, not just yet. She wanted this to last and last. Forever might be out of the question, but at least a little while longer.

"Are you close?" Ian asked.

"Yes." She took her clit between her thumb and forefinger, squeezing gently. "So close, thinking how good you feel against me. I want you inside me. I want you to fuck me."

"No. Not yet. I want to make you come with my mouth first. Then I want to fuck you."

Maura let out breath. "Sounds good to me, so long as I get to come again when you're fucking me."

He laughed. "Greedy girl."

"Always."

"I wish I could see you," she said before she could stop herself.

Silence. Then, "hold on."

Her heart thumped and thundered so hard it almost hurt. A half a minute later, her phone buzzed in her hand with a text from him. A picture. His bedroom in the background, a closeup shot of his belly and the curve of his hip. The picture was fuzzy and dark, but she knew his body so well there was no mistaking him. Her heart skipped in its beating, and she blinked back another threat of tears, moved that he'd given her what she asked for. There'd been times when such a simple request would've been met flat-out with refusal. This picture had more meaning than a simple snapshot, but she wasn't ready to let herself think of what.

"I love it," she told him. "I want to bite that. And then lick it."

"Now you."

Again, she blinked away a sting while her pulse thumped, and cursed her tender heart for letting him ever make her wonder if he really wanted her. It took maneuvering and the light was terrible, but she sent him a shot of her head, turned from the camera, the line of her neck and throat exposed.

"Perfect," he told her. "I know you want me to bite that. And lick it."

She managed to find the breath to speak, even though her voice shook as much as her hands and the muscles on the insides of her thighs. "Leave a mark. I want to remember you."

As if she could ever forget him.

He didn't answer right away, but the hiss of his breath edged toward a groan. She pictured him, eyes closed, brow furrowed with effort as he pumped his cock into his fist. He'd be biting his lower lip by now. Easing himself toward coming. She loved watching him get off.

"I'm licking your clit," he murmured. "Moving my mouth a little lower to taste you. So fucking sweet. You're hot and silky wet, and you can't stop moving under me."

This was true. She was moving, lifting her hips as she stroked her clit. "I'm so close."

"I'm going to make you come, Maura."

Oh, he certainly was. Her hand, but his words. The thought of him. The memory of his touch and scent and flavor, all of those things were sending her over the edge, hurtling her toward climax. There was, in fact, no stopping it now, not that she wanted to. She wanted to give herself up to it, lose herself in the pleasure. Let it consume her.

She still had words, but they were broken by soft, breathy sighs and gasps she couldn't hold back. "Fuck," she said. "Oh, fuck, Ian, that feels so good…"

Ian kept talking, telling her just what he was doing to her, how much he loved the taste of her, how much he loved feeling her when she came. "I have my fingers inside you. I can feel you clenching."

That was it, she was done. Finished. Ignited, combusting, up and over and inside out. Pleasure surged so fiercely all she could do was shake with it.

Quieting, her breath still rasping, she came back to herself. She blinked into the darkness and licked her lips, unable to tell if sweat or tears had painted them with salt. Every muscle felt loose, but pain tightened in her chest with the heavy thud of her heart. She waited to regret this, but she never had and did not, now.

"I love the way you make me feel," she told him. "When you're inside me. I love how you make me come. I love how you fit against me, and how you say my name. I want you to feel good, too."

Ian huffed into the phone. "I am. I do. Getting closer, touching myself. Thinking of you."

"I love that, too." The ache of desire to be with him hit her hard, a fist squeezing her heart. Maura put a hand over her eyes, pressing her fingers into her temples, willing herself to hold her shit together. Not to break down, not now. He wanted her to beg, but not this way.

"Shit, this feels so good. I'm getting close, thinking about fucking you, Maura. I want to be behind you, pulling your hair so your head tips back…"

She shivered, too sated to even get close to another climax but helpless not to be aroused by the image he painted. "I love it when you pull my hair."

"I know you do." Ian's low laugh slid into a groan. "Oh, fuck. So close, now."

"I want you to come, baby. Come so hard for me." The words people said while fucking were always so silly, but she didn't care. She wanted to talk him to orgasm the way he'd done for her. If all she had of him were words, she was going to use every single one she had.

"I'm coming." His voice slurred into silence broken by the harsh, rough edge of his breathing.

She listened, waiting, counting her own in-and-out breaths. After eleven of them, Ian spoke. "See what you do to me?"

He meant it as a compliment, but it tightened her jaw. Maura scowled, knowing he couldn't see her face but that he'd hear anger in her voice if she wasn't careful to disguise it. Did she even want to?

"Well, goodnight," she said abruptly. "Thanks for the mutual jack-off. It was great."

"Wait, what? Hey, hey. Don't..."

She disconnected the call and got up from the bed to stalk to the bathroom, where she splashed cold water on her face and brushed her teeth to wash away the imagined taste of him. It didn't work. You can't rinse away a memory.

Her phone was ringing.

She'd never assigned him his own ringtone—in fact, this might be the first time he'd ever called her phone directly. For so long their communication had been limited to furtive instant messages and phone calls sifted through third-party apps. Now there was no reason for them to keep anything a secret, yet the trill of the phone still set her on edge. The call went to voicemail before she could reach it, but the phone rang again a few seconds later. She answered it, but with silence.

"Don't do that," Ian said by way of greeting.

"Don't do what?"

"Hang up on me." He sounded pissed.

Well. So was she. Maura gripped the phone tight, pressing it to her ear. Naked in the dark and cold, the heat of her anger kept her teeth from chattering even though the rest of her had prickled into gooseflesh.

"You got what you wanted," she told him. "What more is there to say? What? You wanted to cuddle, after?"

She knew how to read him by every huff and puff. Now he gave a low, frustrated mutter. "What's your problem?"

"You're my problem. You've been my problem for three years. Soon it will be four. And five. And someday, ten. A hundred fucking years, Ian, you'll be my problem." She chose her words carefully, determined not to cry. She'd given him a lot, but she wasn't going to give him her pain.

"Maura…"

She waited for him to say more than her name in that defeated tone she hated so much, but Ian didn't say anything else. She bit her tongue and rubbed the sore spot against the back of her teeth to keep herself from speaking. So much to say that couldn't be said, so much that had always remained unspoken and maybe always would.

Ian sighed. "Do you want me to not call you any more?"

"You're the one who said we shouldn't see each other again. You're the one who said this had all been a mistake from the start," she reminded him. "Remember that? It was only yesterday. And then what, a few hours later you're messaging me with your dick in your hand. What, exactly, am I supposed to think, Ian? Am I supposed to be flattered that when you're horny, you think of me?"

"It's not just that, and you know it!"

Maura pinched the bridge of her nose, but

refused to soften. "Tell me then. What is it? Because I can't even pretend to know, any more."

"I don't know what to tell you."

"How about that you want to be with me? You could start there." She wanted to spit the words but settled for swallowing their sour taste. When he said nothing and the sound of his breathing began to hurt her ears as his silence was hurting her heart, Maura disconnected the phone again.

He called back. "Stop doing that."

"It's late," she countered. "I have to work in the morning, and so do you."

In the beginning, they'd spent so many nights staying up too late that for a time she'd walked through most of her days in a sleep-induced haze. She didn't want to do that now. If anything, she wanted the oblivion sleep would bring so that she didn't need to have this discussion with him any longer.

"I'm trying to talk to you," he said.

"And yet, you say nothing. I get it. I understand. You've made yourself abundantly clear. I'm not an idiot," Maura said tightly, "but I guess I sure am dumb."

Ian sighed. "No. You're not. Stop."

"That's all you ever say!" She cried. "Stop. Don't. Can't. Won't. I get it, Ian! You can't give me what I want, and I'm the asshole who just keeps asking. Well. Guess what. I'm done, now."

"Done with what?" He sounded alarmed, and Maura smiled though she found no speck of humor in the conversation. "What does that mean."

"It means I'm done asking you for anything.

And you know what happens when you ask for nothing, don't you? That's exactly what you get. Don't knock on my door if you don't intend to be there when I open it."

"Don't hang up," Ian said hastily, then added, "please."

The please caught her. Maura slid into her covers and tried to warm herself, not even attempting to find her discarded pajamas in the dark. "All you ever do," she said quietly, "is tell me that you can't."

"I'm sorry I can't go all in with you."

She closed her eyes, so tired. "For fuck's sake, Ian. I'm not asking you to marry me. I'm just asking you to give this a real chance. It's been almost three years, and no matter what else has happened, doesn't that mean something? Everything's different now. I'm free to be with you, for real. I thought…goddammit, Ian. I thought you wanted that. I do."

"I never wanted you to leave him for me."

There it was, bold and harsh, the truth she'd already known. It didn't feel any better hearing it from him, but it didn't make her angry or defensive. It only made her sad and resigned and tired.

"Oh, Ian," Maura said. "Don't you get it? I left him for myself. Not for you. It was never for you."

This time when she disconnected, he didn't call back.

Three

What do you do when you can't stop yourself from going back over and over to the same person? No matter how bad they are for you. No matter how much they hurt you. Again and again, always the same. What do you do when you can't stop loving?

It wasn't the longest they'd gone without talking to each other. In the beginning, weeks had passed sometimes before one or the other of them reached out, though it was always as easy to talk to him as though no time had passed at all. At least in the beginning. And there'd been months of silence during her divorce, when she'd been focused on making sure everything she needed to do was done. This time, it had only been three days. A very fucking long three days.

The worst of it was the constant forgetting — she'd see something funny and want to text him a picture, hear a joke and want to tell him, discover a new song and her fingers were on her phone's keyboard all ready to share it with him before she remembered. For three years they'd had to sneak every scrap of contact they had, and now that nothing was stopping them from talking or seeing each other whenever they wanted, they weren't speaking.

She missed him. She would always miss him. That's what love was, sometimes, a big gaping hole in the middle of everything else.

"It's not like I never had my heart broken before," Maura told Shelly across the table. "It's just the first time I ever did it to myself on purpose. I knew better. And yet…"

"You just kept doing it. I know." Shelly made a face and put the menu aside. She'd order the same thing she always did, and so would Maura. They'd been coming to the Black Raven Cafe for ten years. The chicken caesar salad was to die for.

Maura laughed at her friend's expression. "What can I say? His penis is made of magic."

"Riiiiight." Shelly looked skeptical. "That's totally it."

"And I'm head over heels, totally crazy for him. That too. I can admit it." Maura sighed, then rapped the table with her knuckles. "Fucking Ahab."

Shelly looked sympathetic. "He's a pussy."

"Yes. That. Or maybe he just doesn't feel about me the way I feel about him." This was hard to admit, hard to feel. But necessary.

"Bullshit. He's crazy about you, too. He's just being a man about it. He can't give you what you seem to want?" Shelly snorted her derision and wagged a finger. "Bull. Shit. All that means is that he's too scared to try."

Maura stirred the ice cubes in her glass of iced tea, wishing she'd gone for a cup of the Black Raven's famous hot cocoa with a peppermint stick and plenty of whipped cream. Screw the calories. Screw the salad, too, she decided when the waiter came to take their order. "I'll take a bacon double cheeseburger, chipotle mayo on the side. Onion rings. Oh…and an extra large cocoa. Extra whip. Hot fudge drizzle."

"Super cute," Shelly commented about the waiter when she'd placed her own order of the expected salad and he'd walked away. She gave Maura an eyebrow lift. "And, wow. When's the last time you ate?"

"I'm eating my feelings," Maura said flatly. "And I didn't notice him."

"You didn't notice how cute that waiter was? What the hell? I can't even with you," Shelly said. "What happened to your hot dude meter?"

Maura frowned. "It broke."

This earned a second brow lift from Shelly, who could always be counted on to provide comfort and ass-kicking in equal measures. "Ian's an asshole."

"Yeah," Maura said, not meaning it. Because that was the thing. Ian could be a jerk sometimes, who couldn't? She wasn't proud to say she had her moments of outright bitchery. But he was not an asshole.

"I hate to see him get to you." Shelly leaned a little closer across the table. "I mean…you're not regretting anything now, are you? About Chad?"

"God, no." Maura gave a startled laugh and shook her head. "No way. The divorce was the best thing. The right thing. Sometimes things break and you can't fix them. Better to end it than live on in misery and resentment."

Shelly, who'd been married to her high school sweetheart for almost twenty years, pursed her lips. She was the only other person Maura had ever told about Ian. If she'd laid judgment about the affair, she'd never given Maura any sign of it.

"There are days," Shelly said, and paused before saying in a low voice with a furtive glance around the room, as though someone might give a damn what they were saying, "I envy you."

Maura laughed, then covered her mouth apologetically. "Oh, c'mon. You and Rex are like salt and pepper. Peanut butter and jelly."

"Doesn't mean I don't want to toss him out the window sometimes. The one on the second floor," Shelly added, as though she needed to clarify.

"That's normal." Maura chewed on her next words a minute before figuring out how to say what she meant. "When all you do is argue about who forgot to put the cap on the toothpaste or whose turn it is to empty the dishwasher or who should take care of Christmas presents for whose parents…when that's all you've become is nagging each other, that's no good. But I didn't leave Chad because we fought all the time. I left him because I'd stopped caring enough to even argue. One day he asked me why I hadn't bothered to pick up his dry cleaning for him, and all I could do was stare at him like he was talking in a foreign language. I mean, literally, Shelly, I simply could not process what the fuck he was talking about. And he kept on and on about it, just picking away at me, until I realized that I simply no longer cared enough even to defend myself. It wouldn't matter. If it wasn't the dry cleaning it would be about whose turn it was to make dinner, or why I couldn't iron his shirts for him, and I was just…done. All done."

The waiter brought their food then, and both women stopped long enough to dig in. Maura let out a long, low groan of satisfaction at the taste of the burger. Fuck the size of her thighs. This was heaven wrapped in nirvana on a platter of delight.

The conversation turned to other things. Work, family, celebrity gossip. It was exactly what Maura had needed, a few hours of girl time with her bestie, and even she'd been unable to manage any ogling of the super cute waiter, she did feel better by the end of the lunch.

In the parking lot, Shelly hugged her unexpectedly. Maura squeezed back, surprised but grateful for the embrace. A good friend was worth everything in the world, and Shelly was one of the best.

"Hang in there, cookie," Shelly said. "You know I'm here if you need to vent."

Maura straightened and smiled. "Thanks. I know. I'll be fine. I'm sure it's for the best, anyway. I'll get over it…eventually."

Shelly didn't look convinced, but she didn't argue. "Anytime you need me, just call. And hey. If you need someone to go out with dancing with you and play wingman while you score with all the hot guys who will be lining up for a shot at you, I'm your gal."

"Absolutely." Maura had no intentions of going on a manhunt any time soon, but there was no doubt that when she did, Shelly'd be the first person she'd call. Then again, wasn't that how she'd gotten into this mess in the first place? Girls' night out, one too many margaritas, the slow pulse and throb of her favorite song and a man who knew how to dance?

If she'd known then what she knew now,

Maura thought as she got in her car and waved at Shelly, driving away. She caught sight of her reflection in the rear-view mirror, wide gray eyes lined with navy. Today, she wore red lipstick like armor. If she knew then what she knew now, nothing would've changed. She'd have done it all over again.

    Every time.

Four

The message pinged through her phone late enough that she knew he was hoping she'd already be asleep, but not so late it could be considered outrageous. Of course she'd left her phone on, with all the notifications set to alert her if he should contact her. And what had he said, after all this time?

Hey

That was it. Not even a fucking winky emoticon to give the single syllable any sort of tone of voice. Staring at it, Maura shook her head.

If you want to talk to me, she typed, you can call me. Remember?

She waited. The minutes ticked by while she busied herself with her bedtime preparations. Shower, shave, wash her face, deep condition her hair. Brush and floss. Moisturize.

He wasn't going to call.

Bastard.

Well, fuck him then, Maura thought as she opened up her tub of scented lotion and began smoothing it over her legs and belly. Her breasts. Her breath hitched when she held the weight of them in her hands and thumbed her nipples taut.

Her phone rang. Ian. She answered right away, not interested in playing games.

"Hi," he said. "Are you awake?"

"Depends. Am I dreaming this?" She settled against her headboard, knees drawn to her chest.

He laughed, but uncertainly. "I don't think so."

"I'm not sure. It doesn't feel quite real."

"I could convince you."

His flirting tone forced a reluctant smile out of her. "How are you going to do that?"

"Uh…" Ian laughed again, a little more genuinely. "I don't know. How are you doing?"

"Fine. You?"

"Good, I'm good." Pause, an awkward chuckle. "I was going to wait a week before I texted you, but I just couldn't hold out."

God, she fucking hated games. "Maybe next time, you should. Or not bother at all."

"I didn't call to fight with you," Ian said immediately. "Okay?"

She bit back another angry response. "Why did you call, then?"

"I missed you."

Her anger and frustration drained away. She said nothing at first. Then, "I miss you every day."

"I thought about you today when I was at the grocery store. They had Goldfish crackers on sale. I bought three bags."

"…You don't like Goldfish crackers," she said around the rush of emotion threatening to make her voice waver.

"But you do."

"Too bad I'm not there to eat them, then."

"Right," Ian said. "Too bad."

There'd been as much silence as speech in their relationship, hardly any of it awkward. There'd been times when the only communication they'd needed was a smile. A touch. A kiss. The stroke of his fingers along the back of her neck and tangle of them in her hair.

"I guess I'm always surprised to know you think about me at all," she offered after a half a minute and unable, this time, to keep her voice from cracking.

"I think about you all the time, of course," Ian said and broke her heart all over again. "You should know that."

"Why did you call me, Ian? Why are you doing this to me?"

"I don't know." It was an honest answer; if there was anything she knew about him, it was that he'd never lied to her. "I wish I could stop."

Maura pressed her fingertips to her mouth for a second before being honest with him, too. "I don't."

"You should. You should tell me to stop. Never to call you again. You should tell me to go away."

"I can't do that, love." She drew in a shaking breath. Stomach a little sick.

Up and down, back and forth, in and out. Everything changed and everything stayed the same. Who was the fire and who the hand that touched it?

"If I ask you to come over, will you?"

She wanted to say no. "Yes. You know I would. Are you going to ask me?"

"...No."

More than once, when circumstances had meant they couldn't be together, he'd told her he wished she were there. Now she could be, and now he wouldn't ask. Together, they were a tapestry woven of complication and fuckery. But why couldn't that change?

"Let me tell you a story," Maura said.
"What kind of story?"
"Shhh," she told him. "Just listen."

***

I've spent an hour going through everything in my closet. Another mixing and matching outfits, uncertain what to wear. Nothing fits right. Nothing flatters. All I have are clothes I hate, and if I don't feel good about what I'm wearing, how in the hell will I be confident enough when I'm naked?

After all the talk, the hours on the phone or messaging on the computer, after the second time we met at the dance club and ended up making out for hours in his car…tonight, I'm going to fuck Ian for the first time. He doesn't know it; at least I'm not sure he does. He might be hopeful, but uncertain. Maybe even wary. He might even try to tell me no.

But I'm not going to let him.

Naked, I stand in front of the mirror. No woman stares at her reflection and finds herself without flaws, but this…this is horrifying. Every bulge, every stretch mark, every stray hair and lump and bump, leap out at me like I'm looking at a circus mirror. How can Ian want me when I am so clearly imperfect?

And, closing my eyes, I run my hands over all the places I want him to touch. I think of the way he looks at me. Of his smile. I think of the taste of his mouth, the curve of his lips on mine. I think of his fingers curled against the small of my back and the press of his thigh between mine. The first night we met, he pulled me close and danced with me, and my face found the heat of his neck, the sweetness of his shoulder. I lost myself in him that first night for no more than a few heartbeats, but in them, I melted and I've never been the same.

Maybe if I'd let him kiss me that first night, this wouldn't feel like such a big deal now. If I'd taken that leap just over a year ago, done that bad thing back then, I'd never have spoken to him again. Guilt-stricken, I'd have tied up my tiny secret with ribbons of crimson and black and tucked them deep inside, never thought of them. But no, I'd done the right thing and pushed him away.

"I can't," I'd said. I didn't know I had a line until I couldn't cross it.

Now my line is toe-scuffed and faded, blurred into oblivion. Oh, I still have a line, it's still there. At least that's what I tell myself as I powder and lotion and smooth and stroke and paint and primp. When I slide on stockings and garters and pretty lace panties and a matching bra. There is still a line, somewhere. I just no longer care about stepping over it.

We live about twenty minutes apart, but we are meeting for dinner in a restaurant an hour and a half away. Ian is on a business trip, and I have the weekend unexpectedly free. Chad's gone fishing with his buddies to someplace in upstate New York. He left Wednesday night, won't be home until late Sunday. Before he went, he expected me to not only do his laundry but to help him pack his suitcase. We didn't fight about it, because I walked away before we could.

I walked away from him; now I'm running toward Ian.

I take too long with my hair and makeup and the outfit on which I've finally decided. I chose a simple wrap dress in navy with a faint, paler blue pattern of flowers on the fabric. It shows off my cleavage and disguises as it flatters. Paired with a pair of kitten heels and a single strand of pearls — real, my grandmother's, a necklace I never wear, I've done enough. Made enough of an effort without looking like there's more than dinner on my mind. Still, I'm late now. Later still when I can't find my keys. The clock is ticking, stealing away precious minutes of time I could be spending with Ian. There's never enough.

I search the closet hook where the keys are supposed to hang. My purse, the one I'm leaving behind because I've switched to a nicer bag for tonight. The last jacket I wore. I text Ian as I search.

Haven't left yet. Will be a few minutes late.

Take your time, comes his reply. No rush.

He doesn't understand. There is a rush. I need to be on the road. I need to get to him, before my lost keys and worries about my clothes and hair and face all rise up to crush my determination to make this, at last, the night I finish what we began a year ago on a dance floor.

Finally, I find them on my dresser, where I must've left them to reply to Ian's earlier texts with the restaurant's address and the time of our reservation. He's taking me to one of those

Brazilian steakhouses, the kind where they bring you meat after meat after meat and you can eat until you explode. I clutch the keys with suddenly shaking fingers. The metal's cold, or maybe I've grown too warm.

My knees threaten to give way, and the stuff on top of my dresser shakes and rattles when I put both hands flat on the surface. I bought this dresser from a thrift store because of the handles. They look like seashells. The dresser is Waterfall, an Art Deco style with beautiful inlaid laminate and a huge mirror surrounded by intricate scrollwork. It matches nothing else in the bedroom, but I had to have it. I spent hours cleaning and polishing the wood to its original luster, but I haven't really looked at it in a long time. I focus on it now to keep myself from thinking too much about anything else.

In the mirror, my eyes are wide and very, very gray. Is my mouth too red? My hairstyle too fussy? A blemish threatens in the corner of my mouth.

"Breathe," I say aloud. "Breathe."

If I don't leave now, I won't go at all. I push away from the dresser, keys in hand. I take my carefully packed overnight bag, my purse, grab a lightweight trenchcoat from the closet downstairs. There might be rain, later.

In the car at last, I type another quick text to Ian. On my way.

I have an Ian playlist. It's full of songs about lust and fucking, also about longing. Lots of dance music, but there are a few ballads and hard rock classics, too. The song we danced to, that first time. The song I'd like to slow dance to with him, if I ever get a chance. I crank the music loud. I sing and sing and sing as my car chews up the miles, bringing me closer to him. My fingers tighten on the wheel until they ache. Every exit I pass sends another wave of anxious arousal over me. I'm awash with anticipation.

I drive so fast I should get pulled over, and how would I explain to Chad about where I was going and why? I should be more cautious, but it's impossible for me to drive slow. I pass eighteen-wheelers and resist the urge to pump the air with a fist, asking them to blow their air horns the way I did as a kid. I am giddy.

And then, I'm there.

I pull into the parking lot and find a space. I don't see him, though I'm a few minutes late as I'd warned him. My hands shake as I turn off the ignition. The music cuts to silence. I sit with my phone cradled in my palms, knowing I need to text Ian and let him know I'm here and yet unable to keep my fingers steady enough to do it.

I see you, his text says. I'm waiting for you.

Oh god. Oh god. Oh god.

I check my reflection quickly. Run my fingers through my hair. I want to swipe my nose with powder, my lips with gloss, but there's no time now because he's heading for my car. I gather my purse and phone, pull my keys from the ignition. I get out of the car.

First, he takes my hand. Leans in to kiss me, but on the cheek. We could be business acquaintances, long-lost cousins, anything but almost-lovers. Hell, he could be my pastor for all

Perfectly Reckless

the passion in this embrace.

"I hope you're hungry," Ian says.

"Starving," I assure him, though the truth is I'm sure I won't be able to eat a single bite.

We don't hold hands in the parking lot as we walk toward the restaurant. An hour and a half from home, I'm still cautious about being seen. Besides, after that initial brief squeeze, he let me go and hasn't reached for me again. His hand on the small of my back, though, that is typical Ian. Steering and guiding me, making sure I navigate the scatter of broken glass on the asphalt, the smear of rainbow-shimmer oil.

"Careful," he warns.

It's too late to be careful, but maybe I'm the only one who of us who knows it. Inside the restaurant, they take us to an intimate booth in the back. Tall sides guarantee our privacy, the curved seat means we can sit next to each other instead of across. Ian, ever the gentleman, lets me slide in first. The vinyl snags my skirt and the metal clips of the garters on my thighs, so by the time I reach my spot, my hem has crept up far too high for propriety. I don't pull it down.

"Have you ever been to a place like this?" Ian turns his body toward me. The dim lighting turns his hazel eyes brown and hides the glint of silver at his temples.

I shake my head, my voice steady though it feels like it wants to tremble. "Nope. All I know is that it's a meat-a-palooza."

He laughs and tugs the menu toward us. "Yeah. Says here, fifteen kinds. Basically, they give you these cards. Turn the green side up when you want them to bring you meat. The red side when you want them to stop for a while."

"Seems easy enough."

We stare at each other with no more than a few inches on the seat between us. What would the wait staff do, I wonder suddenly, if I were to straddle Ian right here? Fit myself on his lap, unzip him, push him deep inside me and ride him until we both come? I shiver at the thought of it, my nipples tightening, but I know I'd never do it. If anything, I'm a voyeur, not an exhibitionist. I can't even hold his hand in the parking lot, how on earth would I fuck him in a Brazilian steakhouse booth, no matter how secluded?

The waiter brings us drinks, and the parade of meats begins. I find my appetite, at least a little of it, and since no single serving of meat is more than a bite or two, we work our way through a staggering array of the choices they bring to our table before I have to admit defeat and turn my card red side up.

"Just try this one more." Ian slices a bit of garlic-infused steak, rare, from his plate and offers it to me on his fork.

So intimate and sensual, that simple act of taking food from his fork. Flavor explodes in my mouth. I'm way past any kind of physical hunger, but that steak is literally so delicious that I moan. A full-on sex noise, right there in front of him.

"Good, huh?" Somehow we are sitting closer. Touching, now. His thigh pressed to mine. His pupils have consumed most of his iris. Dim light or desire?

I want to devour him and spit out the bones. "So good."

I want him to kiss me. I want him to anchor his hand in my hair and pull me toward him. Plunder my mouth. Take away my breath. I want him so much it's fire.

The waiter, who's probably at least a little used to interrupting cooing and billing couples in this back booth, offers us coffee and dessert. With a look at me to confirm, Ian declines. Neither of us have moved, and the pressure of his knee on mine is enough to send a pulse of desire straight to my clit. Internal muscles clench.

"You want to get out of here?" Ian asks.

"Oh yes," I tell him. "Yes, Ian. Please take me somewhere."

He's staying in a business-suite hotel. His room has a couch, a fridge, a desk. The bathroom is purely functional, no luxury about it, but the bed…oh, God. The bed is enormous and it's really all I can see.

He offers me a drink, but I don't really want to add alcohol on top of all that meat. Plus, I'm already drunk with anticipation and lust. My head already spinning. Here I am in Ian's hotel room. I still have time to leave. He hasn't made so much as a move to kiss me, much less take me on that gigantic bed.

I can't look at him. My gaze will be too hungry and greedy; there will be no hiding the desire on my face. Ian talks enough for both of us, and I realize that he's nervous too. Maybe more than me.

As a kid I used to go swimming at a local lake.

There were several docks anchored far out in the water, one with a diving board set a few feet off the surface. One twelve feet high. To jump off that high dive meant plunging straight down and sinking below the first foot or so of sun-warmed water to the frigid depths. If you were heavy enough or jumped hard enough, it was rumored you could actually touch the lake's bottom, though I'd never known anyone who actually had. Word was a kid had drowned trying and his ghost would grab your feet and hold you under if you ever managed to do it. Kids jumped from the high dive with their hearts in their throats, straight as arrows until they hit the water, when not even the bravest could stop themselves from clutching their knees to their chests to keep their toes from the icy grip of the ghost at the bottom of the lake.

I hated the high dive. I hated the climb up the rusty, narrow ladder. If there was a line, you might have to cling there for a while before you could move up to the platform. I hated the way the earth seemed to tilt away from me when I got up that high. I hated creeping out to the edge, my toes curling over it, and I hated looking down into the water. Most of all, I hated that leap. The final few seconds before leaving the dubious safety of the board and launching myself into the air were always the longest and most horrifying. Worse even than the way my stomach lurched into my throat, or the sting of the water against my bare flesh when I hit. I hated jumping from that high dive, yet I did it every summer.

I hadn't done it in years, never taken any sort of

chance. I'd met and married a man who hadn't asked much of me, at least not emotionally. I'd settled into a career that provided me with a living but didn't challenge me. Still, those far-off summer days of childhood had taught me how to leap, and that's what I do now.

I jump.

Not literally. As a matter of fact, it takes me forever to cross the room toward him, every inch as hard-won as though the carpet is made of tar clutching at my heels. Everything around me goes bright and clear, a picture forced into focus. Every sound amplified. The gust of chilly air from the vent, the sliver of light through the blackout curtains, the faint hiss of static from the clock radio next to the bed.

"Ian."

He turns from the TV, remote in hand, hazel eyes wide and unexpecting, and that's when I finally kiss him.

He puts his arms around me immediately. The remote disappears, dropped or tossed away. One hand goes to the small of my back, the other to the base of my skull. We fit together, every line and curve of my body matching a place on his.

We kiss and kiss and kiss until I break it with a gasp. "I want you so fucking much, Ian, do you know that?"

His answer comes with another kiss. I back him toward the bed until he sits on the edge. And then at last I can straddle him, my dress hiking up so that my stockings snag on his leather belt. Ian's hands slide beneath my dress to palm my ass. The heat of him sears me through my lace panties. He presses me closer, grinding me against his erection.

I cup his face in my hands, holding off the kiss for a moment while I try to catch my breath. I see my face reflected in his eyes. My hair's a mess. My mouth swollen. I lick my lips and the flicker of my tongue against his mouth sends a shiver through us both.

"I want you," I whisper against his lips. Then against his cheek, his jaw, his throat, where I nip and nibble between the words. Then into his ear. "I want you, I want you, I want you."

Ian rolls us so that he's on top. He's strong. I feel the muscles in his arms bunch when he moves me upward on the bed, and I'm not a small woman, but Ian makes me feel tiny and precious.

It's not the first time he's ever touched me, but this is different than grinding on the dance floor or even making out in his car. The weight of him is unfamiliar. The way he moves his hands over me. His mouth. He traces my chin with his lips, moving lower to my throat, where the press of his teeth tips my head back to give him all the access he wants.

I've never asked him how many women he's been with, but this is certainly not the first time at the rodeo for either one of us. And still we fumble, still we hesitate. His watch gets caught in my hair, pulling, and not in the way I like. My stockings run. His cock presses hard in his pants, and I can't manage to get his belt undone. We are ungraceful in our eagerness, and I love every second of it.

He's on top. Then I am. He takes off his button-down shirt, leaving him in a slim-fitting t-shirt.

"Well," I say. "If we're taking things off…"

I wriggle out of the garter belt and toss it away. My knees pressed to his hips, I run my hands up and over the soft fabric of his t-shirt, feeling the muscles of his chest and belly, eager to get at his bare flesh and yet wanting to draw this out as long as I can.

It's going to be the only time, after all.

I inch up his shirt, revealing a sliver of skin. Then a little more. I could lean to kiss him, but I'm too fascinated by this slow reveal.

Ian, on the outside, is a businessman. He wears his dark hair short on the sides, a little longer on the top but only a little. Silver at the temples. He uses glasses for reading. He favors solid-colored shirts and ties with tiny patterns. The first time I met him, he wore a pair of plaid shorts in several shades of brown and a matching white polo shirt — total preppy.

But underneath his clothes…oh, my God. I push the shirt higher and higher, shamelessly ogling what he's got going on. Abs. Not a six-pack, nothing so obvious. Just hard, firm flesh with the ridge of muscle clear beneath it.

His belly button is perfection.

I have to get my mouth on him. First, the tie on my dress. It opens easily enough, and I shrug out of it.

"You," Ian says, "are so sexy."

The compliment sends a surge of heat through me. A blush. I duck my head at first, meaning to deny it, but after a second, fuck that. We are on our way to naked. There's no place here for anything but confidence.

"Thank you."

My hands are on his belt, and this time, I manage to get it undone. Then his button, the zipper, I've got my mouth on his perfect stomach as I ease his cock free, and I'll get my mouth on that as soon as I can get him out of his jeans. We shift, we struggle, I use my foot to push the denim past his calves and ankles, and Ian kicks them off. I have him in my fist when I find his mouth with mine again. I barely stroke, barely move my fingers, but his cock leaps under my touch and his mouth opens on a gasp.

Still kissing me, he sits, murmuring, "take this off."

"Take this off," I order, pulling his shirt over his head.

We keep going and then at last, we're totally naked. On our sides, his knee between mine, no room between us. Our heads on the same pillow. We stare into each others' eyes.

This shouldn't feel romantic. We are not in love. This is lust at its most raw and unrefined, at its most base, and if I'm going to be honest, destructive. I am a married woman. I should not be here. Everything about this is wrong, but when Ian kisses me, all I feel is what's right.

Ian pushes my hair off my face. "Maura."

"Shh." I stop him with my mouth on his. There's no room here for talking.

We've gone too far to take any of this back; I wouldn't want to even if we could. I drink in every second, every moment. I consume every breath in and out, every gesture, scent, sensation. I memorize him in these moments because I believe this will be the only time this happens. Once I fuck him, this has to end.

Because…how could it go on?

I met him in a night club, and for the past year, we've been dancing. Ian pulls me close and pushes me away, and all I've ever done since that first night is try to end this, whatever it is between us.

This will end it. It has to. If we can just fuck each other out of our systems, he can go back to his financial reports and business meetings and visits to the gym, his sterile failures at being matched with single, professional, divorced women with kids. I'll go back to the desert of my marriage and maybe see if things can work out. Maybe not. But one way or another, I believe in my heart that this will be the only chance I ever have for Ian to be inside me.

With the subtlest of shifts, he could be, but neither of us move. I'm wet and hot and ready for him, so turned on I'm not sure I'll be able to last much longer. At the same time, I want it to last, and I know that once he is inside me it will all happen faster than I want.

Instead, push his shoulder gently to roll him onto his back. I straddle him again, knees pressing his sides. I lean to kiss him, and the curtain of my hair shields us.

"Should I get a ponytail holder?"

"No," Ian says. "Leave it down. I like it."

I've kissed his mouth a hundred times by now, but each one is still as fresh and new as the first. I love Ian's mouth. His lips. His cheek and jaw, the spot below his ear. The hollow of his throat. His collar bone. I skim my lips and teeth along every line, every dip and curve. His skin is warm and tastes faintly of salt; he's sweating though the room is chilly.

I kiss his chest and take my time with his nipples until he gasps and laughs, his hand in my hair. I nip at his ribs, counting each with my tongue. I trace his hipbones with my fingertips and follow with more kisses. Down his thighs. The bumps of his knees. Ian's calves make me want to write a song about them.

"Your feet," I murmur. "Oh, my God. Your fucking feet, Ian."

He laughs, shaking the bed. "What about them?"

From my place near his ankle, which I'm worshipping with my kisses, I look up at him. I want to mark this sight in my mind forever, me at his feet and him pushing up on his elbow to look down at me. "They're perfect."

"Oh, God." With a groan, he falls back onto the pillows, a hand over his eyes. "You're crazy."

"About you," I tell him and work my way kiss by kiss back up his legs.

I nuzzle his inner thighs. I bite a little too hard in my eagerness and brace myself for a yelp, ready to apologize, but Ian only jerks and lets out a soft sigh. His beautiful cock is so close, but I take my time before I get to it. As my friend Shelly's fond of saying, if I wanted balls on my nose, I'd be a seal — and yet with Ian everything is so unimaginably perfect and delicious that I use my mouth and hands on every part of him and revel in it.

I can't hold myself back any longer. I need him in my mouth. I want to make him moan and shift and pump his hips. I want to make him lose his mind. I slide my tongue up his length, and his reaction is immediate and gratifying. A soft, hissing sigh that trails into a little growl. I close my eyes at that last moment, when I take him all the way in. Slow, slow, I work my lips and tongue along his shaft as far as I can — which turns out to be all the way until my lips brush his belly.

I add my hand when I slide up, sucking gently on the head of his cock. Down again. I lose myself in the rhythm of fucking him this way. My hair tangles, getting in the way, and Ian lifts it from my neck to hold it in his fist. The gesture is simple and considerate, and I stagger for a moment.

"Feels so good," he murmurs.

"Does it?"

"Can't you tell?" Ian asks with a low laugh.

I kiss his belly, my hand still stroking. I press my face to his warm skin and breath in his smell. "I want you to feel good, Ian. I want you to tell me when I do."

"You are." He pulls me up to his mouth.

His erection's trapped between us when we kiss. I'm so wet for him, all it will take is a tilt of my hips and he'll slide right in. But before that, of course, I need to do something else. My fingers fumble with the plastic package, my poise shaky since it's been forever since I even had to think of using a condom. But I am woman, hear me roar. I sheathe him without too much struggle, and when I look at Ian, his mouth is thin. His brow furrowed.

"It's been a long time," he says, a hand on my wrist as I grip his cock.

"I'll be gentle, sweetheart," I breathe against his mouth, and we both laugh. Thank God for that, for a second I thought it was going to get way too serious.

We both make a noise when I ease him inside me. I lean forward to kiss him, but neither of us move beyond that. Beneath my palm, Ian's heart is beating very fast.

"Maura…" he grips my hips.

"Shhh." I kiss his mouth, urging him to open for me. Our tongues stroke. I kiss him for a long time without so much as rocking my hips. His cock is impossibly hard inside me, even throbbing, something I'd have said was something made up for stories. But no, I feel his nice, thick cock twitch inside me when I suck on his tongue. When I clench my internal muscles, Ian groans.

He rolls me smoothly so I'm under him. Pushing up on one hand, Ian looks down at me while he uses the other hand to hook beneath my knee, easing my leg up. Opening me to push inside even deeper.

We move together. Slow at first. Too slow. I dig my nails into his back, then his ass. Murmur in his ear.

"Fuck me, Ian," I tell him. "Harder."

At first he won't, and I know why. I've grown to understand Ian very well over the past few months. Intimacy grows in strange places, and Ian and I have spent hours in conversation, revealing secrets. There's been an honesty in this relationship, a lack of pretense, because basically, when you both know there's no way this can ever be more than what it is, what's the point in playing games? And maybe because we've both needed someone to be honest with.

I know him. I know he's trying to tease me, and that he's also trying to be in charge, because Ian doesn't like to be told what to do. When I reach up to grab the headboard, he reacts at once, shuddering. His expression goes dark.

I tilt my hips, back arching. Breathy voice. "Harder, Ian. Please."

It's the 'please' that gets him. With a groan, he thrusts a little harder. A little faster. It feels so good, I'm already so close that every press of his belly on my clit sends ripples of pleasure all through me.

"Please, Ian. Please, please, please…"

He fucks me hard enough to move me on the bed. His fingers encircle my wrist, pinning my hand to the headboard. That hurts a little, but so does the fierce thrust of him inside me.

It all hurts, and I love the pain.

I'm looking into his eyes when I come. He sees my pleasure on my face. Maybe feels it in the clutch of my cunt on him, I can't be sure. My body moves all on its own, and I can't control it. I don't want to. I am lost in desire. Lost in his eyes. I'm lost in Ian, and there's no finding my way out.

He puts his face against my neck, and I feel his sweat. His grip tightens on my wrist. More pain, this time making me gasp a little. It sends him over but if this was a game of who's in control, the way he mutters my name when he comes seems to make me the winner.

A minute passes before he loosens his fingers and rolls off me to lay on his back. The soft huff of our mingled breathing is lulling me to sleep when Ian gets up and pads to the bathroom. I hear the toilet flush. He comes out, washes his hands. Rinses his mouth and spits into the sink. I haven't moved when he comes back to bed. I'm not sure I can. The mattress dips when he slides in beside me.

Ian turns me onto my side and pulls me back against him. Spooning. I tuck my hand under my cheek, my head on the pillow, his warmth behind me and his hand resting lightly just under my breasts. I wait for regret and feel only safe and if not loved, at the very least, adored.

For that moment, adored.

Five

"In the morning," Maura said, "you brought me coffee and a bagel from the place next door. Remember that?"

Ian was silent for a few seconds. Then sighed. "Yes. Of course I do."

"We ate in bed, and you said you didn't mind the crumbs because this was a hotel, but when we were in your bed, I'd have to do without breakfast. And what did I say?"

"That you'd make a meal of my…of me." He could be filthy, there was no doubt of that, but at the same time so charmingly shy.

Maura laughed. "Yes. I said that. And you had to go to your meetings, but you walked me to my car and kissed me goodbye. And you know what I thought just then, Ian?"

Another pause. One second. Another. "What?"

"I thought about how I'd truly believed that it would only be once, but when you kissed me there in the parking lot, in the bright light of morning, I knew there was no possible way I could go the rest of my life without kissing you ever again."

He laughed at that. "I never thought it would be the only time."

"No?"

"No. I thought if we did it…if we actually fucked, that it would never end."

Maura closed her eyes, listening. "But it did. It has."

He said nothing, but what had she expected him

to say? That he loved and wanted her? That he would do anything to be with her? The time for that had come and gone, and more than once.

"Do you want this to be over, Ian?"

"I want you to be happy," he said.

She believed him. The words were nice. Yet they cut deeper than if he'd simply answered yes.

"I want you to be happy too," Maura said. "I love you, Ian."

Again, he said nothing, but the sound of his breathing shifted. She imagined him rubbing his mouth. At least if he were holding back words she didn't want to hear, she could be grateful for that.

She tried biting back her own words, but they slipped out anyway. She'd always been honest with him and couldn't seem to stop herself now. "I love you. I want you. I want to be with you, I want to see if we could make it work. For real. Me and you, Ian."

"You just think you want that."

Maura set her jaw. "Don't tell me what I think or what I want. Don't treat me like I'm stupid. Do you think I'm stupid?"

"No. Of course not. You know I don't."

"Actually," she said, "I don't have any idea what you think, Ian, because you don't tell me."

Maura paused, thinking of all the hours they'd spent talking and of the things he had said. Why was it always so much harder to hang onto the positives? So much easier to believe him when he told her 'no' and 'don't' and 'stop.'

"Doublethink," she told him when he stayed silent. "You know doublethink?"

She heard the soft huff of his breath. "Yes. From that book you gave me. 1984."

"Yes. Doublethink is the act of accepting two mutually contradictory beliefs as correct, simultaneously. I doublethink with you all the time. Because there's a part of me that knows without a doubt you love me and want me as much as I want you. Part of me knows this as complete truth, that there is no possibility for it to be any other way."

"And the other part?"

Maura sighed. "That I mean nothing to you and never did. That I have left no impression on you whatsoever. I think I'm immeasurably important to you and insignificant at the same time. Two totally opposite feelings, and I believe them both."

"What do you want from me?" Anger hard-edged his voice, but that was ok. Better fury than apathy.

"I want you to be miserable without me!" She could be angry, too. "I want you to wake the fuck up and get your shit together."

She'd pushed him too far. "Get my shit together? The ink's barely dry on your divorce papers! You said yourself you hadn't been single since you were eighteen years old. What the hell makes you think I just want to be the next in line?"

That was the trouble of telling someone all your truths. They could use them to tear you apart. Maura drew in a breath, biting her tongue, counting to ten before she could answer him without screaming.

"And why should you ever, ever trust me?" She asked him. "After all, I'm a cheater."

Ian made a low noise. "I didn't...that's not what I said. Don't put words in my mouth."

"But it's the truth, isn't it? Goddammit, Ian, can't you even just...tell me that? If it bothers you?"

"Yes!" He cried. "Fine. Yes. I think about that. How could I trust you? If you did it with me, maybe you'd do it to me. Right? And how do I know that you're just not afraid of being alone? That I'm not just convenient. Here I am, you already know me —"

"I do know you," she told him softly. "I know every part of you."

"What if it just doesn't work out?"

Maura swiped the tears that had crept unbidden down her cheeks and struggled to keep them from her voice. She'd already given him too much. "How will we ever know if we don't try?"

"I don't know if I can."

"You think that I don't really want you. That I don't know what I want, that you're just some fantasy for me. Is that it?" She lay back on the pillows and wished the world away. His silence was her answer. "You think I should...what? Be with someone else?"

"Maybe."

"Ian!" She cried. "Do you want me to be with someone else? You can think about that and not be bothered?"

"It bothers me. Of course it does," he admitted, and sent her heart leaping into her throat.

"Because you're worried that I haven't dated enough?"

"You just got divorced. You shouldn't leap into anything long-term or serious right away."

She frowned. "Just because you fucked your way through the dating scene when you got divorced doesn't mean I want to. Or have to."

"You should have some time to be with yourself," he told her firmly. "Find out what you want. Not just jump into the first thing that comes along."

Maura's eyes narrowed. She listened to the spaces between his words. The things he didn't say. And, she held onto hope. She doublethought as hard as she could.

I mean everything. I mean nothing.

"Fine," she said finally. "Then here's what I'm going to do. I will date other people, if that's what you want. I will open myself up to the possibilities of finding someone who is not you, or the possibility of ending up alone. But you're going to do something for me, too."

"What?" Ian asked, sounding wary.

Maura glanced at the clock. 11:11 Wishing time. She closed her eyes and put out her desire to the universe.

"You're going to listen to me tell you about every single one of them," she told him, "until you can't stand it any more."

Ian made another of those low noises, discontent. "And then what?"

"Then," she said, "you'll either never speak to me again, or you will realize you can't live without me. Either way, Ian, the way things are right now is going to change."

Six

Whoever had set up Luvfinder must've been a huge fan of Monty Python, Maura thought as she sorted through her email notifications. Seven winks, eight nudges. Too bad there was nary an Eric Idle or John Cleese in the bunch.

Not that the selection was terrible. She'd made her parameters pretty narrow, wary of the dating site's claim to have a "ninety-eight percent match rate!" As far as she could see, anyone who waded through the ten page questionnaire and made it to the end without stabbing anyone already deserved at least one date.

So far, she'd been on thirty-seven.

"It's serious business," she told Shelly as they settled into their favorite booth, the one toward the back so they could people watch. "I have a spreadsheet."

Shelly snorted laughter. "Oh. My. God. No, Maura. No, you can't."

"I do." Maura nodded and held up a finger. "Color coded."

"Sweetie, this is supposed to be fun. Not like studying for the bar."

Maura shrugged. "I'm trying to maximize my membership, that's all. I only paid for the three-month intro package. After that it's a staggering twenty-nine ninety-five a month unless I want to commit to six more months. And honestly, kind of like losing twenty pounds, if I haven't managed to get a good start in three months, I'm probably not gonna."

Shelly shook her head and stirred some sweetener into her coffee. She had a fruit cup in front of her, but eyed Maura's thick slab of chocolate cake with unabashed lust. "If you keep eating that sort of thing, you're not going to lose twenty pounds."

"I listed my body type as curvy." Maura stabbed the cake with her fork and took a bite, savoring the fudgy icing. "God. So good."

"Have you heard from him?" Shelly sounded hesitant, almost afraid to ask.

"Nope." Maura stabbed her cake again, but didn't take the second bite. The first had been so good she was afraid to ruin it by overindulging. She'd learned a lesson about that, hadn't she? Something about leaving while the party was still fun.

"Have you called him?"

"Nope."

"...Texted?" Maura smiled and shook her head. Shelly sighed. She reached across the table and took a chunk of Maura's cake with her own fork. "Are you going to?"

"Oh, yes. Definitely. I just wanted to be sure I had something to tell him when I did, that's all. That's part of the deal." Maura sipped her own coffee, relishing the warmth of the mug in her hands. Outside, the leaves were changing early, predicting a terrible winter. It had been two agonizingly long weeks since she'd spoken to Ian. Every day when she woke, she figured she might finally stop missing him. So far it hadn't happened.

"Do you have something to tell him yet?"

The best part of having a best friend was being able to tell her all your secrets. Maura grinned, but said nothing. The other best part was being able to tease her with them.

"Bitch." Shelly shook her head. "C'mon. You know I have to live vicariously through you. I want details. I mean, if you're keeping a frigging spreadsheet…"

Maura laughed. "I have to or else I'll never keep it all straight. For example, Saturday, I met Matt in the morning for coffee. I had lunch at the Taj Mahal with Jordan. He's an investment banker. I'm not sure why I thought that's why he'd pick up the tab for the four-ninety-nine buffet, but nope. He fully supports women taking the lead in a relationship, which apparently included not only me covering my own bill — which I'm fine with, by the way. But also paying for his. Also would've been fine, I guess, if it hadn't been our first date, and if he hadn't been the one to be so insistent about it. I'd already turned him down a couple times before I gave in. The food was good, though."

"Yikes!" Shelly said, too loud, then giggled. "Wow."

"Yep." Maura nodded. "Dinner that night with Robert, a total sweetheart with two kids under ten. So. No to that."

Shelly wrinkled her nose. She had teenagers, and that was as close to kids as Maura'd ever come. "Hmmm."

"Drinks later that night with…hmm. I'd have to check the spreadsheet. It was either Bill or Brad.

Either way, he met me at some jazz club. I wanted to poke my eardrums out before I finished my first martini. It was an early night." Maura leaned back in the booth. "Sunday, I got up early and went to the flea market with Jacob. He's got grandkids. Somehow that bothers me less than Robert having young children. Does that make me weird?"

"Wait a minute. Hold on. All of that in one weekend?"

"Yep. And," Maura leaned closer to say in a triumphant half-whisper, "You'll never guess who looked me up on Connex and asked me out. I mean, like out on a date, out."

"Norman Reedus!" Shelly's shout turned heads.

Maura guffawed. "Don't I wish? That's a Do Not Pass Go, Go Directly to Bed situation, right there. No, it's someone real, actually. Daniel."

Daniel Petruzzi, six-foot-three, blond hair, brown eyes. Wide, friendly smile and a habit of tilting his head to one side when you talked to him. Hands that could palm a basketball. Fingers that could make a girl lose her mind.

"No." Shelly looked stunned. Then both brows went up. "You said yes, didn't you?"

"Of course I said yes. I haven't seen Daniel in what…eighteen years?" Maura paused, thinking of that long-ago hot summer when she and Daniel had nearly eaten each other alive. "There's something about your first real sexual relationship, you know? The one where you stop fumbling around and start to get it right. At the very least, I want to see how he looks in real life, not just in his Connex profile picture. Which looks pretty damned good, if you must know."

"And he just happened to get in touch with you now? Now after all this time? What a strange and happy happenstance." Shelly's brows waggled.

Maura laughed, heat tinging her cheeks. "He friended me a few years ago, but we never messaged or anything. He was out of the country for a while. He…um…well, he said he saw my changed relationship status."

"And he asked you out on a date. Woo hoo!" Shelly made guns of her fingers. "Pow, pow! Take that, Ian dingleberry."

Maura laughed so loud she clapped a hand over her mouth. More heat flooded her, a little guilty this time. "Don't call him that."

"Well," Shelly said. "That's what he is."

Shelly wasn't wrong, which was both hilarious and sad. More doublethink. Maura shrugged.

"I'm having dinner with Daniel Saturday night. Tonight, I'm meeting James at the gym for a complimentary weight training session. On a Friday night. I think that tells you how well it's going to go. I've got a plan to meet someone for drinks later. Can't remember who, but it might be a second date. I'll have to check my spreadsheet."

"You're going to burn out!"

Maura shrugged again. "I told you. Serious business."

"Why, sweetie?" Shelly frowned. "Why does it have to be so serious?"

"Because." Maura thought hard about what to say for the rest of her answer, but that was the best she could come up with.

The conversation turned to other things, which was something of a relief. They hugged in the parking lot, and Shelly squeezed her hard. When she pulled away, she searched Maura's face with her gaze.

"Call him," Shelly said. "You want to."

"Of course I want to. I want to every day." Maura's mouth twisted. "I'm crazy about that kid."

Shelly laughed and rolled her eyes. "So. Call him. Or at least text him."

"I can't. Not yet. All I've done is go on lame dates with people I have no interest in seeing again."

"Isn't that kind of the point you want to make to him?" Shelly pulled her jacket closer around her neck and looked up at the gray sky with a shiver. "That you don't really want anyone else?"

It was the point, but it hadn't quite been made yet. Maura knew him too well to believe that a few coffee dates and some funny stories equalled what Ian thought she needed. "I haven't even tongue-kissed any of them yet, much less had rampant, wild sex."

Shelly made a face. "Are you really going to sleep with someone else just to prove your point?"

"Maybe." Maura lifted her chin. "Why not? I'm a woman empowered by her own sexuality, ready to take control of my passion. If I want to go out and get laid, why shouldn't I?"

Shelly didn't say anything.
Maura sighed.

Seven

As it turned out, she didn't have to call or text Ian, because Saturday night her phone pinged while she was in the shower. Once upon a time, the sound would've been like the bell to Pavlov's dogs. Now, head bent under the hot water washing away the feeling of Daniel all over her, Maura seriously considered not even looking at the message.

She did, of course, though not right away. Let him stew for a little while, she thought. Let him wait. Let him pace and ponder and fret.

She dried herself carefully and smoothed her body with lotion, remembering Daniel's hands. Here. There. She pressed her fingertips between her legs and felt herself, still slick. Her still-tender nipples tightened under her next touch. She rubbed her hair briskly to dry it, then combed through it and stared at herself in the mirror while she brushed her teeth, all the while waiting for her phone to make that sound again.

It did, finally, when she'd slipped beneath her covers and lay in the dark with her phone pressed to her heart. She hadn't yet checked Ian's message, but the fact he had indeed sent another message meant something. Didn't it? She could read it and find out for sure, but what if he'd said something she didn't want to read? Something like he'd met someone else, fallen in love. Maybe that he'd finally fucked that girl who always wore yoga pants, the one forever making eyes at him in the coffee shop. Patty, her name was. Yoga Pants Patty.

And what would Maura be able to say to that, considering what had happened less than two hours ago?

She needed to read his message and couldn't bear to read it. Doublethink, doublethink, she'd grown too adept at the concept of holding two contrasting ideas simultaneously. Pick one, Maura. Read the fucking message or delete it, but do something.

She thumbed her phone's screen to bring up the text and took a deep breath, readying herself for disappointment.

All it said was hi. Then, hello.

Maura let out a long, streaming burble of humorless laughter. She typed quickly.

Hey

She'd probably missed him. It was late, after all. But no, within seconds came a reply.

Yo

"Oh, God, Ian." This time, she burst into real laughter and clutched the phone to her chest again like a schoolgirl with a love note. She loved him so fucking much it hurt. She dialed his number and waited, breathless, for him to answer.

"Joe's Blowhole, best discount blubber on the East Coast."

Maura didn't miss a beat. "I'd like twenty pounds of your most gourmet blubber, please."

"Hi," Ian said.

"Hi. It's late." She snuggled deeper into her blankets and looked up. She'd covered the ceiling with plastic glow-in-the-dark stars. Why? Because she could. A few of them had started to fade, but the ones closest to the overhead light were still bright.

"Were you sleeping?"

"No," she told him. "I just got in."

A pause, a breath. She imagined his look of surprise, but maybe he wasn't. "Oh."

She waited for him to ask her where she'd been. He didn't, the bastard. He said nothing, leaving it to her to move the conversation forward.

"What's up?" Maura said finally in a too-bright voice when an eternity had passed with them both playing the waiting game.

"Nothing much. What's up with you?"

Games. Always the games. Maura sighed. "Ian. Don't do this."

"Don't do what?" Predictably, he sounded disgruntled she'd called him on it.

"It's been weeks since we talked, but that doesn't make us strangers. Can we not pretend we're chit-chatting at a cocktail party? Can you just talk to me? Can't you tell me that you missed me?"

"Did you miss me?" Ian asked at once.

"Every day," she answered honestly. "All day long."

Ian sighed. "I missed you too."

She smiled, relieved but hating herself, just a little, for letting what should've been such an easy, no-brainer of a sentiment make her heart leap so high. "Talk to me, sweetheart. Tell me all about it."

"All about what?"

"Everything," she said. "What's been going on?"

The heat between them, that chemistry, the way a simple look from him could make her nipples hard and her clit pulse. That had always been great. But this was what she loved the most. The way they could talk about anything and everything, for hours and hours. She loved the rise and fall of Ian's voice, the faintest drawl that came from who-knew-where, since he wasn't from the south.

He told her about his job. Not the work part of it — she'd have listened, of course, if he'd needed her to. No, Ian told her about the people he worked with. She'd never met any of them, but hearing so many stories about his co-workers had made her feel like she had. Good old Merv, the office custodian, full of advice on Ian's dating life as well as confidential asides about who left rubbers in their trash and who'd been known to hide a bottle in the desk drawer. Perky Peg, the receptionist with crazy eyes who baked cookies every week that Ian suspected might just have weed in them. He had Maura laughing so hard with his stories that at first she didn't hear the question he'd asked her.

"What, honey? I missed what you said."

"I asked you," Ian said, all traces of good humor aside, "where you were tonight?"

Oh.

Maura cleared her throat. This was what she'd wanted, wasn't it? To give him what he'd said he wanted? To make him know it?

"I was on a date."

Ian said nothing and was so silent, not even the sough of a breath in her ear, for such a long time that Maura was convinced he'd disconnected the call. Finally, he spoke. "I see."

"I've been on a lot of dates." She kept her voice

flat and neutral, wanting no hint of triumph or dismay though in truth, she felt a little bit of both. "Close to forty, as a matter of fact."

"I see," he repeated. It was what he said when he was pissed but didn't want her to know it.

More games. Maura's jaw went tight. "I'm doing what you wanted me to do. Right? Going on dates. Making sure I know what I want."

"And this one, tonight? How…how was it?"

"Well, Ian," Maura said slowly. "Let me tell you a story."

***

Time hasn't been unkind to me. I'm vain enough to admit that. Practical enough to see the lines and creases, that stubborn silver hair that insists on coming back right there in the front by my part. I don't have an eighteen-year-old body anymore, but on the other hand, I sure know what to do with the one I have.

Daniel, however, is even hotter than he was that summer before my first year of college. The years have polished him like a diamond. He's so gorgeous it's hard to look at him dead-on because I'm terrified I'll simply blurt out something stupid like, "please let me sit on that perfect mouth and ride until one of us breaks."

His smile when he sees me is like a supernova. When he leans to kiss my cheek, one big hand on my upper arm, he smells so good my mouth literally waters. Vanilla sugar. What man smells like vanilla sugar unless he wants to get eaten?

"So good to see you," he says. "Wow. You look fantastic, Maura. Your pictures don't do you justice."

I find a smile for him. "That's saying something, considering the only ones I post are the ones where I'm sure I look ten times better than I do in real life."

"No." He looks serious, shaking his head. "You're so much prettier in person."

What answer can a woman have to something like that but a blush? Heat radiates from my toes to my forehead, bathing me in the warm, golden glow of being complimented. In all the dates I've had over the past couple weeks, nobody's told me I'm pretty. A few of the men told me I looked "great." A few dingleberries, to use Shelly's terminology, had said I looked better than my pictures, but somehow the way they'd said it had conveyed reluctant relief and not Daniel's seemingly genuine appreciation.

I remember now why I liked him so much. Daniel is a veritable fountain of praise. He likes my hair, my dress, the shoes I picked out at the last second and had been second-guessing. He likes the restaurant I suggested and the cocktails we order. And all of it, every positive comment, is accompanied by one of those mega-watt smiles that melt the panties off every woman within a ten-mile radius.

The conversation with him is easy. We haven't kept in touch the way we each have with other friends from that long-ago summer, but we still share mutual acquaintances. And we didn't end badly, Daniel and I. No hard feelings. It's not hard to see him again. Not at all.

"Wow. It's been so long," he says when the waiter puts our food down in front of us. We're sharing an appetizer tray and will share the hotpot entree too. Daniel's never been to a hotpot restaurant, but this is one of my favorite places. "How've you been?"

My life is boring compared to his; I give him the brief rundown, but I'm more interested in hearing about him. "What about you?"

"Guatemala for the past five years. El Salvador before that." Daniel designs and oversees the construction of infrastructures for companies building up their businesses overseas. I'd never known what he studied in college; we'd never delved that deep during our relationship, when the only engineering I'd ever known him to do was how to fuck me hard against a wall without dropping me. He'd been very good at that; I'm not surprised he's won awards for designing bridges.

"I haven't done anything nearly as exotic. Or exciting."

"Do you still write songs?"

I sit back in my seat, stunned that he remembers. "Oh. Wow. Um...well, I haven't in a long time."

I wrote a song for Ian, but I'd never played it for him. It had been too long since I'd played or sang. I'd been embarrassed.

"That's too bad. You wrote some great songs. I still have the tape you made for me." For a minute he almost looks shy. "The one with the song on it."

"Oh, wow, Daniel. Wow." I blush again, even hotter than when he'd said I look pretty. I had written him a song. Not a love song, really, because nothing we'd ever done had been quite big enough to be called love. But I'd meant every word at the time.

"It broke. The tape I mean. I listened to it too much, and one day it wore out I guess." He scratches his fingers through his golden hair, rumpling it. The twist of his mouth is totally endearing. "You're the only girl who ever wrote me a song. And sang it. And played the piano."

I slap a hand to my embarrassed face. "Oh, God. That was terrible."

"It wasn't terrible. It was great." He grins and leans over the table a little toward me. His eyes are very, very blue. The lines in the corners make him exponentially hotter. "Very sexy. You were always so sexy."

Trip-trap-trip, the beat of my heart bumps in triple time. There's an answering pulse and flutter between my legs. My clit's so easy to please. I shift in my seat, the pressure of my thighs sweet and tantalizing. My eyes go heavy lidded for a second at a memory of Daniel's tongue against me there. Even at eighteen he'd been a champion pussy eater, willing to go down and stay there as long as it took to get me off multiple times. Once, a memorable five in a row.

I wonder if he's remembering the same thing? The look in his eyes tells me he might be. Or that he'd need only the vaguest of reminders. Suddenly, there's a heat between us that's not from my blush or the burner in the center of the table that is now cooking our food.

I've been on enough dates the past few weeks to appreciate how effortless our conversation is. My memories of Daniel have never been about his brain, but I'm pleased to discover that he's smart and not just pretty. He's got a good sense of humor, too. He makes all of this so easy.

He makes it even easier to say yes when he asks if I want to go back to his place. The movie we'd intended to see is sold out, and none of the others appeal. We could, Daniel says, stream something from Interflix or watch a DVD, if I want.

"I'd hate to end things so early," he says. "It's been so great catching up."

Our relationship had not been of prom and backyard barbecues. I'd never met his parents, but I'd snuck in and out of their house a few times at three in the morning. Daniel's parents had moved to Florida a few years ago. He's left with the cute Cape Cod nestled in the woods not far from where my own parents still live, but he assures me as he unlocks the front door that he no longer sleeps in the basement.

Not much else has changed. Photos of him and his sister as teenagers still hang in the hallway to the kitchen, where he takes me first to make us both some coffee. He pulls a cheesecake from the freezer. Caffeine AND sugar? This guy gets me, all right.

We settle onto the lumpy, beflowered couch to watch a cheesy horror flick that sounds perfectly unwatchable. Daniel stretches out long legs to prop his feet on the coffee table, one arm snaking along the back of the couch but not touching me. We make it through the credits and the first mangling, and finally, just when I'm thinking I'm going to have to make the first move, he kisses me.

It's not the best first kiss, even if technically it's not our first. It's certainly not as good as the first time we ever kissed, when I'd taunted him into it until he pushed me up against the wall and plundered my mouth until I couldn't breathe. This time, I'm turning to say something snarky about the movie and he's leaning forward. Our noses bump and teeth clash. My mouth is open though, which allows the slip of his tongue inside. His hand slides from the back of the couch to my shoulder, easing me closer. The kiss deepens for a moment before he pulls away.

"Sorry about that." He touches the corner of my mouth. "Are you okay?"

I touch my tongue to it. There's no blood. "I'm fine."

The second kiss works much better. We move in at the same time, heads angling. I slide into the open space between his legs. We tangle up together as the kiss gets harder. When Daniel lets out a low moan, something deep inside me twists.

At least Daniel wants me.

Desire makes desire, as the saying goes. So does memory, and all mine of Daniel are flaming hot. When he nudges my chin upward with his mouth so he can get at my throat with his teeth, it's my turn to moan. He pushes me back against the couch and fits himself between my legs, the bulge of his belt buckle pressing just right on my clit through the barrier of all our clothes. Pillows scatter. His hands roam. I'm wearing a tank top and a cardigan sweater along with a short, pleated skirt that allows for easy access — though the winter-weight sweater tights beneath are a real cock blocker.

Still kissing me, Daniel murmurs sweet words of admiration. "You smell so good, Maura. Your mouth is so sweet. You feel so good against me. God, I want to taste you."

Shifting a little to the side, the couch not nearly big enough for both of us, he runs his hand over my breasts. Over the cardigan at first, but my nipples are so hard he can definitely feel them through the thin material of the tank top and sweater. He tweaks one, and sudden sensation stabs me. I arch under that touch.

It's been too long since a man has touched me this way. Sure, I've had many orgasms, but all by my own hand. I crave this…affection, because that's what it feels like. This affection, desire, this adoration. I crave it as much if not more than the sex itself.

"You are so pretty." Daniel pauses in kissing me to say it against my mouth. His fingers roll my nipple taut.

I catch my breath. Swallow hard. "Thank you. You're not so bad yourself."

For a second, something flickers in his gaze. His mouth turns down a little at the corners. But just for a second, and just a little, because then he's kissing me again. His hand slides under my sweater. Under the tank top. Over the sensitive skin of my belly, tracing the edge of my shirt before moving up to tug at the neckline. The tank top is form-fitting, easier to access from the top than bottom. My breast pops free, and before I can think to say or do anything, Daniel dips his head to take my nipple in his mouth.

Electric pleasure, oh fuck. Oh, wow. His tongue flickers against my tight flesh before he sucks gently. Pleasure arcs straight from there to my clit. I've always loved having my nipples played with — I've come close but never quite been able to manage an orgasm from that alone. Under Daniel's skilled mouth, I'm starting to think I might make it this time.

He pulls my shirt lower so he can get to my other nipple. My fingers thread through his hair as he sucks my skin. His hands move lower, over my belly. My hips. One slides between my legs, pressing against my tights, his thumb hard on my clit.

I break the kiss. "Daniel."

He looks up at me. "Hmmm?"

I hate myself for saying it, but I do. "I should probably go."

He sits up, but slowly, letting his mouth and fingers linger. He runs a hand through his hair. His face is flushed, mouth wet. Eyes bright. "Yeah...yeah, I'm sorry, I got carried away."

"It's not that." I pull my shirt back over my breasts but move closer to him. I don't want this to be weird. It isn't, after all, that I'm ashamed. "But

I'm not here for the right reasons."

Both his brows go up. He's let me link my fingers through his, and he looks down when I squeeze. Then at my face. "Are there wrong reasons?"

"I think so." I laugh. I'd kiss him again, if that wouldn't be totally counterproductive.

"I really did just want to catch up on old times," Daniel says suddenly. "I don't want you to think I meant for this to turn into something like…well. Like this, I guess."

"Like making out on your couch?" I tease a little.

He smiles, and again there's that flash of something, quicksilver, in his gaze. "Yeah. I mean, of course I kind of hoped you'd let me kiss you. You were always such a great kisser."

"Hey!" I punch his arm lightly. "Was?"

"Still are," he assures me. His eyes travel over my face, and though you'd think the time for blushing was past, heat slides up to cover my cheeks and throat. He leans a little closer, hesitant.

The kiss this time is sweeter. He presses his forehead to mine for a moment, his eyes closed. I cup his face in my hands and kiss his mouth again. The kiss gets a little harder.

We had fucked fast and furious back in the day, and the chemistry's still here. Potential. I did set out to prove a point, after all.

But I can't do it.

"I'm sorry, I can't just use you, Daniel."

He looks surprised. Then laughs, shaking his head. "No?"

"No." I sit back a little on this lumpy couch, probably the same one that's already seen us naked and fucking on it a few times. "See, there's this guy…"

"There's always a guy." He says this with such a put-upon sigh, such a lift of his shoulders and roll of his eyes that I have to laugh, even if it's a sad little chuckle and not a full-on guffaw.

"It's kind of a mess."

"It always is." He pauses. "Your ex?"

I flinch. Grimace. "No. No complications there."

"Ah. Someone else. I'm too late, huh? Waited too long to ask you out?" He's clearly teasing, but it's still a nice thing to say.

I'm not sure how much to tell him. I haven't said a word to any of the other men I've gone out with, I guess because even though I'm sure more than one of them wouldn't have minded ending up on a couch someplace, so far none of the dates have even headed in that direction. I'd told Shelly it was a serious business, and I meant it. But that didn't mean I was going to simply jump into bed with a stranger. Serious business, and also tricky.

"He doesn't think we're supposed to be together," I say.

"Is he an idiot?" Daniel looks serious. He pushes my hair over my shoulder.

I want to cry because he's so sweet. I don't believe him, not utterly. But it's so much nicer to be told yes than an everconstant no.

"Yes. My friend Shelly says he's a dingleberry."

Daniel made a face. "Wow."

"He's cautious," I amend.

"Scared." Daniel says this with authority. "Men are assholes about relationships, Maura. He's scared shitless."

"That is probably true." I shrug. "Doesn't make it feel any better."

"So…" He studies me. Moves a little closer. He traces my chin with a fingertip, a totally cheesy move that nevertheless has me melting as thoroughly as it did when I was eighteen.

I kiss him a little more, because, defiantly and triumphantly, I can. The kissing turns to petting, the petting to his fingers moving under my tights and pulling them down to leave my thighs bare. I'm ticklish there, squirming and giggling. Breathless.

Daniel looks at me. "Maura, listen. I'm only home for a couple months, then I'm heading to Malaysia. I'm not saying this just to get in your pants.…"

"You're in them, pretty much," I point out.

"What I mean is," he says seriously, "is that I've always had great memories of you, and I really did want to just catch up on old times. But this is great too. And if you only want to use me to get back at that other guy, I'm totally down with it."

I burst into laughter that he joins until the couch shakes. I cup his face again; kiss him. Look into his eyes.

"It's not about that, exactly. He wants me to go out with other people. He thinks I need to, in order to be sure he's the one I want."

Daniel's mouth twists. His fingertips tickle on

my inner thigh until I squirm. Heat has pooled low in my belly. I could stop his fingers from creeping higher, closer to the edge of my panties, but I don't.

"What do you want?"

"I guess it doesn't matter what I want," I say irritably. Angrier than I meant to.

Daniel pulls away. "It should."

"You've grown up, Daniel. I mean that in the best way."

He smiles and kisses me again. Soft brush of lips on my jaw. My throat. A little lower, over the swells of my breasts. He's down between my legs before I can stop him — not that I've tried. At the press of his mouth on my inner thigh, already sensitized from the circling patterns of his fingertips, I let my head fall back against the cushions.

I have never been a fan of denying pleasure. Chocolate cake is a gift from God, as far as I'm concerned. A good book and a warm blanket on a rainy day instead of an hour on the exercise bike? Sign me up. I pet all dogs, coo at all babies, taste all the hors d'oeuvres at the party. And sex…oh, well. Sex is one of the biggest pleasures of them all.

When he pushes his hands underneath my ass to slide my panties off, I let him. When he pushes up my skirt, I let him do that too. When he kisses each inner thigh and then moves to my cunt, his hot breath caressing my already swollen clit…Oh, yes. I let him.

Daniel slides his hands under my butt again, this time to lift me closer to his feasting mouth. His lips and tongue expertly find my clit, first flicking softly. Then stroking with the flat of his tongue in smooth, steady strokes that within a couple minutes send me up and up, but not quite over. My hips roll, pushing my body against his kiss. It feels so good I want to cry out, but bite my tongue. His parents aren't here, but old habits die hard.

There's not enough room on this couch for both of us. Daniel shifts me so that he can kneel on the floor in front of me. He spreads my legs wide, and before I can protest, puts the right one over his shoulder. I'm open, exposed, bare to him.

It's fucking amazing.

Daniel was the first guy to ever go down on me, and while I remembered his skill, I thought maybe it had just seemed so great because at the time I'd had no comparison. But now, years later, with half a dozen lovers since him, Daniel's still proving he's a pussy eating champ.

Soft and slow, then a little harder. Licking, sucking, never too hard. Just hard enough. The slide of fingers inside me makes me tense — at eighteen I hadn't worried much about my body or being self-conscious about it, but I'm quite a few years past that now. I haven't had children to ruin me, as Shelly likes to say, but still, time leaves a mark.

"You taste amazing, Maura," Daniel murmurs against me, and the soft sound of my name makes me lose any worries.

I'm getting close. I can't stop shifting under his tongue. I grip the cushions, then slide a hand into his hair holding his mouth against me. I don't mean to be rough, but Daniel gives a muffled groan and makes no move to pull away. His mouth works faster. His fingers fuck into me, curling upward a little in a "come here" gesture that has me rocketing toward orgasm. In these last minutes, I am not ashamed to say I can think of nothing but how good these feels. Everything else falls away. The only thing that matters is getting off.

I cry out when I finish. No words, just sound. The couch creaks as we rock it. Against my flesh, Daniel hums and moans; the sensations sends another round of orgasm rippling through me before the first has even had time to fade. A few seconds later it's too much. I pull his hair to lift his mouth from me. I can't speak.

Daniel rests his head against my thigh while my body twitches and finally quiets. He kisses my clit quickly, then moves up my body to kiss my mouth. I hold him close to me for a second or so longer when he tries to pull away.

"Wow," I tell him. "That was great."

There's a shuffle of clothing and rearranging of cushions, and we end up curled together on the couch with my head pressed to his chest. Arms and legs tangle. He kisses the top of my head. The movie's long since over.

He's being very quiet, and I wait for him to suggest we go to the bedroom, or that it's my turn to go down on him. Something. But Daniel's breathing slows and I realize he's falling asleep.

"Daniel? Do you want me to go?"

He blinks awake, looking confused for a moment. Then smiles and scrubs at his face. "It's late. You can stay if you want?"

I have Sunday morning coffee plans with a new

guy who doesn't seem very promising. I could cancel them without feeling too bad, though it's been my policy so far to keep any dates I make as a matter of pride and courtesy. "Well…"

"You don't have to. I just didn't want you to think I was running you off."

"I don't." I sit to look at him. "Hey. Are you okay?"

"Great." He grins. "You?"

"I'm…sated." I make a show of lolling against the back of the couch for a second or so before sitting up again to study his face. "But…what about you?"

It hasn't been my experience that many men bring a woman to orgasm without trying to get a little something for themselves. Certainly when Daniel and I were together before, even after he'd made me come with his mouth, he was always ready for me to do the same for him. But there's something going on here. An undertone I'm not sure of. I'm not positive I'm ready to have intercourse with him — with anyone. But I'd be willing to do something for him, at any rate.

Daniel looks uncomfortable. "Ahh…I'm fine."

"Really?" I eye him, then slide a hand up his thigh to cup his crotch. "You're not…you don't want…?"

He shifts a little when I touch him. Then he takes my hand and puts it up higher on his belly. He holds it there with his.

"I can't right now," he says after a few awkward seconds. "I wanted to. Thought I might be able to. But I'm sorry, Maura, I can't."

Blinking, I sit back, but I can't take my hand from his without making this a big deal, and I don't want to do that. "Okay? That's fine. I didn't want you to think I was so selfish I'd take without umm…giving."

His grin would look genuine if I hadn't been familiar with it. Now it seems the tiniest bit forced. "From what I remember, you're pretty damned good at giving."

"Even better now." I buff my nails on my shirt. False bravado. I'm not fully convinced of that at all. "…Are you sure?"

Daniel clears his throat. The easy closeness we've had since within minutes of our meeting tonight becomes tension. He sits up straighter on the couch, putting an inch or so of distance between us. It's enough to make me feel awkward. We sit for another minute without saying anything.

"I've been having a problem," Daniel says. "Umm. With that."

I chew my lower lip for a second, not sure what to say. "With…sex?"

"With getting an erection. And keeping it." It pains him to say this. I can see it on his face, hear it in his voice.

I try to think of what to say carefully, so carefully, because it seems to me this is the equivalent of a woman feeling like she has fat thighs and an enormous ass…only ten times worse. No. A hundred. I don't need a dick to know how much of a man is often tied up in how well his works.

In the end, I say nothing. I kiss him instead.

Then I snuggle up next him, head on his chest, and listen to the sound of his heart slow.

After a few minutes, his hand strokes my hair. His voice is low. "I was married to a girl I met in Guatemala. She found out she had ovarian cancer a few days before the wedding. She died just before our first anniversary."

"Oh, Daniel. I'm so sorry."

He clears his throat again. He won't look at me at first, then does as though defeated. He shakes his head.

"It was only last year. I guess I'm not...it takes time."

"Of course it does. Of course." I snuggle him again. My heart aches for him. I'm embarrassed now that I let him make me come, and so hard. It feels so...shallow.

"I wanted to make you feel good," he says in a low voice, like he can read my thoughts. "You looked so pretty tonight, and it's been a long time since I went out with anyone I didn't feel like I had impress. Not that I didn't want to impress you," he adds hastily, though I haven't taken offense. "But it was different."

"I understand." I'm pretty sure I do. "I was thrilled when you messaged me, to be honest."

His arm around me tightens. "This guy. You love him?"

"Yes." Such a tiny word with such a vast meaning. "I love him."

"I hope he figures his shit out, then."

"Me too," I tell him with a sigh. "Me too."

Eight

Ian was silent when she'd finished speaking, and Maura let him stay that way for so long she almost fell asleep with the phone pressed to her ear. When he said her name, she opened her eyes. "Yes, Ian."

"You never told me you wrote me a song."

"It was in the beginning," Maura whispered. "Before I felt like I could tell you how I really felt."

"Will you play it for me?"

She smiled, sleepily. "No."

Ian made a small noise. "It's late. You should go to sleep."

"You should, too." She yawned.

"I want to see you," Ian said in a voice so low she almost missed it.

Maura didn't answer right away. He could mean he wanted a picture. Or that he wanted her to get in her car and drive to him.

"Dance with me?" Ian whispered. It had been their code for a long time, meaning that he wanted to see her on video chat.

"If I see you, Ian," Maura said, "I'm going to want you."

Ian made a noise. "Ah. Well. Best not, then."

"Goddammit, Ian! You can't keep doing this. It's not fair."

"I know. I'm sorry."

"Have lunch with me tomorrow," she said impulsively. "Just lunch. We can go to that Thai place you like. Maybe a movie, after."

"No. I don't think so."

"C'mon, Ian. Why not?"

The rustle of his phone had her picturing him shaking his head. "Because if I see you, I'm going to want you."

Maura scowled, wide awake now. "You want me to dance with you, but you keep changing the song."

"Maybe you should find someone else to dance with, then," Ian said.

"I don't want someone else."

"You wanted someone else tonight," Ian said in a tight voice. "Seems to me, you wanted him enough."

"Fuck you, Ian," Maura said, and hung up on him.

***

"Boy, someone's in the doghouse." Madge, the woman who worked down the hall, held aloft a glass vase of flowers with a balloon attached to it. Grinning, she settled it on Maura's desk, turning it to show off the card. "They left it in my office by mistake. Thought I'd walk it down to you."

"Thanks, Madge." Maura didn't bother to open the card. She knew who the flowers were from.

"You know, my George always sends me flowers when he's done something he knows I'm going to scold him for." Madge leaned an ample hip against Maura's filing cabinet. "Not that I have to very often, of course."

"Of course not." Maura smiled. George was as close to perfect as a man could get, according to Madge. Having met him, Maura was inclined to agree — at least that he was perfect for Madge.

"So…" Madge lifted her chin toward the plant. "New beau?"

Madge was one of the few in the office who knew any of the details about Maura's divorce. Not about Ian. Maura hadn't told anyone but Shelly about him. But Madge had been there to listen more than a few times when Maura'd been down about her marriage. Even before she'd met Ian. Madge had taken Maura to lunch and listened to her vent, had always offered advice but never judgment.

"No. Not quite." Maura untied the balloon, which was bouncing annoyingly in her line of vision, and let it float up to the ceiling. Maybe it would pop.

Madge laughed. "How's the dating going?"

Maura's laugh was more rueful. "It's…going."

"Well," Madge said with another lift of her chin toward the plant, "Whoever sent you that must be trying to apologize for something."

"Can I ask you something?" Maura swiveled in her chair. "How many times can someone hurt you in the same way before you just…give up on them?"

At this, Madge pulled up a chair and settled into it. "Oh, dear. I guess it depends on how important they are to you."

"Very important."

Madge nodded, not looking surprised. "Did you know that George wasn't my first husband?"

"No!" The way Madge always talked about him, Maura'd assumed they'd been childhood sweethearts.

"No. I was married once before I met him. In fact," Madge added after a second, her brightly painted mouth thinning for a moment, "I was married when I met him."

"Oh. Oops?" Maura offered, keeping her expression neutral.

"I'm not proud of it," Madge said.

Maura found a stray paperclip to unbend so she could keep her hands busy. "No. I guess not."

"But...I'm not sorry." Madge sat a little straighter. "Does that shock you?"

Maura smiled slowly. "No."

Madge laughed a little sadly. "It shocked my mother, let me tell you. She loved my first husband. Thought he was the best thing that would ever happen to me. Honestly, she thought he was the best I could do."

Maura had heard plenty of stories about how difficult Madge's mother could be, and how much she hated her son-in-law. "That's why she doesn't like George."

"Yes. But that doesn't matter, does it? Because I like George." Madge grinned.

Maura twisted the bit of metal in her hands, thinking about last night's conversation with Ian. "So, how'd you two end up together?"

"I left my husband when I found out he'd spent all the money from our checking account at the track. I had to work two jobs to make ends meet after that, and one of them was as a waitress. Let me tell you, sweetie, there might be days when this job has me run ragged, but it's nothing compared to working the nightshift in a truckstop diner." Madge shook her head. "When George found out where I was and what had happened — he was a friend of my best friend Jill's husband. That's how we met. At Jill's house. Anyway, when George found out where I was working, he started showing up towards the end of my shifts. Two in the morning, when he had to get up for work the next day! Can you imagine it?"

Maura's throat tightened. "Wow."

"He said he had insomnia. I believed him at first, too." Madge laughed. "And he's such a bad liar, Maura, I was just fooling myself. He'd show up, order the same breakfast every night. Two eggs over medium, hash browns, sourdough toast. Then he'd be there to walk me back to my car. He said he wanted to make sure I was safe."

"George is awesome."

"He is. Do you know, the first time I ever saw him, I thought, 'I bet that man could kiss my socks off.'"

Maura put a hand over her mouth to cover the guffaw. "Yeah?"

Madge nodded. "Yes. Of course, I didn't do anything about it for a long time. Except one night at Jill's house, she was having a Christmas party. We were all a little toasted. And Keith, that was my first husband, he'd already gone home because he didn't like Jill's husband, because he'd once told Keith he needed to stop spending so much time with the ponies and more with his beautiful wife."

"Sounds like Jill's husband's a keeper, too."

"Oh yes," Madge said. "Definitely. He and George have been friends forever. And…quite honestly, I think Mark knew that George was interested in me. That's why he hung the mistletoe."

"That was your first kiss?" Maura leaned her chin in her hands to look at Madge. "Romantic!"

"Yes. The room was all lit up from the tree, which had this lovely star on top of it, all different colors in a disc that spun faster and faster the longer the light was on. It was the seventies, so you can imagine what it looked like."

Maura laughed, thinking of childhood Christmases. "Yes. Like a disco ball."

"Yes! Exactly. So we'd been topping off our eggnogs all night long, and George was looking so handsome. He wore a mustache back then. I can't believe I ever liked that, but you know, it was the style." Madge laughed, shaking her head. "Lord help us. Anyway, we were the only two in the room…though I'll tell you, Maura, there could've been a hundred people there, and me and George would still have been the only two in the room."

Maura knew how that felt. Not a disco ball Christmas tree star, but the swirling lasers and flashing strobes of a dance floor. Hundreds of people, and the only one she'd been able to see was Ian.

"Someone had put on that Kenny Rogers' album, the greatest hits one that so many people were listening to. And Jill told me there was something I needed to do for her in the living room. I didn't know Mark was telling George the same thing. We both ended up in the doorway at the same time, right there under the mistletoe." Madge paused. "On purpose for both of us, I'm sure, though I've never asked him."

"I'm sure." Maura swallowed against the tightness of more emotion. "And then what?"

"Oh. Well. I kissed him," Madge said matter-of-factly. "It was a terrible first kiss. A peck, really. But I'll never forget it. How the world sort of swam all around me. The smell of his cologne. The tickle of that awful mustache."

"It sounds lovely."

Madge gave Maura a knowing look. "It lasted a million years and only a second or two. Something tells me you know a little something about that."

"A little." Maura laughed.

"Lucky women do." Madge leaned forward a little. "But I guess that didn't answer your question, did it? About how many times someone can hurt you in the same way before you give up on them."

Maura hadn't forgotten.

"I broke off with George at least seven times before we got engaged. I was sure he wasn't the one for me. I was sure I was making a big mistake, that he was making a bigger one. And I wasn't nice about it, either," Madge said. "Once I told him I never wanted to see him again, that his face made me sick."

"Madge!"

"I did. I was lying, of course. I thought it was the only way to get rid of him. To hurt him so much he wouldn't want to come back. Of course it broke my heart. But I did it anyway."

Maura shook her head and toyed with the paperclip, working it free of the kinks and bends. "But he forgave you."

"Yes. You know what finally ended it? Well," Madge laughed. "It didn't end it, obviously. But it would've if I hadn't swallowed my pride and gone back to him."

"What?" Curious, Maura asked.

"I told him I loved him."

Maura's brows rose. "And that's what ended it?"

"Yes. We were arguing about something silly. It's always something silly, isn't it? But it doesn't matter, when you're so angry you'd rather spit than kiss him."

"I can't imagine you ever being that angry with George," Maura said.

"Believe me, it happens. George might be close to perfect, but he's still a man. And I'm a woman," Madge said. "Oil and water, men and women are. Lord knows why on earth we ever fit together the way we do, being so different. I was angry with him because he'd brought me flowers. Roses, as a matter of fact, my favorite. Long-stemmed red roses, a dozen. Plus a white one in the middle. It was the most beautiful bouquet of flowers I'd ever received, and I was angry with him because I'd told him we weren't going to celebrate Valentine's Day together. It was a day for lovers, that's what I'd said."

"And you weren't…?" Maura coughed delicately, insatiably curious but not wanting to get too personal.

Madge burst into gales of delighted laughter and clapped her hands together. "Oh! Oh, my. Yes, we were. Like bunnies! Constantly. Lord, lord, there were days I was sure I'd broken something. But I was trying to convince myself that all we had was just…" Madge lowered her voice. "…You know. Sex."

Maura nodded solemnly.

"That it wasn't love," Madge continued. "I didn't want to be in love with George. Not so soon after leaving Keith, anyway. I mean, I'd loved Keith, and that had been a mistake. What if I was making the same sort of mistake with George? And an even worse one, really, since Keith and I had never heated up the sheets the way George and I did."

"What did George think about it?"

"I didn't know, because I never asked. Now he'd tell you he was sure it was love from that first kiss. But he was just as nervous and scared as I was. He won't admit it, but he was. And I knew it then, which is why I threw those flowers in the trash, told him I loved him but I never wanted to see him again. I left him in front of the restaurant and walked away. I was sure that was it, that I'd just made the biggest mistake of my life, but you know what, sweetie? Walking away from him, I felt more relief than I had when I signed those final divorce papers. " Madge's eyes had welled with tears during this part of her story, and her voice trembled.

Maura, eyes stinging in sympathy, handed her a tissue. "God, Madge. Why?"

"Because I'd told him the truth, at least there

was that. And if the last words I ever said to him were "I love you, well…at least I'd said it. And meant it."

"If you loved him," Maura asked slowly, "why did you tell him you never wanted to see him again?"

"First of all, I was stupid." They both laughed. Madge wiped her eyes. "But also…I knew I needed some time to think and cool down. I'd told George I didn't want to celebrate Valentine's Day, and he'd brought me those flowers anyway. To me, that seemed a lot like what Keith had always done. That what George wanted was more important than what I did. Even if my reasons for it were stupid, I wanted to know that he'd listened to me. That what I thought and felt was important."

Maura nodded. "Yes. That makes sense."

"I was proud." Madge touched the tissue to her nose and sighed. "But walking away from him, I thought, 'well. At least it's over now. At least my heart can stop breaking over and over again.'"

"Oh, Madge." Maura had to take a tissue for herself at that. "What did you do? How could you stand it?"

"I didn't see him for two weeks. Every time the phone range, I prayed it was him even though I told myself I wouldn't talk to him if it were. It never was. And the days stretched on and on, and I knew I'd lost him for good. And I was miserable. Just miserable. So. One day I just put on my best dress and did my hair and makeup, and I went on over to his house with a bouquet of red roses, one white one in the middle. And I told myself I was only going to apologize for throwing the flowers away. I wasn't going to cry or beg for him to take me back or anything like that. I was going to say I was sorry, because flowers were very expensive, you know. George had spent a lot of money on them. He was always surprising me with little treats."

He still did, Maura knew that, because Madge often came in with a new pair of earrings or a bracelet, and her desk so often had fresh flowers on it that seeing it bare was unusual. George was the type of husband who showed up on a Friday afternoon with a packed bag for both of them and whisked Madge off to some fun-filled weekend as a surprise.

Ian had never bought her anything. For a long time, obviously, it was because it would've been difficult for her to explain away new jewelry or other lovers' gifts. Maura had never minded that he hadn't showered her with presents, not even when she'd made a special point of surprising him with packages on his birthday and holidays. She'd never bought him something out of obligation — it was always more because she'd been thinking of him when she saw a funny card or t-shirt, and picked it up with him in mind. It had always been because she was thinking of him all the time.

She looked at the flowers, now. The card, scrawled with her name in someone else's handwriting, not Ian's. Would she even know his handwriting, she thought suddenly, trying to remember if she'd ever seen it. He'd never sent her a card or a letter or a note. Maybe he had written this card, and she would never know.

"What did you do when he answered the door?" Maura asked with a dry tongue, forcing herself to pay attention to Madge's story and not the boring, silent tragedy of her own.

"I jumped into his arms and kissed him all over his face," Madge said. "And I took him into the bedroom and we didn't come out until the next day."

Maura laughed. "Hooray!"

"But we spent a lot of that time talking. About my fears. And his. We talked and talked and talked, oh, my goodness. We laughed. We cried. A few times we shouted at each other, and I thought about leaving again. But I didn't. We talked it through until we'd figured out what we both had been fighting all along. That we couldn't live without each other, and there was no better way to start our new lives than together. So. That was that. We went out the next day, when we finally couldn't survive a minute longer without coffee and eggs…George, being a bachelor, didn't have anything stocked in the kitchen, you see." Madge laughed again. "We staggered outside and had breakfast. Then he took me to the jeweler's and we picked out a ring. We were married two months later."

Maura let out a sigh so hard her shoulders lifted. "I can't believe you never told me that story before!"

Madge winked and got up from her chair. "I guess it never was the right time before."

"That would make a great romance novel." Maura threw her tissue in the trash but kept the straightened paper clip.

"The man who sent you that plant," Madge said, gesturing. "He's trying to apologize to you for something. Isn't he?"

"I don't know if it's an apology."

Madge paused in the doorway on her way out. "Maybe you should read the card. Find out."

When she'd gone, Maura pulled the card from the plastic holder stuck into the pot. The envelope wasn't sealed, and it opened with only the slightest press of her fingertips. She pulled the card from inside it — plain white, single-sided, with a beveled edge. Different handwriting from the outside, and she knew instinctively upon reading it that it was Ian's. It looked like him.

She pressed the card to her lips without reading it. Closed her eyes against the threat of spilling tears. She breathed and breathed again until she could be sure she wasn't going to dissolve. The card trembled in her shaking hands when she looked at it. One word.

Lunch?

She didn't need to look at the clock to know she'd already almost missed it, not to mention that she had a ton of work to get through today, and her chat with Madge had taken up so much of her time she'd be lucky to get out of here with even half the workload finished today. He hadn't mentioned a place or even a time.

She wasn't going to go. She'd asked him Saturday night, and he'd said no. Now he was asking her, and she was supposed to give in, because it was what Ian wanted? What about when it was something she wanted?

No.

Maura tossed the card into the trash can, along with her tear-damp tissues. The paperclip had become a thin straight strip of metal. She could bend and twist it, but it would never be a paper clip again.

Some things, she thought as she tossed the piece of metal into the trash, could never be put back the way they'd been before. No matter how much you wanted them to. No matter how hard you bent. Sometimes, you ruined things and couldn't fix them.

Nine

Of course she went to lunch. Late enough she could be half-sure she'd have missed him, late enough that if he'd stayed, that would mean something. Mean what, Maura refused to tell herself. When it came to Ian, so much could mean so little.

He hadn't said a time or place, but she'd assumed he meant the restaurant she'd asked him to. They'd been to this place dozens of times, never for the food but for the privacy. Dim lighting, secluded booths, a part of town neither of them normally frequented. It was a bad choice today, a reminder of secret meetings. Furtive kisses. He'd told her once that he loved her sitting in his car in the parking garage that she could see now from the restaurant's front door, where she was still hesitating about going inside.

Chin up, she thought. Chin. Fucking. Up.

Inside, she blinked and blinked to adjust to the dramatic change in light. The hostess, a perky blonde in a white shirt with a few too many open buttons, gave her a bright smile. Maura clutched her coat a little tighter around her throat, scanning the room.

"I'm meeting someone," she said before the woman could ask her. "He'll be seated in the back room."

The hostess stepped aside with a nod. Maura moved through the restaurant toward the back. There was a booth near the back they'd always preferred because it was set back into a small alcove hung with curtains that shielded most of the table from the rest of the room.

"Hi, Ian." Her relief at seeing him was enough to weaken her knees. She put a hand on the table to keep herself from crumpling or worse, hurtling herself across the table to get to his mouth.

If he'd looked smug, she told herself she'd have found the strength to turn around and walk out on him, but Ian looked as relieved as she felt. He stood to let her slide into the booth. For a moment, Maura thought he meant to kiss her. She moved past him, not giving him the chance.

"Did you eat?"

"No." He paused, gesturing at the array of glassware. "Drank a lot of iced tea. I was waiting for you."

"I'm not hungry," she told him. "It's almost three o'clock. I was sure you wouldn't be here."

"I was sure you weren't coming."

"How long were you going to wait?" The question slipped out before she could stop it.

Ian looked at the table for a few seconds before meeting her gaze. "I don't know. I'm glad I didn't leave, though."

"Me too." The truth was always so much easier than lies with him, even when she hated herself for giving him too much.

"Do you want something? Are you hungry?"

"No. I'll have coffee."

"Dessert?" Ian asked with a small smile. "Key lime cheesecake…?"

Maura raised a brow. "I'm not that easy."

"Yes, you are." Ian moved a little closer and lowered his voice. "You know you want it."

She shook her head. "Nope. Trying to cut back."

"Well, I'm going to have some. Key lime cheesecake and coffee. Two, please. Cream and sugar." He turned to her when the waiter left. "I'm glad you came."

Her heart skipped. "Are you?"

"Yes." He moved closer again so that his knee barely brushed hers. He reached for her hand. Their fingers linked.

Maura kept her hand very still, though the impulse to squeeze him tight was hard to resist. She wanted to rub her thumb along the back of his hand, to feel the familiar pattern of his tendons and veins. She wanted to press each of his fingers to her mouth.

They looked each other in silence for some long minutes, and again she kept herself from kissing him although the need for his mouth had become a hungry, desperate thing in the pit of her belly. Ian traced a figure-eight on the back of her hand, sending shudders all through her that she hid by straightening her spine.

He let go of her hand when the waiter brought the dessert. One plate. Two forks. He poured the coffee and left the sugar and cream, which Ian pushed toward her. Two creams. Three sugars. He didn't even have to ask how many she wanted.

"In the last days of my marriage," Maura said quietly, "I went with him to a diner so we could go over some final paperwork. Do you know, he had to ask me how I took my coffee? Ten years we'd been together, and he didn't know."

Ian said nothing.

"He didn't care enough to know, really. That's what it came down to." She emptied the cream into her coffee and stirred. Then the sugar. She sipped, relishing the warmth and the slowly spreading glow of caffeine.

After that, they talked. Not the easiest conversation they'd ever had. She gave everything she said a second thought before she spoke to be sure there could be no misconstrued innuendo. No accusations that she was trying to lead this in any sort of direction. She let him talk, and she gave answers. Sometimes, his knee bumped hers, but he didn't take her hand again.

"You want the last bite?"

She'd eaten only a single bite of the cheesecake, and shook her head. "No, thanks. You eat it."

She watched him lick the fork clean and had to look away. Fucking Ian. Fucking mouth.

The restaurant was filling with a dinner crowd. Ian paid the bill and stood. Helped her with her coat. In the restroom, Maura ran the cold water over her wrists until she could stop shaking. She gripped the sink and stared herself down in her reflection.

"This means nothing," she whispered so low the sound of rushing water covered up any sound, though she was alone in the ladies' room and it didn't matter. "This means nothing."

He waited for her by the hostess stand. He took her elbow as he pushed the door open for her. On the sidewalk outside, his hand went briefly to the small of her back.

"Where are you parked?" Ian asked.

"The garage." She pointed vaguely.

"Me too."

They walked together without discussing lunch. Or anything. They walked in silence along the sidewalk, past the coffee shop where once he'd made her laugh so hard she'd nearly choked on the whipped cream of her drink. Past the stationary store where she'd bought him a birthday card — a unicorn vomiting rainbows. Memories, memories, they threatened to choke her.

In the elevator, she stood to one side. Ian to the other. He pushed the button for four and looked at her. That was where she'd parked, of course. Fourth floor. Theirs.

The garage had emptied a bit since she'd parked there. She'd been distracted earlier and hadn't seen his car before, but now there was no missing it. "Oh, Betty," Maura said automatically. "Has she missed me?"

It was a joke, but didn't taste funny. Black Betty, like the song. Maura had always teased that the car was a BMW with the heart of a 1964 Mustang. That Ian should soup her up, take her to the races, instead of keeping her so pristine. Betty was a girl, like the car in that horror novel, Christine, but she approved of Maura.

So many little stories, Maura realized with another pang. So many jokes. She was walking toward Ian's car before she knew it. She ran a hand over the door handle and turned to him.

"Do you want me to get in?"

For the most fleeting of moments, she thought he was going to say yes. But then, "Nah. Better not."

Her fists clenched automatically; if he noticed, he didn't show it. Chin up, Maura, she reminded herself. She put her hands in her coat pockets. If it was this cold in September, she could only imagine what they were in for this winter.

"Thanks for coming to lunch with me," Ian said when she didn't speak again. "Even if you did get there late."

He was trying to tease, to keep this light and meaningless. Maura answered with a shrug, unwilling and frankly incapable of making any more jokes. She bit at the inside of her cheek to keep her expression as neutral as she could, but Ian wasn't fooled. He'd never been.

"C'mon now. Don't make the sad face." Maybe he'd like her angry face, better, but she couldn't quite manage that one. Ian rocked a little on the balls of his feet and cupped the back of neck for a moment before meeting her gaze. "Maura. Please, don't."

"Don't what?" She demanded at last. "What do you want from me, Ian?"

"I thought we could have a nice lunch. Just lunch, that's what you said."

"And that's all we had, didn't we?" She kept her back straight. Shoulders squared.

"Barely," Ian muttered. "You were so late."

She gaped at him for a few seconds before she managed to smooth her expression again. "You're lucky I showed up at all. But then, I remember when you told me you were lucky I ever gave you any time at all."

He remembered saying it. She saw it in his eyes, which narrowed. The hand on her shoulder, pushing her back against the car, surprised her into a gasp. His knee between her thighs, another. At the last minute she could've turned her head to avoid his kiss, but really, was there ever a chance she would do such a thing?

It was an angry, bruising kiss that left her with the taste of blood. Breathing hard, Ian broke it and pushed away from her. He wiped his mouth. And once again, he broke her heart.

When she moved past him, Ian grabbed the sleeve of her coat. Maura snatched it from his grip and turned on him. Whatever he saw in her face must've been intimidating enough to back him up a few steps until he was the one pressed against the car, though she didn't touch him. She looked him up and down, no longer trying to hide her feelings from betraying her all over her face.

"It happened right there. In your car." She pointed past him and was angry enough to get some cold satisfaction in the way he flinched a little, like maybe he thought she was going to hit him. "Remember that, Ian? If you don't, then let me tell you."

***

The night is hot enough that we're both sweating. Sticking to the leather. The radio's on low, and the air conditioning hasn't kicked on yet. We've just finished dinner. It's getting late, but I don't have to be home. Chad is on a business trip, so there's nobody there waiting for me, but Ian doesn't know that because I haven't told him.

I'm going to end this tonight, but Ian doesn't know that, either.

He tempted me into his car, or at least he thought he did. I wouldn't be here if I didn't want to be, no matter what he offered. This time it's an excuse to get out of the heat and still steal a few more minutes together with a little privacy, an excuse to continue for just a little longer with the flirting we'd been doing all through dinner.

Lingering glances. The brush of my foot along his calf. Sharing a dessert, eating from his fork. The touch to the corner of his mouth to catch a bit of whipped cream I sucked clean from my fingertip. Lover's gestures, each one of them the last I think we will ever have.

Ian fiddles with the CD player, and a familiar song comes on. I gave him this song to listen to, a long time ago. In the beginning, before things became more than they were supposed to. If I'd known then what I know now, I never would have added it to the CD, but at the time it was just a song I happened to like. Now the lyrics and meaning have become something of a touchstone between us, the words he sometimes whispers in the dark when it's easier for him to pretend it's not real.

I want to turn off the song, even though there

could be no more perfect soundtrack to the end of us. "I have to go."

"I know."

Neither of us moves at first, and then…mouths open. Tongues sliding. My hand anchors at the back of his neck. His finds my breast and cups it, thumbing the nipple through the thin material of my summer-weight dress.

I am kissing Ian. He is touching me. I'm the one who leaned toward him, one hand on the center console to support myself since there isn't enough room for me to slide onto his lap. That's where I want to be. On Ian's lap, straddling him, his belt and button and zipper undone. His cock in my fist, or better yet, inside me.

"I have to go," I whisper. "It's late."

"Not yet." It's exactly what I want him to say.

My kiss lingers, my mouth moving on his when I speak. "Just one more."

"Always." That little growl, the way he slips a hand between my legs, his fingers on my bare thighs…I'm undone.

I am always undone.

"I love your mouth." I nibble him. Suck and stroke and love him with my tongue and teeth and lips until we are both gasping for breath. I taste salt when I lick my lips, because even with the air conditioning on, the car is getting hot. "I love the way you taste. I love the way you touch me. I love you, Ian."

"I love you, too."

I sit back from him a little, stunned at what I've said. More stunned at how he's responded. I don't know what to do or what to say. I hadn't meant to tell him. I wasn't sure it was true.

"You don't have to say that." I'm hugging him awkwardly over the center console, my mouth near his ear. "Shhh, Ian. Don't."

He holds me. One hand in the center of my shoulder blades. My skin is bare there, too.

I am not crying. I am not crying. I am not crying.

"I am so lucky," Ian says as his fingertips stroke my skin. "So lucky that you ever bothered to give me any of your time at all."

And there it is. The perfect way for this to end. But it doesn't, because although I'd arranged to meet him tonight, fully prepared to tell him this had to be the last time, the very last time, I am unable to do it. Because I love him.

"Take me somewhere, Ian," I say into his ear. "Just take me somewhere."

And he does.

***

"Because," Maura told him, "for the thirty seconds it took for you to say it, I believed you meant it."

"Maybe you should've ended it then, if you wanted to so much." Ian was stung.

She could see it all over him, and it hurt her to know she was the cause, but not enough to keep her from saying, "I was going to. I thought it would be the right thing. The best thing. But when it came right down to it, I didn't want to. I still don't. I still think you are amazing and wonderful, and I still love you."

She waited for him to say something. Anything. To give her the tiniest crumb, and yes, fuck, she would take whatever scrap he tossed her because right now it was all she could do not to get on her knees right there in front of him.

"Ian…" Maura said, the dual syllables of his name breaking between them.

But Ian gave her nothing. Maura backed away from him. He took a step toward her, but no more than that.

"How many times do you let someone hurt you in the same way," she asked him, "before you become the asshole who keeps allowing it?"

"I don't want to keep hurting you."

"Well you are," Maura told him. "Over and over again, Ian, and I am the asshole who keeps letting you."

This time, when he reached for her, she let him pull her close. She fit so right against him. He kissed her hair.

"You're not an asshole."

"Then you are," Maura said in a low voice. "And I'm stupid."

Ian huffed a warm breath against her hair. "You're not stupid."

"Take me somewhere, Ian."

His entire body tensed against her when she asked. His fingers tangled, snagging, in her hair. "Maura…"

She pushed away from him. "Fine. Never mind. Forget I asked."

"I want to."

"I know you do," she said, "so why are you making this so fucking hard?"

"If I take you somewhere, I'm going to want to kiss you. And if I kiss you, I'm going to want to touch you. And if I touch you, I won't be able to stop. I'm addicted to you. I won't be able to quit." He said this without a trace of a smile, without reaching for her.

She twisted inside. "I fail to see the problem with this."

"I hated hearing about you and that guy."

She smiled, just a little. "Good. You're supposed to hate it. It's supposed to make you want to Hulksmash things. I want it to keep you awake at night, tossing and turning while you gnash your teeth and pound your pillows. I want the thought of me with someone else to drive you fucking insane."

Ian laughed and looked away from her. He covered his mouth with a hand and shook his head, but not like a denial. "It does."

"I want to be the last thought on your mind before you fall asleep." It was from that song, the one he'd stopped whispering to her. It was the truth. "But you know, Ian, right now all I can think is that you are my nicest thing. And I am your…nothing."

She turned her back and walked away, then thought better of it. One last thing to say, while she still had the chance. Their relationship had been made up of too many last times; here was one more and she'd be damned if she missed her chance to tell him how she felt.

"I was never addicted to you. Addiction is about being unable to choose, and you were always a choice for me." Maura paused, chin up, back straight. "Maybe you were a bad choice. But I've never regretted making it."

"Even now?" Ian asked.

"Even now." She turned again, hoping but not really expecting him to call out after her. Maybe to chase her. Take her in his arms and kiss her.

But of course, Ian let her walk away.

***

She didn't cry. Not on the drive home. Not when she got in the door. Not even when she stripped down and crawled into the shower, where she curled into a ball on the floor and stayed there until the water ran cold. It would've been better if she'd been able to sob and scream she thought as she got out, shivering, and dried her hair with a towel. But all she had was a sick and twisting emptiness in her gut and a throbbing ache in her chest.

In bed, she thumbed open her calendar to check her week's schedule. The number of dates was too daunting to think about just now, especially without her spreadsheet to categorize them neatly. On her phone it was simply name/location/time, name/location/time until she had to close out of the calendar before she started to have a panic attack. She had something schedule every day, sometimes more than one. How long could she keep doing this?

Maura closed her eyes, willing herself to let go. Let go. Let him go, she told herself fiercely, hating herself for holding on so tightly to what no longer served her. Ian does not love you.

Not enough.

Her phone vibrated with a message, the notification a small red one like a single devil's horn. She almost didn't bother to check it. If it was from Ian, let him wait on her for once. Let him wonder if she was going to answer. But, just as there was really no way she'd have been able to deny him his kiss in the parking garage, it was unrealistic of her to expect herself not to read his text.

It wasn't from Ian. It was from Daniel. Maura stared at it for a long moment, trying to figure out if she were disappointed or relieved.

Hey. I was wondering if you'd like to get together for dinner and a movie sometime this week. I'd love to see you again before I leave. Give me a call.

Maura looked at the clock. Though the day had seemed to last forever, her late lunch and the argument after with Ian lasting a million years, it wasn't even nine pm. Still early enough to call someone, especially if he'd asked her to. She dialed.

"Daniel," Maura said. "Hi. I'd love to go to dinner with you."

Ten

I haven't been this nervous about a date in a long time. Heath's profile on Luvfinder was totally intimidating. First of all, he's gorgeous. Six foot three, black hair, brown eyes. Tall, dark and handsome epitomized. Second, he's a plastic surgeon who spends his free time climbing mountains and running marathons, when he isn't volunteering in homeless shelters and providing free facial reconstructions to children born with cleft palates.

He's pretty close to perfect.

What would a man like that see in me? I check my reflection again and again, wondering what it was about my profile picture, my carefully chosen questionnaire answers, that prompted him to make a connection with me. I turn my head from side to side, sucking in my cheeks to give my face the appearance of cheekbones. It's the most effort I've put into any of these dates so far, and it's not Heath who prompted it as much as my renewed desire to simply…I don't know. Make a fucking effort. Give all of this a real chance. So, I've plucked and powdered and primped, even going for a spa manicure and pedicure. My brows are freshly waxed, and so is everything else.

Everything.

I'm not used to be being bare there. Sure, I groom regularly, but for my own satisfaction, not some media-fueled idea of what women should do with their pubic hair. I'm not sure I like the sensation of my silk panties rubbing me so intimately. Everything feels so much more sensitive that, two days after I had it done, I still find myself shifting my thighs together when I walk.

Looking in the mirror, I cup myself. The pressure of the heel of my hand against my clit shouldn't make me squirm, but it does. I press a little harder. Giving in to temptation, I slip my fingers into the front of my panties and rub, rub, rub. I've mesmerized myself, watching, and the pleasure mounts until I'm so quickly on the edge I'm going to surprise myself into orgasm...except that my phone trills from my dresser, and I pull my hand out of my panties with a guilty furtive look as though whoever's calling me could possibly have seen what I was doing.

"Hello?" I sound breathless. Guilty.

"Hi," Ian says. "What are you doing?"

I look at my flushed cheeks and my nipples peeking through the lace of my bra. They've gone instantly tight at the sound of his voice. "I'm getting ready to go out. On a date. We're going to that new Asian fusion place for dinner, and then to the hookah lounge next door."

He knows exactly where I mean, because he's talked about taking me there. Leather chairs, dark corners, a bar. Once he told me how he'd fantasized about using his hand to get me off on the leather couch tucked away in a shadowy alcove, the two of us in a room full of haze.

"Oh," Ian says. "I guess I'd better let you get to it."

"No, it's okay," I tell him breezily. "I'm still getting ready. I have time to talk."

"I don't want to interrupt —"

I laugh like he's Shelly. No, more like he's a casual acquaintance I barely see, not Ian, my sometime lover. Not the man I'm so desperately in love with it hurts to even think about. "Don't be silly. I can get dressed while I talk to you."

"You're not dressed?" There's a perk of interest in his voice I find utterly arousing and also infuriating.

"Not quite." I smile at my reflection, imagining his face. "Just panties and a bra."

"...Oh." Ian clears his throat. "Wow."

My voice dips low. Husky. I run a finger along my collarbone and in the valley between my breasts. "Yep."

"What color?"

"Emerald green satin with black lace." He's seen me in this bra and panty set. Once he told me it was what he imagined me in when he stroked himself in the shower. Even if I hadn't been wearing it, I'd have said I was.

Ian mutters something that sounds like a very soft and concerned, "fuck."

"What're you up to?" I ask, like I care about anything but getting him to think about what he'd like to do to me.

"Umm...I was...well, I was just catching up on some old episodes of..." Ian coughs. "Nothing much, really."

"Not busy tonight?"

"Not really."

I give an exaggerated sigh and put oodles of oozing, cooing charm into my tone. "No big plans?

Just hanging out by yourself, all alone?"

"Yes." Ian's tone is clipped. I'm pissing him off or turning him on, I can't be sure which.

"Well," I breathe, sexier than Marilyn Monroe ever was singing Happy Birthday, Mr. President. "Have fun with that."

Then I disconnect. I have to grip my phone extra-tight in my shaking hand, my palms suddenly sweaty. The pale skin of my chest and throat have gone crimson, but I breathe and breathe until the color fades.

Dinner is amazing. Heath is the perfect date, pulling out my chair, consulting me about my choice of wine. He looks into my eyes during our conversation, which he effortlessly leads in a number of different but intellectually stimulating directions without ever once making me feel like I didn't know what I was talking about.

He is so fucking pretty I can hardly stand it. I've never seen such perfect eyebrows on a man. I want to trace them. Thick but groomed, arched just right over those thick black lashes framing deep brown eyes in which I want to drown. His mouth is made for kissing. No.

His mouth is made for my cunt.

So far, Heath has made no moves toward anything but dinner and the cigar lounge after. He asks me, sounding slightly anxious, if I'm sure I want to go there. He doesn't want to make me do anything I don't want to do.

"I've heard a lot of really cool things about it, that's all."

He's so tall I have to crane my neck to look up

at him. "No, I've always wanted to try it out. It will be fun."

Nodding, Heath reaches for my hand to hold as we cross the alley between the restaurant and the hookah lounge. It feels funny, holding his hand, even so briefly. It's so much bigger than mine. I'm suddenly overcome with an image of him on top of me. Inside me. He would engulf me, and thinking of it, I shiver. Turned on and a little put off at the same time.

"Have you read 1984?" I ask suddenly as he holds the door open for me.

"Huh? Umm, no. I don't have a lot of time to read." Heath waits until I go into the lounge, then follows so close on my heels he gives me a flat. "Oh. Sorry."

It's awkward to hop a little while I fix the back of my shoe, so I grab his sleeve for balance. His other hand covers mine, helping me, and when I look up at him from this silly, bent-over position, I mean to laugh at how funny I must look. His stare stops me. His dark eyes are alight, that mouth slightly open. I catch the flash of his tongue, darting out to taste the center of his bottom lip, before I straighten.

"No problem," I tell him. He hasn't let go of my hand on his sleeve, and this is more awkward then my little "fixing my shoe" dance.

"Two?" The hostess wears a lot of dark eyeliner and pale lipstick. She leads us to one of the tables near the back.

I see the leather couch in the alcove Ian coveted. It's occupied. A man and a woman sit close together, sharing a hookah pipe. His hand casually imprisons her knee against his, and the way she leans toward him tells me she doesn't mind. Not at all. Again, I am aware of how bare my cunt feels, how the press of satin and lace on my sensitive flesh has been teasing me unexpectedly for the past few days. As I watch, the couple kisses. His fingers press a little higher on her thigh.

I want that to be me.

"Hmm?" Heath has said something while I was distracted.

"I asked if you read a lot." He pulls the menu of different flavored tobaccos toward him.

I sneak another glance at the couple on the leather couch. She passes the pipe to him so he can draw in a long pull of smoke. It curls from his nostrils a few seconds after that, and she tips her head back in laughter. From this angle, the table in front of them shields his hand. I wonder if he's moved it higher.

"Oh." I pull my attention back to my date, who's looking at me curiously. "Yes. I do. Not as much as I used to, sadly. But I love to read. You don't?"

"It's not that I don't like it," Heath tells me. It's obvious, though, that he doesn't like it. "I'm just too busy, I guess. Always something else to do."

From what he's told me about his schedule, I'm not surprised. "Well. You always find time for things you enjoy, and reasons to put off the things you don't."

Heath gives me a funny look and says again, "It's not that I don't like it."

"No worries," I tell him. "I frankly can't quite wrap my head around the idea of strapping myself to a harness and dangling hundreds of feet over an abyss. But the good news is, the world's a huge place with lots of things in it to love, and we don't all have to enjoy the same ones."

For the first time tonight, tension sprouts between us. Heath orders an apple-flavored tobacco without asking me what I'd like. I don't care, really. Never having been here before, I have no preference. But I notice how he looks at me from the corners of his eye and how his mouth works, as though he wants to say something to me but hasn't decided what.

On the leather couch, the couple is kissing.

I close my eyes for a second longer than a blink. My clit pulses against the insistent press of my panties; crossing my legs is a sweet torture I'm not ready to end. When I open my eyes, Heath is looking at me intently.

"Why did you ask me if I read that book? Which one?"

Over his shoulder, I can still see the kissing couple. His hand is definitely moving, his shoulder lifting and falling so slowly it would be impossible to tell if I weren't looking for it. I force myself to look at Heath. "1984?"

"Yeah. I think I read it in high school."

"You probably did. It's a good book." I wish desperately for something to drink. My mouth has gone too dry.

"So…why did you ask me if I'd read it, just out of the blue like that?"

He sounds way more concerned about it than is necessary, so I smile to ease this growing weirdness. "It was a throwaway comment, that's all. Something made me think of it, that's all."

The server brings the tobacco and sets up the hookah for us. Unlike the couple on the couch, Heath and I each have our own hoses, tipped with disposable plastic tips, to use for the smoke. He grins at me.

"Ready?"

"Sure." I bend forward and draw the smoke into my mouth, letting it seep through my nose and settle in my lungs for a few seconds before I blow it out.

"You've done this before?" He looks surprised. "I thought you said you'd never been here."

"I haven't. My..." I hesitate, not sure what to name Ian. Ex-boyfriend? Ex-lover? He was barely either of those long enough to be called an ex anything. "A friend of mine wanted to bring me here, but we never managed to find the time."

"Oh. Good." Heath draws in smoke, but coughs it out in a second or so. He waves a hand in front of his face, eyes red-rimmed. He laughs, though, not embarrassed.

The momentary strangeness that had threatened to turn this date from great to terrible has eased. Heath again leads the conversation the way he had at dinner, but I'm quieter now. Not as much to say. The hookah smoke is making my head spin a little, or maybe it's the couple on the couch. I'm convinced he's got his fingers inside her by the way she wiggles and sighs, the way she looks at his face.

"...So we should definitely do that," Heath is saying.

Once again he's caught me not paying attention. I don't want to seem insufferably rude, so I nod. He tilts his head a little, studying me. Those perfect brows knit for a moment.

"Were you listening to me?"

"I'm sorry, I didn't catch what you said. It's so loud in here." I wave a hand through the haze hanging between us and give him a smile he hopes thinks is sincere.

Heath leans back in his chair. "I said, we should get together again next week. Maybe check out a movie? The new Quentin Tarantino looks good."

Frankly, I'd rather poke out both eyes with plastic picnic spoons than see a Quentin Tarantino movie, but when he stretches to grab the menu again, my gaze is snared by the sight of his forearms below the rolled-up sleeves of his dress shirt. Maybe I could suffer through it for a chance to get my hands on those forearms, because sweet mother of mercy, it's like they came from a catalog of all things that get Maura hot and bothered. I want to bite the tendons in his wrists.

Heath notices me staring and gives me another of those curious but somehow inscrutable looks. "You wanna get out of here?"

"Yes." I do. Never mind the slightly off vibe. The man in front of me is everything any woman should ever want, and that's why I'm going on all these dates, isn't it? To find myself someone I want more than Ian? As I stand from my chair, the floor tips a little under my feet, and I laugh. "Whoa."

"Hookah smoke isn't supposed to make you high." Heath says this with a twist of his mouth and a sideways glance down at me. "It's not like pot."

I laugh a little as I turn so he can help me with my coat. "I've never smoked pot."

"Good." He smooths the fabric of my coat over my shoulders and down my sleeves. He's standing very close behind me, and for a moment his hands circle both my wrists. I note again the size of them — he easily holds me still even with the bulk of my sleeves.

We don't move for what seems like far too long for propriety, Heath aligned along my back and holding me still. My heart thumps a little harder…is he…smelling me? I hear the intake of breath. I watch the couple on the couch, the man with heavy lidded eyes, his partner staring seriously into them. She's going to come. I'm sure of it. He's going to make her come, right there on the leather couch, and I'm the only one watching.

Involuntarily, I tense internal muscles. I can actually bring myself to climax without touching myself by doing this — a trick I learned in long, boring sociology classes with a super hot professor. It would take more effort and time than I have right now, standing here with Heath at last stepping away from me. But the sensation is there just the same, weakening my knees so that when I turn to face him, I reach for his arm to keep myself from stumbling.

"Steady," he says. "I got you."

In the parking lot, he walks me to my car while

we talk about where we're going next. I have no suggestions. My head is filled with images of the couple on the couch and how she must've felt with his fingers easing her toward climax. All the colors seem bright. The air too cold on my hot cheeks.

Ian said he'd kiss me there. Ian told me he would take me on that couch and make me come. Ian, Ian, Ian…

"You're not listening to a word I'm saying, are you?"

I pull myself from my reverie and give Heath an apologetic look. "I'm sorry."

"You know, Maura, I picked you because I thought we'd be compatible. I liked your answers. I liked the way you look. You're very pretty." Heath shakes his head, then looks me up and down. "But you already know that. Don't you?"

I'm not sure how to answer this. I've been told I'm pretty, but there've been plenty of times I've been shown up as plain, too. "Pretty's relative, I guess."

"Not beautiful," Heath continues, as though I haven't spoken. "Your eyes are too wide for that. Your jaw's too square, and your mouth isn't quite full enough."

I'm not sure what to say about this dissection. It's honest and accurate, and it's not necessarily cruel. Before I can say anything, not that I'm sure what to say, Heath smiles and turns to look at my backside.

"But your ass…your ass, Maura, is perfection."

I can't help laughing at that. "Thanks? I didn't have any pictures of my ass in my profile. Thank goodness it's not a disappointment."

"No. Your manners, on the other hand. They're a disappointment."

He's serious. Both my brows go up, and I try to take an automatic step back, but Heath snakes out one long arm to keep from moving. By the rules of polite society, I'm expecting an apology, but that's not at all where he's going with this.

"You're off in your own little world, aren't you?" He tugs me closer, one step. Another.

We are in a public parking lot, and I'm not afraid of him, but I'm wary. "Yeah, I guess…"

"You're with me. I'd like it if you're focused on me."

"I'm sorry," I say stiffly.

Heath leans so close to me his whisper easily carries to my ear. "You were watching that couple on the couch, weren't you."

"Yes." I turn my head a little, and Heath's breath gusts over my neck. My heart's pounding again.

"That was hot. Him getting her off like that. Oh, I saw it. You liked that?"

I push away from him to look into his face. This evening has gone from pleasant to awkward and back again, and now I'm not really sure what the fuck is going on. I don't feel menaced, but my body tenses anyway. "Yes. I liked it. Did you?"

My question seems to take him by surprise, because first his eyes go wide. Then narrow. His smile twists. "No. Because it meant you were distracted from our date. I find that unquestionably rude. In fact, if you were my girl, do you want to know what I'd have to do about it?"

"What?" I spit the word like a challenge.

I could resist when he turns me, firmly but gently toward the car. I could fight, kick, scream or push him away. But again, I don't feel menaced or afraid. I'm not quite sure I feel turned on, but it's a possibility. My hands go automatically in front of me on the hood of the car, like I'm being frisked by the police.

Heath presses himself to my back and says into my ear, "yeah, like that. I knew you had it in you to be a good girl."

"You did?" I hold back hitching laughter I'm sure he would take the wrong way. "I thought you just said I was insufferably rude. But with a great ass."

His hand palms it. "You have a perfect ass…for spanking."

There I am in the parking lot, bent over the hood of a car but not so obviously that anyone is going to come running unless I start to scream, with a man rubbing my butt. This could go a hundred different ways, more than one of them scenarios I'm sure I've seen in porn. I look at him over my shoulder.

"Would you like that?" Heath asks me.

I only have one answer for that, and I give it with a grin. "I guess I don't know until I've tried it."

***

At two in the morning, I should be scared by a shadowy form waiting for me on my front porch, but I know who it is. In stygian darkness, I would know that shape. Ignoring him, I push past and into my living room but leave the front door open behind me.

Ian closes it after himself. Locks it. He must be planning on staying awhile.

I take off my coat and hang it carefully in the close. I slip off my shoes and, letting them dangle from my fingertips, climb my front stairs without a word to him. Without looking back. In my bedroom, I loosen the first few buttons of my blouse before Ian appears in the doorway. Only then do I turn.

"Did you fuck him?" Ian asks.

I'd guessed it was what he'd want to know, but I hadn't expected my soft-spoken Ian, my gentle-demeanored Ian, to be so vociferous in his questions. Facing him, I put my fingers to another button and slip it free. I watch his eyes go there. Watch his tongue press his lower lip as he bites down.

I shrug out of my blouse and toss it to the floor. Then I ease my skirt over my hips and down my thighs. I let it fall, stepping out of it. I stand in front of him in the emerald green satin and black lace bra and panties I'd so cleverly described to him earlier.

Ian is on me before I can move away, not that I've even tried. His mouth skates along my throat as he breathes me in. "I can smell him on you."

My head falls back. I make no protest when he

shakes me a little. My smile makes him angry, and I don't care.

"Answer me, Maura. Did you fuck him?" Ian puts a hand between my legs. He finds my panties. Beneath, my bare cunt. His brow knits, his pupils wide and dark. His thumb strokes me. "Oh. Shit. When did you do this?"

"Few days ago." I'm not drunk, but my words slur a little. I am woozy from his touch. "You like it?"

Ian pushes me a step or two toward the bed, then onto it. He pulls my panties down. He stares between my legs and runs his hands up my thighs. His thumb finds my clit; my head falls back as I sigh. When I look at him, he still looks angry.

"You did this for him?"

"I did this," I say on a little gasp as his thumb circles my clit the tiniest bit faster, "for myself."

"Answer me."

I push his hand from me and sit up. Now I'm at the perfect height for my mouth to get at his cock, but I stare up at his face, instead. "What do you want the answer to be?"

"Damn it, Maura!"

"You want it to be no," I say in a slow, thick voice. "But you told me to go out and find someone else, Ian. So maybe, I don't know. Maybe you want it to be yes."

He moves away from me to pace. I push up on my elbows to watch him. He is angry. So am I. I'm also incredibly, indescribably turned on.

"He wanted to spank me," I say as I get up. I turn, watching Ian over my shoulder as I bend over and put my hands on the bed. Legs spread. "Like this."

Ian makes a low, grinding noise from low in his throat.

I rock my ass a little and lean a little closer to the bed. Eyes closed. I wait for him to touch me, and I don't have to wait long. He's there in a moment, one hand sliding over my ass and then between my legs to stroke along my already slick cunt. The other grips my hip.

Ian has never spanked me. Never tied me up or blindfolded me. He's never asked, I never offered. We've shared fantasies, but this was never one of them. Yet here, naked but for my bra, bent over the bed, all I can think about is how sweet the sting would be if he slapped my ass. Hard.

Ian rubs my ass cheek with the flat of his hand while the other works my clit. It feels so good I push back against him. He stops.

"Do you want me to spank you, Maura?" He says this so low I almost don't hear him. "Is that what you want?"

"I want whatever you want to give me, Ian."

He doesn't hit me hard at all, but it still stings. I don't yelp. I moan. I bury my face in the bed, my fingers clutching the bedspread into wrinkles.

"You want me to hurt you?" Ian rubs the flat of his hand over the heat his slap left behind. "Is that what you want?"

It's not about that, but I'm not sure he'd understand. "I just want you to…own me."

I think he will spank me again, but instead Ian pulls me upright. He spins me to face him, his hand between my legs. "Did you let him spank you?"

My voice catches as he finds my clit. "...No, Ian. I didn't let him."

"Did you fuck him?"

"No, Ian."

"Why not?"

"Because he wasn't you."

His kiss is too soft. Too tender. I want it to bruise and sting and hurt; I want the taste of blood. Ian slides his hand into my hair and yanks my head back, exposing my throat to him. He bites me there, at last giving me the pain I so unexpectedly crave.

"Did you kiss him?" Ian asks against my skin.

"No. Not even that."

He lets out a shuddering sigh. His fingers ease inside me. His thumb presses my clit.

I have been on edge for most of the day, and this is Ian. My Ian. I'm coming before he fucks into me more than four or five times. Shaking, I dig my fingers into his shoulder as the pleasure surges through me. My orgasm is sharp and hard and fierce, the sting of it sweeter than the slap had been.

He kisses me again, not hard. His tongue strokes mine. He holds me while the aftershocks shake me, until I'm finally still. Then he takes my hand and puts it to the bulge in his crotch. He moves it along the ridge of his erection, and I discover I'm far from finished.

I work open his belt, his zipper. Our mouths fused, I get Ian's cock from his pants. I break the kiss with a small gasp at the heat of him in my hand.

Somehow, we are on the chair next to my bed.

Ian's so deep inside me it hurts. My knees press his sides. His hands cup my ass. Mine are on his face. We are not kissing, but our mouths are so close we might as well be. We breathe together. In and out. We move, slowly at first. Then fast and faster, each thrust inside me bringing me closer to another climax. We finish together, and I'm not at all ashamed that the noise I make at the end is exactly the sound of his name.

"Stay," I say against his mouth as he throbs inside me. "Please, Ian. Stay with me."

Eleven

The park was a beautiful place to be in mid-October. A little chilly, but the changing leaves had not yet started to fall and the trees were full of red and orange and gold. Ian shifted on the bench, a paper cup of coffee in his hand. He hadn't lifted it to his mouth once, not in all the time she'd been talking.

"Too bad that's not how it happened," Ian said.

Maura smiled, then shrugged. "A girl can dream, can't she?"

"The first part of it. That was true."

It was. He had called her while she got ready for her date. She had been wearing the panties and bra she had described. She had gone on a date with the perfect plastic surgeon, and they had ended up at the hookah bar.

At last, Ian sipped his coffee. It had to be cold by now. He'd barely taken a drink all the time she'd been talking. "The rest of it, though. When does it become fiction?"

"When do you want it to?"

"I know I wasn't waiting for you when you got home," he said.

"So. Back it up. Do you want the rest of it to be fake, too?" Maura had her own coffee, but hers was almost gone. She'd needed the caffeine and sugar to get her going, though once the story began she'd found it surprisingly easy to tell him.

On the park bench, they had to sit side-by-side, but both of them were turned in toward each other.

Knees barely touching. Ian had a bad habit of bouncing his knee, and now Maura reached across and put her hand on top of it to stop him from jostling. Ian shrugged.

He'd agreed to meet her here today. At least there was that. It was better, seeing him in person, than it could ever be on the phone or video chat. She kept herself from leaning in to smell him only because she did have a tiny shred of pride.

"Do you want to ask me if I fucked him?"

Ian shifted at that. His coffee sloshed from the small hole in the lid of his cup, spilling over his hand and onto his khaki pants. "No. I don't want to know. It's not any of my business."

"No, not really. But I'll tell you —"

"I said I don't want to know!" Ian got up and stalked to the trash can, where he threw his cup so vehemently it was like it had done him wrong.

"That was the deal, Ian!" Maura called after him.

He turned, brows knitted, and came back to the bench to stand over her. "All I ever said was that I thought you needed to see other people, spend some time making sure you knew for sure what you wanted…"

Maura stood. Ian didn't move back, so they were toe-to-toe. "And I told you that you were going to have to listen to me talk about it until you couldn't stand it any more. One way or another."

Her heart pounded at the way she pushed him. He could walk away from her, forever. He could have decided he was done with this, with her, with everything. And then what would she do?

Learn to live without him, Maura thought as she watched his expression twist. What other choice would she have?

He stared at her without saying anything for as long as it took her to count to fifteen in her head. Kiss me, she thought, but Ian didn't. Touch me. But he didn't do that, either.

Instead, he took her hand and pressed it between them, inside his long trench coat, to the bulge in his pants. He rubbed her hand slowly along him, staring into her eyes without looking away. Then he curled her fingers gently around him and held her hand still. That was all it took to send her heart thumping in her throat. To weaken her knees, make her clit pulse.

"Ian," she murmured when he didn't say anything, "I didn't fuck him. I didn't even kiss him. The stuff about spanking…all made up."

That's when he let her go, and stepped away. "But you did with that other guy."

Her mouth opened and closed a couple times before she could find words. "Yes. I did."

"Are you going to see him again?"

"Heath?"

"Him. And the other guy. The one you used to fuck in college." Ian's face held no expression, and his voice was cold.

Maura lifted her chin. "Heath, probably not, though if he asks me, I might go. Daniel? Yes. Definitely. Friday night, as a matter of fact. We're going to dinner."

Ian took a few more steps backward and put his hands in his pockets. The hem of his coat flapped a little in the suddenly chilly breeze that also pushed his hair over his forehead. "Have fun."

"All you have to say is 'don't,'" Maura told him, but Ian shook his head and walked away.

***

Maura's phone pinged with a text she didn't bother to check for some thirty minutes or so — busy with work and not expecting anything important, she registered the message when it came in but promptly forgot to check it when her boss peeked around the edge of her cubicle with a new folder of work for her go through. Thirty long minutes before she saw the message was from Ian and her heart leaped. Thirty minutes, she thought, in which maybe he'd been waiting on pins and needles for her to reply.

It was a photo, taken with one of those phone apps that add effects and filters to turn any mundane snapshot into brilliance. Ian had always been derisive of those pictures and the online services that showcased them, yet here it was, a squared picture of an artificially bright landscape. A tree, bare of leaves but for one still stubbornly clinging to the dark branch. The grass below it, very green. The tree itself black. The leaf, a gorgeous, glowing red.

The text below the photo said, "thought of you."

Damn him for making her want to cry at work. Damn him for taking this beautiful picture — and despite the pretentious use of filters and effects, the shot was beautiful. It was art. Ian had made her something beautiful and sent it to her, and Maura actually clutched her phone to her chest for a moment before heading down the hall and out the back door to the smoking area so she could have some privacy to talk to him.

"I love it," she said without preamble when he answered her. "But it surprised me. Why did you send it?"

"I told you. I saw it and thought of you."

She paused, scuffing her toe along the concrete while she thought of what to say. "Why?"

"The one leaf. It won't let go of the tree, no matter how hard the wind blows."

She closed her eyes against the spark of tears. "Oh."

"Eventually, though, it will have to give up. Fall down." Ian's voice got a little rough. "Eventually, the leaf will let go. When it starts to snow, it won't have a chance."

"Maybe," Maura said, "we'll have a mild winter."

They shared the silence for a minute or so. The sound of his breathing comforted her. The fact he was there, real and alive somewhere out in the world, even if it could not be beside her…well. It had to be enough, didn't it? And if it wasn't, she would have to find a way to make it be.

"Will you…have dinner with me?" Ian asked. "At my house? Tonight? Forget it. You probably have a date already —"

"I do. Two, actually."

He paused before answering. "How do you have two dates in one night?"

"I have a spreadsheet," she told him, and burst into semi-hysterical, on-the-verge-of-tears laughter. She pressed a hand to her mouth and looked around to make sure she was alone, but there weren't many smokers left in the office.

"Can you squeeze me in?" Ian laughed, too.

It was so good to laugh with him. "I miss you so much," she said impulsively.

"I miss you, too."

"I will have dinner with you," she told him. "Absolutely."

***

What do you wear to dinner with a not-quite-former lover? Should she dress for seduction or comfort? It all came down to the shoes. She could wear the six-inch, black patent leather ankle breakers, or she could go with the low-top Converse embroidered with skulls.

Comfort won. At this point, if she wasn't able to seduce him wearing jeans and a concert t-shirt, no amount of heavy duty feminine artillery would matter. Besides, she had a tiny shred of pride. She didn't want it to look like she was trying too hard.

So. The jeans that made her ass look magnificent, a form-fitting concert tee that showed off her tits and whittled away her sides to emphasize her hips. Sneakers. Hair pulled on top of her head in a messy twist designed to look as though she'd barely bothered with it, but more importantly, to show off the line of her neck and collarbones exposed by the t-shirt's neckline, because Ian loved her neck.

She wasn't totally giving up on the idea of seducing him.

She brought wine, too. The kind he liked. Earthy and rich and red, too heavy for her. She'd also picked up dessert, chocolate-peanut butter cake with an inch of thick fudge frosting. Cake like that was almost as good as sex, so...just in case.

She'd been to Ian's house a few times, but it felt so different to park in the driveway and walk to the front door as though she had nothing to worry about. Cake in one hand, wine in the other, she used her elbow to push the doorbell and willed her hands to stop shaking. She couldn't do anything about her insides twisting up like pantyhose in a washing machine, but she put a smile on her face and lifted her chin.

Deep breath.

He opened the door for her, a kitchen towel slung over his shoulder. Fuck her life, he looked better than any chocolate cake ever could. He wore khaki pants and a pink dress shirt, open at the throat and rolled up to show off his forearms. He knew what he was doing all right, and they shared a look as she crossed the threshold.

"I like your shirt," Maura said. She'd bought it for him, dared him to wear it. She'd told him only men totally confident in their masculinity could get away with wearing pink.

He smiled. "Thanks."

"Wow, something smells amazing." She handed him the bottle of wine as she followed him into the kitchen, where she put the cake on the center island. She took another deep breath, this one not to center herself but to enjoy the delicious odor. "What are you making?"

"Beef bourguignon." Ian pointed to the crockpot on the counter. "I had a recipe."

She'd bought him the crockpot, too, certain he'd never use it though he complained often about having to decide what to make for dinner. The fact he was using it now, just like he was wearing the shirt she'd bought him, could mean something. Or nothing. Or everything.

"Yum," was all she said. "What can I do to help?"

They'd never shared any sort of domesticity, but they worked together easily. Setting the table, checking on the boiling egg noodles, pouring the wine. Once, moving from the fridge to the table, they almost collided. Ian stopped her with a hand on her upper arm before they could hit, and they stood face-to-face for a few seconds longer than necessary. She thought then he might kiss her, but he didn't.

"Careful," Ian murmured.

She wanted to eat. Had been starving, as a matter of fact, but now could only push the succulent chunks of beef around in the gravy and nibble gingerly at the noodles. It meant the wine went to her head sooner than usual, so she could blame that for the slightly woozy way she walked after dinner when Ian told her to leave the dishes and follow him to the den. She'd been in that room before. On the couch, she remembered that, though nothing else about the room.

Maura looked around as though seeing it for the first time, then at him with a laugh. "None of this looks familiar."

"No?" Ian looked around, then back at her. "Do you want some more wine or anything?"

He had to remember the only other time they'd been in this room. Hands roaming, mouths kissing, the soft gasp of his name when he entered her. It had been dark, the only light coming from the hallway outside. It had been the night she ran here, desperate to get away from a house where even breathing had become too oppressive. At the time she'd worried that she tasted of sweat, but it hadn't much mattered.

They'd fucked on that couch and when it was over, she'd told him she loved him. Ian had not said it in return. He'd given her a ride home though, dropping her off a couple blocks away. The silence in the car had been thick and uncomfortable, and they hadn't kissed goodbye. That had been the last time she'd seen him before her divorce and the long, silent months during it.

His silence in the face of her declaration of love had been the reason she'd gone ahead with the divorce. Because she'd realized in that moment that it didn't matter if Ian loved her or not. She didn't want to be with anyone else. Didn't want to love somebody else. If she couldn't be with him, she didn't want to suffer being with anyone.

"No, I'm good. Thanks." Maura sat on the end of the couch.

Ian sat on the loveseat, so far from her it might as well have been on the other side of the world. "You sure? Water? Anything?"

"If I drink anything else, I'm going to float away." Maura shifted to the edge of the cushion, more uneasy now than she'd been before ringing the doorbell.

"So," Ian said. Then nothing.

Maura tensed. "So."

"I have to talk to you."

"I guessed that much," she said. "Do I want to hear what you have to say?"

Ian wouldn't look at her. Everything about his body language screamed denial and distance, which was answer enough. Maura stood on shaky legs, her stomach churning, throat dry. He was going to tell her he'd had enough. He'd found someone new, or maybe worse than that, simply that he no longer wanted her.

"No," she said when he didn't answer her right away. "I guess I probably don't. Thanks for dinner, Ian, but I'll show myself out."

She was already in the doorway before he managed to catch her by saying her name. She stopped but didn't turn, one hand on the doorframe to keep herself steady. Everything had gone the opposite of woozy, everything had gone completely crystalline. She wouldn't even have the benefit of hazy recollection, later. She'd be able to remember every single second.

"Maura," Ian said again. "Wait."

Still, she didn't turn. She owed it to him to listen, she supposed, but how could she look at him while he broke her heart again? Her fingers gripped the wood, and she took a deep breath. She was the asshole, here. She was the one who kept running after the football, only for him to pull it away at the last minute.

"I love you," Ian said.

A single sob burst out of her before she bit it back. And still, she couldn't face him. Could not look at his face. Not even for this, what she'd been waiting so long to hear. If only he would touch her, she thought. Kiss her. But he didn't.

"It's Room 101," he told her.

This turned her, though only halfway toward him. "Loving me is Room 101? The worst thing in the world?"

So he had read the book, George Orwell's 1984. Like the shirt and the crockpot, it had been a gift she was certain he wouldn't use. Room 101 was where the Thought Police took you in order to break you. It contained the worst thing in the world.

Ian stood. "No. Losing you is what's in my Room 101. The thought of it, Maura. I can't stand it."

She'd have run to him, if she thought he would take her in his arms, but even with those words coming from his mouth she wasn't convinced that he wouldn't push her away. "You don't have to lose me."

"But I could."

"Anyone could lose anyone, Ian, it's…it's the risk you take when you love someone." Her breath shuddered. She watched him look away from her, unable to meet her gaze. "And I love you."

"I know you do. For now."

She was helpless to respond to this with anything but the truth. No false promises. He wouldn't bear them, and though Maura could never claim not to be a liar, she had never been untruthful to Ian. "Yes. For now. And I have for a long time."

"Love," Ian said, "ends. It doesn't last. No matter how much you want it to. It all ends."

How could she argue with that? He wasn't wrong. Pessimistic, but not wrong. She crossed the room to him, finally, because waiting for Ian to do it meant it would never happen.

She kissed him.

And again.

She cupped his face in her hands and looked into his eyes, and she kissed his mouth over and over until at last he yielded to her. His arms went around her. His mouth opened. He sighed into her and filled her with his breath.

"Ian. I love you. I want to be with you. I know it's complicated fuckery, but…it always is. With anyone. And I want to try to make this work with you, how can I make you believe me?"

"I believe you. I just don't believe it will last."

Honesty stings, and though she knew he had every right to feel that way, it still felt like a slap. "You think I don't worry, too? I changed my whole life —"

"Not for me," Ian said roughly, almost panicked. "You said -"

"No. Not for you. Not because of you, except

that you became a part of me. You are so much a part of me, Ian. You are amazing and wonderful, and I love you. I want to be with you."

"It's reckless," he said.

She smiled. "Perfectly."

"I don't know why you think that," he said harshly.

The answer to that was another kiss, this one lingering. She looked into his eyes, desperate to find a way to convince him and knowing there was nothing for her to say that could. "Because it's true."

This time, Ian kissed her. Soft at first, then getting harder when she sighed against him. His hands moved over her back to grab her ass and pull her against him. And just like that, like a match to gasoline, they ignited.

Ian dragged his teeth across her throat to nip at her collarbones, and the pleasure-pain forced a small cry from her. Both his hands came up to cup her breasts through her thin t-shirt and the lace bra she wore beneath. Her nipples jutted instantly, and he pinched them as hard as he knew she liked.

Maura went to her knees, her hands already working at his belt. She went too fast, jerking at the leather hard enough to move his entire body, but in moments his cock was free and in her fist. Her mouth seconds after that. She drank in his moan was she took him as far as she could, then let her mouth slide along his shaft to tongue the head of his cock. Gripping the base of him, she sucked harder, adding a twist of her hand. He grabbed her hair at that, sinking his fingers deep into it. Pulling.

"I love that," she breathed against him before sucking a little harder, hard enough to make him mutter a curse. He pushed into her. She loved that, too. "Oh, Ian, Ian. I love it when you fuck my mouth."

She knew his triggers. What to say and how to say it. How hard and fast to work his cock until he twisted his fingers tighter in her hair and pulled her head back. On her knees, head tipped back with her hand still stroking him, Maura looked up at him.

"I ache for you," she told him, not caring how much she gave and how much it could hurt when he took it without giving her anything in return.

He didn't pull her to her feet. Instead, Ian got on the floor with her. His mouth sought hers as he tugged her shirt off, breaking the kiss long enough to get it over her head before he was kissing her again. He anchored her to his mouth with a hand on the back of her neck. His other hand slid into the front of her jeans and found her already slick and ready for his fingers. He teased her clit, not enough room for him to push inside her without undoing her jeans. It made his touch all the more deliciously torturous.

He pushed her onto her back on the soft thickness of his beige carpet. Cradling her against him, Ian kept up the steady, circling pressure on her clit while he made love so thoroughly to her mouth, she was left breathless. Mindless, the way he always made her. Maura lifted her hips, struggling toward more sensation.

"Shh," Ian told her. "There's my girl."

She fucking loved it when he called her that,

but there was only so much she could take. "Stop. Teasing. Me."

"You want to come?" Ian mouthed against her ear. He worked open the button of her jeans, making more room but doing no more to get her over the edge.

Maura laughed, breathless. "Yes. God. Yes. But I want you to be inside me when I do."

He might think he had the upper hand, but the way he groaned when she said that told her he was as close to the edge as she was. She had no problem giving up to him. Giving in. He was the one who fought it, but times like this proved he was as helpless against her as she was to him.

"Inside me," she whispered in his ear as he moved his fingers inside her panties to find her heat. "I want your cock inside me."

They worked together as seamlessly as they'd worked together earlier in the kitchen. Her jeans and panties off, his pants. Her bra after that. His shirt, a button pinging off the edge of the wooden coffee table in their haste. Then he rolled them both so she was on top, his cock nestled against her clit. All it would take was a small shift to get him inside her.

Maura leaned to kiss him, the shift in angle giving him access to her cunt. Ian pushed inside her with a single fluid motion, seating himself so deep they both groaned. She rolled her hips as he thrust. He slid a hand between them, letting his knuckles provide her with the perfect amount of pressure on her clit.

Her climax rolled over her in long, slow waves

that didn't fade but built and built until they overtook her. Her fingers dug into his chest as she rode him. He fucked into her harder, pushing her forward. She kissed his mouth, but her lips skidded from his from the force of their motion. Burying her face into Ian's neck, Maura came for what seemed forever. Ian shuddered beneath her.

When the pleasure had faded enough for her to move, she rolled off him and lay on her back, staring up at the ceiling. Her knees were rug burned. Her shoulder pressed his, and so did her hip, but she was too drowsy and sated to move. Beside her, Ian started to snore.

Maura pushed up on her elbow to look down at him. There might come a time when she was no longer overcome with love at the sight of his face, or when her love might become something soft and faded and worn. But to stop loving him? Impossible.

"How would I live," she murmured, "without my Ian?"

Tenderly, she stroked the hair from his forehead and kissed his mouth. He woke with a start, looking guilty. Maura sat, thinking she should start looking for her clothes. She was getting a chill.

Ian sat, too, saying nothing as she pulled on her panties and bra, then her t-shirt. She watched him carefully as she turned her jeans right-side out, but didn't put them on. She knelt beside him.

"Ian?"

"It's getting late," he said. "We should go to bed."

She'd never been in his bedroom, though she'd

seen it often enough in their video chats. The easy compatibility they'd shared while making dinner and the synchronicity of their lovemaking stalled here. Ian pulled a pair of boxers and a t-shirt from a drawer to give her.

"You can use the bathroom first," he offered. "Umm…I have an extra toothbrush for you."

In bed, she curled on her side, facing out. Ian lay on his back beside her. The soft, slow rasp of his breathing soothed her, but she couldn't sleep. All this time, and they'd only slept together once. She didn't know if he liked to be cuddled or preferred his space; she didn't know if he would mind if she tossed and turned for a few minutes while she tried to get comfortable with a pillow she wasn't used to.

"Are you sleeping?" His whisper eased over her in the darkness, so quiet it made her smile because he was clearly trying not to wake her, if she was.

"No."

The bed shook as he moved closer to her, pulling her against him. His breath warmed her neck. His hand fit naturally just below her breasts.

"It will be okay, Ian," Maura said sleepily, relaxing against him. "Everything will be okay."

But it wasn't. She fell asleep with his arms around her and woke when he moved away from her. When he swung his legs over the edge of the bed, she sat up too.

"Don't do this," she said. The only light came from the moon shining through the window. It made him a shadow, indistinguishable from all the others except that he moved and the others stayed still.

"Go to sleep."

"I can't sleep."

She scooted closer to him. He didn't cringe from her touch when she put curved her body around his and put her chin on his shoulder. She put her arms loosely around him, linking her fingers at his chest. She gave him her warmth and the beat of her heart. According to George Orwell in 1984, if you loved someone, that's what you gave him even when you had nothing else. Love.

Maura gave Ian her love, and somehow, it wasn't enough.

"It's just that...I'd rather it end now than later."

Maura sighed, weary, but giving him the room to say what he needed to say. "Why?"

"So I can be ready for it."

"Are you ready for it?" She asked a little too harshly. "Is that what you want, Ian? For me to go, now. For this all to just...end?"

"Before it leaves scars," Ian said in a low voice.

Maura snorted softly against him and kissed the back of his neck. "Too late, sweetheart. Way too late for that."

He half-turned. He could've kissed her mouth, had he twisted just a little more, but she didn't press forward. "I've never felt this way about anyone. That's all. I just don't think I can do it."

You're doing it, she wanted to say. You've already done it.

Instead, she withdrew from him. Quietly, without fanfare, she gathered her clothes and stripped out of his. She dressed and pulled her hair up again. Ian sat on the bed, watching her, though how much he could see in the dark she didn't know. When she'd finished, Maura went to him. She took his face in her hands and tipped it up so he had to look at her. There was enough light for that, at least.

"I love you," she told him. "But you're right. Eventually, that leaf has to let go."

"I'm sorry, Maura."

"Me too." She thought about kissing him, this her last chance, and couldn't bring herself to do more than brush her lips on his. Straightening, she let go of him. "I'll let myself out."

"I'll walk you —"

"No," she told him, too sharply. Too fierce. "I don't want you to."

She couldn't let him. She would break down and he would see it, and she'd be ashamed. Or worse, she would cling to him, weeping and begging. She would lose herself utterly in this grief already threatening to claw its way up her throat and out her mouth in wails and cries.

No. She would walk herself to the door and let herself out, and she would get in her car and drive herself home. There she might break down, in the safety of her own shower where she could scream and pound her fists. But not here.

In his kitchen though, as she gathered her keys, Maura paused to write a note. Simple. One sentence. She didn't sign her name.

She left it on the table, and she left him.

Twelve

I've always believed you can't predict love. You can't qualify or quantify it. Can't dissect it. Love hits you like a truck or the flu, coming up from out of nowhere to knock you to your knees.

Love burns you up alive.

Having said that, I should also be honest and say that I've been in love four or five times, six if you count my high school boyfriend, and we might as well, because just like the flu, love comes in many strains and just because some are milder than others, that doesn't make it any less, does it? Seven times, seven, if you count the time with Daniel. It was short, it didn't last, but that doesn't mean it wasn't love, in its own way.

What I'm getting at is that I've been in love more than once, and every time was different. I've never been a woman who holds back on emotion or builds walls. When I love, I love hard, but that doesn't make me soft.

Ian makes me soft, but that doesn't make this love. So…what is it then? We are friends. That's for sure. Lovers? Not yet, not quite, though I've thought about it a lot and I'm sure he has, too. I hope he has. I know I shouldn't, but I do.

I tried not to love him, I really did.

After all, what were the chances? I met him in a dance club on a Saturday night. I was out celebrating Shelly's birthday. Ian was there with some friends having a bachelor party. There were five guys, five girls, none of us seriously looking to get hooked up but ready for a good time.

We've been talking for about an hour, our conversation punctuated with rounds of drinks and increasingly inebriated carousing from both the birthday girl and the groom as they play a game of Never Have I Ever. The ten of us had arrived around the same time and found spots in adjoining booths. The more we drink, the more it seems natural enough for the two groups to mingle and squeeze into one booth. The flirting commences, because let's face it, it's always more fun when there's flirting, even if nobody has any intentions of going further. Ian and I have ended up on the outer edge of the booth, both of us leaning against it rather than sitting. It's easier to talk that way, and right from that first night, we've both figured out we like talking to each other.

But the first time he asks me to dance, I say no. "I'm with my girlfriends."

"I'm with my friends, too." He looks at our group. Someone's bought a round of shots.

I look out at the dance floor, where clusters of men and women wriggle and writhe to the music from the live band. I shake my head with a smile, lifting my whiskey sour. "I have a drink."

"When it's finished," Ian says.

Since I plan on nursing this drink for the rest of the night, I agree. Ten minutes later, the band switches from covering Lady Gaga to playing Kings of Leon's Use Somebody. Ian takes my drink and puts it on the table. He takes me by the hand and leads me to the dance floor, where he pulls me into his arms as though I'm meant to be there for my entire life.

Love doesn't lend itself to lists, but if I had to make one, that moment would be in the Top Ten Reasons I Fell In Love With Ian Douglas.

Later, when things were slipping sideways, I'd cling to that moment. Replay it over and over. The brush of his breath against my neck, making me shiver. The press of his fingers, sliding now and then from between my shoulder blades to the small of my back or my hip. Sometimes, I'd allow myself to imagine how it might've been if I hadn't turned my face at the end of the night. If I'd let him kiss me then, how different it all might've been.

When the song ends, Ian and I look at each other, still swaying though the music has gone fast again. Colored lights paint his eyes so that I can't tell for sure if they're gray or blue or green. He says something I miss because of the noise, but that's fine because it gives me an excuse to lean closer to him. For his lips to brush my ear as he speaks.

"Thanks for the dance," Ian says. His hand has found mine and he squeezes it gently, lifting it to look at my wedding and engagement rings. Then he looks at my face.

I step out of his arms with a laugh and toss of my hair, self-conscious. Heat rises in my throat and cheeks. The warmth and pressure of his hands on me lingers even when I put distance between us, and he says nothing else as he leads me back to our group. We are separated after that, our friends taking up our attention, but I catch him looking at me more than once. Well, I guess that meant he catches me looking, too.

At the end of the night, I'm still mostly sober and herding the rest of my group like a kindergarten teacher trying to get her class in from recess. Shelly's what she likes to call shit-hammered drunk, and the other girls, Terri and Lisa, aren't much better. Terri, as a matter-of-fact, who's spent the latter part of the night making out with one of the guys from the other group, is now trying to orchestrate a sort of twenty-one kiss salute for the groom.

"C'mon, ladies!" She yells at everyone who passes. "Line up, give the groom a lucky kiss!"

His face is covered with lipstick.

"What's his fiancée going to say?" I ask Ian as we watch a bar full of drunk and giddy women line up to take their turns.

Ian laughs. I think he's mostly sober too, but I don't know him well enough to be sure. He rubs at his mouth, then the back of his neck as he gives his friend a bemused look.

"She won't know. He's going home with Steve tonight. What's her story?" He lifts his chin toward Terri, who's back to making out with…I think it's Steve, actually.

"Recently divorced." I don't know her that well, she's Shelly's friend more than mine.

Together, Ian and I try to get our friends into cabs. And there in the parking lot, we stare at each other with goofy smiles on our faces that won't go away no matter how hard I try. There isn't time for this, we both have to get in the cabs and drive away from each other. And that's the right thing, the best thing. It's the only thing.

"It was nice meeting you, Ian." I hold out my hand.

Ian presses it with his. Step by incremental step, we move toward each other. Shelly is shouting something rowdy from the back seat. Steve is begging for Terri's number.

The whole world is Ian.

But I can't do it. I can't let him kiss me. The rings on my finger have begun to pinch and bind and weigh me down, but that doesn't mean I can ignore them. At the last second, I turn my face. Ian stops a scant breath from the corner of my mouth. I feel his breath there and close my eyes for a second or two to keep the world from spinning.

"It was great meeting you, Maura." Ian lets me go. Backs away. He gets in the front seat of his cab, but he turns to watch me from the window as it drives away. He waves.

I wave back.

Two nights later, while I'm toodling around on my Connex page, a notification pops up that I've been tagged in a photo taken by Terri. Ian's been tagged, too. I stare at it for a long time, that picture I didn't know was being taken. In it, we stand by the edge of the booth, blurry in the background, looking very serious and deep in conversation. We'd been talking about the differences between fast and slow zombies, and if they weren't really dead but sick with a virus, could they, in fact, be truly called zombies. A moment, captured forever.

And then, dear reader, I friended him.

***

Would it be weird, Ian types, if we talked on the phone?

The cursor blinks in the little square box on my computer screen. We've been messaging back and forth for a while now. Not every day, but when we catch each other online, the conversations go for hours. There's very little flirting, certainly nothing inappropriate. I'm allowed to have friends, I tell myself. And that's all we are.

Except for the memory of his hands on me. His breath on me. Except for the helpless way I curse myself for having passed up the chance to discover the taste of his mouth.

No. That would be okay. Right now?

Can you?

Sure.

I know that Ian is divorced. No kids. One dog. Good job. I know where he went to high school and college, the name of his first girlfriend and of his ex-wife — they had the same name. He knows about my penchant for science fiction and horror movies, my allergies to bees, my fear of heights. We don't talk about my husband or my marriage, though I can feel the subject hanging between us. I tell myself I'd answer any questions he asks, but Ian never asks.

My phone doesn't ring, though I watch it like it's a snake about to bite me. When it does, finally, I almost drop it in my haste to answer. My hands are shaking, and so is my voice when I manage to say, "hello?"

"Hi." His voice is deeper than I remember it. Rougher.

I clear my throat and take a deep breath. "How's it going?"

"Good. You?"

"Good."

Silence.

"So," Ian says. "Do you know why the big sale at the strip club was so unpopular?"

Surprised, I say warily. "…No?"

"Everything was only half off."

I start to laugh, and it spirals up and up while Ian joins me. It's a stupid joke, but utterly endearing for all that. It's been a while since I laughed so hard. It's cathartic.

We spend two hours on the phone until both of us, bleary eyed, agree we need to hang up or else we'll be useless for work in the morning. But though I'm so tired I can barely keep my eyes open and certainly can't manage to hold a coherent conversation, I don't want to end the call. I listen to Ian's soft breathing and wonder if he's fallen asleep.

"You should hang up," I whisper, half-hoping he won't hear me.

"You hang up."

"No," I say with another laugh. "You hang up."

"Where's your husband?" Ian asks, and suddenly I'm as wide awake as if someone stuck a pin in me.

"He's upstairs. Sleeping."

"Ah."

"He has a sound machine." It feels simultaneously necessary and pointless to say that. Doublethink, the way they did it in 1984. I wonder if Ian's ever read it.

"Well. It's late. It was great talking to you. Goodnight, Maura." No longer easy and light, Ian's tone has gone formal. Bordering on cold.

"Right. Goodnight, Ian." Before I can say anything else, he's disconnected, leaving me to sit in the dark and stare at my phone and wonder what in the hell just happened.

I don't hear from him for close to two weeks after that. He's more active than I am on Connex, posting comments on news stories and quirky status updates that show up in the news feed I normally wouldn't even check, so I know he's been online even if he's not logged into his messaging program. I tell myself not to care, but of course I do.

Then, one night when I'm up late because I can't sleep, his name appears in my contacts list. I wait, breathless, my cursor hovering over it. Thinking I should send a message, but not quite able to do it.

Because what if Ian doesn't want me?

Why should he, after all? What point could he have in pursuing me, when it's so clear there isn't anything to pursue? Still, I open a chat window. I type a message, then delete it, start another.

I shouldn't send him a message. I know it. So I delete it and push away from my desk. I should go to bed. It's late.

And then, just before I make my computer go to sleep, a chat window pops up. It's from Ian. My heart leaps, then drops. I feel a little sick to my stomach, waiting to see what he ways.

Hey, is what he typed, and I return his message within seconds.

Hey.

***

Daniel pushed the bottle of wine closer to Maura across the top of the kitchen island. "Connex is the devil."

"Hey. You found me through Connex." She laughed and filled both their glasses.

"See what I mean?" Daniel leaned back in his chair, swiveling it a little. "So then what happened?"

"We kept talking. We became friends." Maura shrugged and went to the stove to stir the shrimp in garlic butter she was planning to toss with some linguine. "Isn't that what you do there? Send cyber pinches and look at pictures of each other's cats?"

"Does he have a cat?"

She shook her head. "No. Ian has very bad dog named Rowdy who eats stuff he's not supposed to."

Daniel looked around her kitchen. "You should get a dog."

"I don't want a dog. Hey, can you grab the garlic bread out of the oven?" Lots and lots of garlic, she thought. It could make kissing him later interesting. If they kissed at all. Never mind the night on his couch, they hadn't yet established what was going to happen going forward.

At the table, they drank more wine while Daniel was properly appreciative of her cooking prowess. There was something eminently satisfying about making someone happy with good food, Maura thought, watching him dig in like he wasn't going to eat again for a month. She blushed at the sight of his mouth glistening with butter, the swipe of his tongue across his lips. He caught her looking and smiled.

"To good friends." Daniel raised his glass.

She clinked it with hers. "To good food."

"Health and happiness," Daniel added, then looked briefly sad. He shook it off, focusing on her again. "So you met him in a dance club and became friends on a social network. What happened after that?"

Maura hesitated, feigning a sudden interest in her plate. She twirled her pasta on her fork, though she'd eaten too much already and felt like Violet Beauregard after she ate the Thanksgiving dinner pill. She shrugged and tried to spear a shrimp.

"I met my wife during an online board meeting with the group that had hired me to come in and do some basic city planning work for a small village in Guatemala. She was the accountant for this really small non-profit group. Mostly volunteers. It was one of the few non-denominational ones I worked with, which I liked. It meant there was no religion pushing on the people, not trading souls for clean water." Daniel sounded a little venomous about it, but then shrugged. "Anyway, the connection was bad and we were both really frustrated because the picture kept cutting out. I gave her a really hard time about the budget. She accused me of being greedy. I told her she was cheap. A week later she was sitting across a table from me, and I fell in love with her instantly. It was her smile."

Maura smiled at that. "You believe in love at first sight?"

"I believe in recognizing something in someone else right away, yeah." Daniel sipped some wine and studied her. "Sometimes, people just…fit. No matter what you do or don't do. That person just fits you like a piece of your puzzle, and there's nothing you can do about it."

Maura drew a hitching breath at that. "Yeah. That's exactly it. It's like…I had this empty space that I didn't know about until I met him, and when I did, I realized it had been Ian-shaped all along. And maybe, if I'd met him just a few months later…"

"What would've been different?" Daniel ran a piece of garlic bread through the butter on his plate and bit into it with a sigh bordering on orgasmic. "This is so, so good."

Her own meal had grown cold without her eating very much of it. "Well. If I'd met him when I wasn't married, I mean."

"Would you have left your husband if you hadn't met Ian?"

The question was honest, if a little blunt, but she had a truthful answer for it. "Yes. Things weren't great already. I mean…happy people don't cheat."

Daniel held up his hands. "No judgment from

me. I'm sorry you weren't happy."

"Things happen. I mean, we had plenty of money. No kids. A great house. We took vacations every year. We both loved our work. But we didn't fit together anymore, if we ever had. I'm not trying to revise history," Maura added. "I'm not saying I never loved him or anything like that. But things changed. I did, and he didn't. Or maybe it was the other way around, who knows. But I never set out to be unfaithful. I resisted for a long time."

"No judgment," Daniel repeated quietly. "I promise you, Maura. I don't think you're a terrible person for falling in love."

She gave him a sad smile. "Ian does."

At that, Daniel got up from the table and came around to kiss her on the mouth. Sweet pressure. No tongue. He looked into her eyes. "Want me to beat him up for you? I know a guy. A couple guys, actually. Tough ones."

She burst into laughter. Daniel sat back in his chair with a satisfied nod and refilled both their glasses of wine. "Thanks. I'll think about it."

"No problem. It's good to see your smile." Daniel smiled, too, then glanced at the clock. "Shoot. We're not going to make the movie."

Maura shrugged. "We could just watch something here?"

"You sure?"

She nodded, studying him. Thinking about the night on his couch. About puzzles with missing pieces. "Yes. I'm sure."

***

Her phone rang and, bleary eyed, Maura plucked it with fumbling fingers from the dock on her nightstand. She dropped it with a clunk loud enough to wake the dead before putting it to her ear. "...'Lo?"

"Hi."

Maura sighed and scrubbed at her eyes, not daring to look at the clock. "Hi."

"Everything okay?" Daniel mumbled from beside her.

"Yes. Fine. Go back to sleep," Maura said and swung her legs out of bed, hating the cold. Hating being woken at asscrack o'clock. She grabbed a sweatshirt from the chair next to her bed and headed out of the room, closing the door behind her.

"Who..." Ian said. "You're not alone."

"No. I'm not alone." In the living room, she bundled herself into the sweatshirt and then under a blanket on the couch, tucking her freezing feet beneath her. Her teeth chattered.

"I'll let you go, then."

"You woke me up, Ian," she said sharply. "Don't you dare hang up on me now."

Ian said nothing for a moment. Then, "I shouldn't have called you, I guess."

"But you did. So talk to me." She yawned behind her hand, waking up a little more. Sleep would be next to impossible at this point. "What's going on?"

"Won't your...friend...miss you?"

"He's sleeping. He has to get up early." Maura paused, but she didn't owe Ian an explanation about how it had gotten late while they watched movies, how they'd drunk another bottle of wine. How she could've made Daniel sleep on the couch but the comfort of a warm body next to hers had been too tempting to pass up.

Let him wonder what had happened.

Let him ask.

But Ian didn't ask. "I want to see your face."

"Now? God." She groaned. "I look terrible."

"You never look terrible."

She laughed at that. Bittersweet. "Ian, Ian, Ian. What am I going to do with you?"

"Get on the computer. I want to see you."

What had happened to her pride? "Fine. I'm logging in now."

In another minute, her screen brightened with an image of her own face and the sound of ringing. She disconnected the phone call and waited for him to answer the video call. Another few seconds passed. Her face got smaller, and Ian's filled the screen.

It had been a mistake to agree to it, she realized that at once. Ian was sleep rumpled and sexy, and when had she ever been able to resist that face? Also, he had "the look."

Oh, she was a goner.

"What do you want, Ian?"

"Missed you." He ran his tongue over his bottom lip, leaning close to the screen. "I couldn't sleep."

Maura bit the inside of her cheek to keep

herself from responding right away. When she didn't speak, Ian ran a hand over his chest and down to his belly. He tugged his shirt so the hem lifted slowly, showing just the hint of his belly.

Fire warred with ice inside her. The sight of him was enough to peak her nipples and make her cunt clench, but Maura squeezed her thighs together and crossed an arm over herself. She kept her expression neutral.

"Go back to sleep, Ian. I'm exhausted, and I have to work in the morning."

For a moment he looked uncertain, and that was when she understood how love can turn to hate in a heartbeat. He'd thought this would be easy, and she couldn't blame him. It had always been so easy for him to come back to her, before.

He held up the note. Her own words scrawled there. The paper had been folded and creased, crumpled and smoothed. She hadn't written them large enough to read at the distance he held them, but she remembered what she'd said.

We will meet in the place without darkness.

She'd been tired when she wrote that. Overwrought. Two weeks later without a word from him in between, all she could do now was stare at the screen and say nothing.

"What does this mean?" Ian asked.

"Fuck if I know," Maura said. "I was stupid to write it. I guess I was stupid to think it you'd figure it out or know what it meant. I was stupid to think anything."

"You're one of the least stupid people I've ever met."

"Thanks." He meant it as a compliment, but she was too tired to feel great about it.

He had the grace to look self conscious, but only for a moment. "I missed you."

She looked at the clock finally, against her will. "Well, Ian, I have to say, three a.m. is a shitty time to figure that out."

"Especially when you're not alone," he retorted with a twist of his mouth that made it look like he wanted to spit.

"I don't have to explain myself to you. You made your feelings, or lack of them, very clear to me." She drew herself up. Shoulders straight. Mouth thin. She probably looked like some kind of hardcore bitch, but that was how she felt. Hard fucking core. "But now what? Now you miss me, so you come to me with your dick in your fist, and I'm supposed to just leap for it, mouth open wide?"

Ian said nothing.

"You call me at three in the morning because you can't sleep," she cried. "Because you're horny and you're alone, and you have nobody else! That's all!"

She dared him to say differently, but he didn't. He stared at her, not moving. Barely blinking. He didn't look away from her, at least there was that, but it was cold comfort when she couldn't read his expression.

"What did you mean by that note?" he asked.

Maura rubbed at her burning eyes and squeezed her thumb and forefinger to the bridge of her nose to fend off the impending headache. She had to be up for work in a couple hours, and she would be miserable all day if she didn't get enough sleep. Fuck that, she thought and looked at him. She already hadn't had enough sleep. She would already be miserable, waiting for Ian to call or message or email her during the day, knowing he wouldn't but waiting anyway.

Like a fool.

"I'm not a yo-yo, Ian. And I'm not a robot. I'm a real person, with real feelings I have never hidden from you. All I've ever done is try to be good to you. Even when I shouldn't have been, I was anyway. And don't get me wrong," she said, "I'm not blaming you. Anything I ever did was because I wanted to."

"And now you don't want to, any more?"

It was starting to feel that way. Or maybe it already felt that way and had for some time, but she'd refused to see it. "I want you to stop fucking with me. That's all. I don't think that's too much to ask, is it? That you be consistent? If you don't care about me —"

"Stop that," Ian said sharply. "You know that's not true."

Maura leveled a look at him. "Actually, I don't know that it's true. You tell me one thing, but words mean nothing without actions to back them up. When you do this, when you push me away only to pull me close again, over and over, it leaves me incapable of trusting you. I don't trust you anymore, Ian, and that makes me so immeasurably sad."

He frowned. "Me too."

"And what's worse, what's so fucking worse, is that now I no longer believe any nice thing you ever said to me."

He looked startled at that. "Maura…"

"Why should I?" She shook her head. "You say one thing, do another. You tell me you love me, and you fuck me, but then you push me away. Really hard. It hurts me when you do that."

She waited for him to say he was sorry, not because she demanded an apology, but because she'd have said it if he'd told her she hurt him. Ian looked away, hand over his mouth in his familiar way that meant he had words to say but was holding them back. Maura swallowed around her emotions.

"Sometimes," she said, "people fit each other like pieces of a puzzle. No explanation that makes sense. You can call it chemistry or kismet or coincidence. You can call it whatever you want, but the universe put us together for a reason."

"You believe that," Ian said with a small laugh. "You believe in horoscopes."

"I read horoscopes," Maura corrected. "I don't necessarily believe them."

"So, what's the reason?"

She shrugged, so far beyond tired now it was starting to hurt. She got up, turning the computer so he could watch her making coffee in her single cup maker. She put the coffee pod into the receptacle and turned leaned against the counter, arms crossed.

"I don't know. You're a blessing or a lesson, one or the other. Maybe both. All I know is," she said as the coffee hissed and spit into her cup, "I can't do this any more."

"I understand."

"You don't." Her laughter sounded like the

grind of rusty gears. She warmed her hands on the mug.

"I don't want to hurt you," Ian began, but more of that grinding laughter stopped him.

"But you do, Ian. Over and over again, you do. And I just keep letting you."

He sighed. "Maybe you should stop."

"There is no more maybe about it." The coffee burned her tongue, but she drank anyway. "You want to know what that note meant?"

"Yes."

"We'll meet in the place without darkness. It's what O'Brien says to Winston in a dream," she said, relaying part of the plot to 1984. "The place where there is no darkness is the Ministry of Love. Where the Thought Police take you when you've committed thoughtcrime."

"To Room 101," Ian said.

"Yes. To Room 101. The place where there is no darkness is Room 101, and what's inside that room is the worst thing ever you can imagine." Maura put her mug on the counter. The floor seemed very far away; like Alice in her Wonderland, she was either growing or shrinking. Things had shifted sideways, yet she stayed steady on her feet. "What's in your Room 101?"

"Losing you," he whispered.

"We'll meet in the place without darkness," Maura repeated. No tears. No gasp for breath. Nothing but ice where once he'd given her fire. "Goodbye, Ian."

Then she disconnected the chat.

***

Things end. Good, bad, indifferent, that was how the world worked. Maura had known from the beginning that her relationship with Ian would probably be short and fraught with woe, but there had been a time, albeit brief and completely delusional, when she believed they might actually be able to make it work.

Oh, heart. Why you gotta break so hard?

She'd deleted his contact information from her phone and computer, along with every way she'd ever been in touch with him. The instant message program that had been their first method of communication. The phone app that had come after that. She'd deleted him from Connex, as stupid and petty as that might seem, but it wasn't to keep him from seeing her updates. It was to keep her from giving in, breaking down and seeking him out.

"All gone," she said to Shelly, showing off the phone. "Nothing left. I blocked his screen name so even if he does ping me, I won't get the message."

"What's to stop him from just calling you up? Or texting you?"

"Nothing," Maura admitted. "But he hasn't. And he won't. I know that kid, Shelly, and he won't do it."

Shelly snorted softly and swirled the clear, greenish liquid in her glass. Maura had made margaritas. It was girls' night in. Tacos, nachos, margaritas and every soft core erotic movie they could find. The Red Shoe Diaries, Lake

Consequence. Old favorites she and Shelly had watched many times. Until Ian, Maura had never quite believed the kind of sex in those movies existed.

"What will you do if he does?"

Maura shrugged. "I don't know. I don't have a backup plan, really. At least, not beyond margaritas and Mexican food. Oh, and Billy Wirth."

"I'd back up on him for sure," Shelly said a little dreamily. "Back, front, upside down, whatever he wanted."

Maura burst into laughter that felt a lot like sobs. She covered them by drinking, then set the glass down to pour more from the pitcher. She licked salt from the rim of the glass and dipped a chip in the melted queso. Shelly watched her, but though they'd been friends long enough that there was no way she didn't sense Maura's emotions, she didn't call her on it.

"So...Daniel," Shelly said. Apparently that topic wasn't taboo.

This time, Maura's laugh felt a little more natural. "Uh huh."

"Don't you uh huh me. Spill it. I want to know it all." Shelly leaned forward with a gleam in her eye, ignoring the movie. "Every last freaking detail."

There'd been so many things Maura had never shared with Shelly. Details about Ian, the things he did to her and how he made her feel, specifics about his taste and how he moaned — she'd shared similar details with Shelly lots of times about other guys, but never about Ian. Everything with him had been different than anything she'd ever done.

She didn't want to think about Ian any more.

"That's not creepy at all," Maura teased.

Shelly pretended to take offense. "Listen, who's the one who helped you use a tampon for the first time? Who held your hand when you had to take that pregnancy test?"

"Longest three minutes of my life," Maura said. "You, of course. My bestie."

"And you're going to hold back now?" Shelly sniffed. "Fine. At least tell me if you're going to see him again!"

"I'm going to see him again. I have seen him again," Maura said. "He's not leaving the country again for another month. We have dinner every couple of nights. Hang out, watch movies. Stuff like that."

Shelly looked impressed. "What about all the other dates?"

Maura shrugged. "I don't see the point in that any more, do you?"

"Now more than ever," Shelly said. Maura laughed. Shelly shook her head, looking serious. "Listen, you can't let Ian put you off dating."

"I'm not put off dating. Just the sheer quantity of it. It's exhausting, Shelly. And technically, you could say I'm dating Daniel." Though it was more like friends without benefits. They hadn't fooled around since that first night, not even when he slept in her bed. She thought he was too embarrassed to try, and she hadn't yet worked up the courage to initiate anything.

"So…what's it like? C'mon, Maura. The two of

you were volcanic together. You told me once you'd never been with a man who'd ever made you come as hard as Daniel could."

That had been true. Until Ian. Maura frowned, concentrating on her drink for a few seconds. Then she sighed. "Okay. So we've fooled around a little. But we didn't fuck," she clarified when Shelly's expression brightened and she looked like she was about to say something. "He just went down on me."

"Just?" Shelly cried and wriggled on the couch until Maura had to burst into laughter. "Nobody 'just' goes down on someone else."

Maura gave her friend a confidential smirk. "Well, he does eat pussy like it's an Olympic sport."

"Guh." Shelly fell back with a sigh.

"Yeah." Maura laughed too. On the TV screen, the couple writhed around naked on the bed in slow motion. She watched for a few seconds before turning back to her friend. "I like Daniel a lot. More than I did when we were younger, I think. I mean, back then he was sexy and so sure of himself, and we had a lot of fun. But we never really talked, you know?"

"And you do now?"

"Yeah." Maura thought about that for a moment, turning over the conversation they'd had a few nights before about politics. "I mean, he's grown into a man, and I remember him as a boy."

"You're not a girl any more either, you know."

"I know. And I think that as much as we set each other on fire back then, we have the real potential to be close friends now." Maura chewed on that thought, trying to make herself clearer, but the margaritas were getting in the way. "Like…we have a lot in common, opinion-wise. We like the same movies and music, the same kind of food. He's easy to talk to. And he's a good listener. I really like him."

Shelly was silent for a moment. "And you're worried about that?"

"I am." She hadn't thought of it quite that way until now, when the blur of booze had worn away some of her inhibitions.

"Because of getting hurt?"

"Because maybe it means I'm not meant to be with Ian after all," Maura blurted. "If I could fall for someone else, and so soon. Maybe what I felt for Ian wasn't real."

"Oh, sweetie." Shelly scooted over on the couch to put an arm around her shoulders. "Don't do that to yourself. It was real."

Maura swallowed tears to give her friend an honest look. "Does that make it better, really?"

"Maybe not. But it's the truth. Honey, I've known you a long, long time. When you talked about Ian, and even the once or twice I saw you with him, you lit up."

"When we were together, everything shined," Maura whispered.

"Yes. That. It was real. What you felt for him. That doesn't mean it was meant to last, you're right. But it also doesn't mean that if you find out you like someone else that what you felt for Ian wasn't real, or true. Nothing you feel for anyone else would negate that."

She knew it intellectually, of course. Loving Ian had not cancelled anything she'd ever felt for anyone else, including her now ex-husband. "I know that. But…"

"No buts," Shelly said firmly. "Ian had his chance. He blew it, spectacularly. You gave him every opportunity, Maura. Just because you love someone doesn't mean you have to let them ruin you."

"No," Maura said. "No. I don't."

Thirteen

I haven't worn this dress before, and the fabric clings to my body in a way I find a little distracting. The wind licks at the hem of it, the fluttery, gauzy fabric tickling my knees and my thighs when it floats a little too high for propriety. My legs are bare beneath it. So's my pussy. I can't recall a time when I went without panties, but today when I pulled this dress from the closet, the sheer fabric meant even my sheerest silk and lace left their lines and ruined the look. No bra, either. My nipples are diamond hard. My clit a tight knot.

I'm looking for Ian.

He's here, somewhere in the crowd. I know he is. The bass beat of dance music throbs between my legs, vibrates my chest. My heart is already skipping beats as I scan the throng for the sight of his face. Overhead, the night sky winks at me, bright with stars. The dance club is miles away from the sea but has a floor made of sand, and I'm glad I'm wearing a simple pair of sandals instead of the stilettos so many of the other women have. I'd take my shoes off altogether and walk with bare toes on the cool and gritty sand, but this isn't the ocean and the sand itself is surely filthy. So instead, I imagine the rush and press of the ocean and look for my Ian.

"Buy you a drink?" The man in front of me is handsome enough. His smile tempts mine, but I shake my head. "C'mon. One drink."

"I'm waiting for someone."

The man looks around. "Any man who'd keep you waiting is a bedamned fool."

Something seems off in his tone. His choice of words. Frowning, I watch him back away from me and wonder if he's right, if I shouldn't wait any longer. I've lost track of the time, and though I squint hard at my watch, the numbers are too small. The hands too fine. I can't tell the hour, how long I've been here. I have no idea how long I'll have to wait.

And then, there he is. There's nothing so silly as a shining ray of light or a chorus of angels, but the crowd does seem to part around him. Maybe it's just that in a sea of faces, Ian's will always stand out to me.

We dance.

Ian turns me so my back aligns with his front, my ass snugged up against his crotch. His hands on my hips. I turn my face to feel his breath on my cheek, and one arm goes behind his head so I can feel his hair with my fingers. We move with the music and the crowd, like we've all become some wild, writhing thing. I don't care about the song, the crowd, the heat rising so my skin begins to sheen with sweat. All that matters is Ian's hands on me, and he turns me to face him.

His kiss, oh, God. Ian's mouth. I fucking love his mouth so much I think I might be unable to bear it. He tastes of salt and beer and his own flavor; I would know the taste of him anywhere. His cock is hard on my belly as the people around us push in closer. My arms go over his shoulders. This close, his face is a bit of a blur, but I don't need to see his every feature with clarity to know the sight of him.

His tongue strokes mine as his hand slips

between us. His knuckles press my clit through the filmy hem of my dress. He doesn't have to move his hand because the crowd moves me against him.

Ian kisses me. Over and over, the slide of his tongue on mine, the nibble of his lips. The press of him against me. I pull him closer, closer, breathing him in. Tasting him. There are people behind me, all around me, but everything is Ian. The entire writhing, grinding crowd is Ian touching me.

"Maura, Maura, what am I gonna do with you," Ian says in my ear in a voice so low I shouldn't be able to hear it over the music, but there's magic in his tone. It vibrates deep within me, subsonic. Strums me internally, resonating on some frequency reserved for him alone.

"Anything you want. Everything you want." My breath is rough in my throat, the flavor of him thick on my tongue.

I want him the way you want to breathe when you've been underwater for too long. The way you crave the kiss of winter after an inferno of a summer. I want Ian without hesitation, reservation, accusation, condemnation. I want him with everything I am and have ever been. Everything I will ever be.

His knuckles rub and rub until I shake with the pleasure of it. I want him inside me, but there's no way for that happen here, in the middle of a crowd. My body strains, yearning toward that release. There's no stopping it. I can't hold it back, until at last the pleasure breaks me.

I'm looking in his eyes when I come.

"Ian," I manage to say as the crowd fades and

leaves us alone, and in front of me, Ian begins to vanish too. "Ian, please don't leave me."

***

Maura woke with a start, her heart pounding, every muscle tense. The memory of the dream's pleasure still coursed through her, though there were no physical signs of her orgasm beyond an extra slickness between her legs. It had been entirely in her head.

Still, she must've moaned or said something in her sleep, because Daniel pushed up on an elbow to look down at her. "Mo?"

She'd grown out of that name a long time ago. In fact, he might've been the only person to ever call her that. She shifted in the bed, seeking the comfort of his warmth even as the uneasiness of having him in her bed made her want to curl away from him.

"Bad dream?" His breath wafted over the back of her neck. His hand pressed flat to her belly. This was the third night this week he'd slept over.

"No." She couldn't lie to him, even if it felt shitty to be dreaming about another man and climaxing so hard it woke her up. "Not bad."

He nuzzled against her, and Maura relaxed into his affection. They'd been spending so much time together over the past month, they'd fallen into the habits of a long-term couple. Hand-holding. Kissing upon greeting and leaving. Most everything but the sex part. They hadn't talked about exclusivity, and Maura had never asked if Daniel was seeing other women when he wasn't with her. Maybe knowing that even if he was, he surely wasn't fucking anyone made it easier for her not to worry.

Or maybe she didn't quite care enough.

Either way, she hadn't opened her spreadsheet in a couple weeks. She still answered texts she got from the few men she'd liked enough to exchange phone numbers with, but she hadn't even logged in to her Luvfinder account to check if she had any offers. She'd thrown herself into work and catching up on the myriad home projects she'd promised herself she'd finish…she'd given up quickly enough on the crocheted afghan she'd wanted to make using all the leftover yarn she'd inherited from her grandmother, but she was the proud owner of completely reorganized cabinets.

There was a sense of relief, she couldn't deny that. She couldn't compare it to ripping off a bandage. It was more like the cessation of a long-term pain that had grown so deep, become so much a part of her, that she only noticed when it was gone.

It hadn't left her unscathed, of course. Like a bruise she couldn't leave alone, the memories of Ian still ached…so long as she pressed them. That was the hardest part. Getting herself to stop.

Daniel helped.

"Want to talk about it?" Now his quiet tone twitched her back from the edge of sleep.

For a moment, Maura lay quiet with his arms still around her. "It was about Ian."

"I figured." His mouth brushed the back of her neck, sending a chill through her that had nothing to do with the cold air pressing down on them outside of the sweet cave made of her comforter.

"I'm sorry."

He laughed a little. "Don't be sorry. You can't help what you dream about."

Except that she thought about Ian, too. Almost all the time. Before she went to sleep. When she woke up. Random moments during the day reared up like snakes and bit her, poisoning her with memories.

"It must've been a good one."

Maura cringed a little. "Was I…?"

"Moaning? Yes. A little. That's why I couldn't tell if you were having a nightmare or not." Daniel paused. His fingers made a slow, small circle on her belly, and she realized he was touching the sliver of bare skin between the bottom of her pajama shirt and her pants. "I guess it could be a nightmare, even if it was good. If you were dreaming about him and you woke up to remember you weren't with him any more."

Maura tensed a little, not sure what to say, but Daniel continued.

"I dream about my wife a lot. Not…um, not dreams like the one you were having. Stupid things, mostly. Sometimes she's in the background. Sometimes she's part of what's going on, sometimes not. I don't always even realize it's her or think about it, sometimes I wake up and only remember it later. But that's the worse, I guess. When I wake up and remember she was in the dream, but I didn't talk to her. I missed my chance. Because dreams are the only place I'll ever see her, you know?"

Maura put her hand over his and wriggled her bum closer into the curve of his body. "I can't compare missing Ian to that. I mean…"

"I know what you mean," Daniel said against the curve of her shoulder. His fingers drifted across her skin. "She's dead. He's not, you just broke up. Does it feel any better?"

"Well, knowing he's out there in the world somewhere, that I might see him again. That I could see him again," she amended. "That it's at least possible. How can I compare that to you losing your wife forever?"

"You didn't answer my question." He kissed the back of her neck.

"No," she said finally, sort of hating herself. "It doesn't feel any better. God, Daniel. I'm so sorry."

He laughed against her. "I told you. Don't be sorry. I'd rather have you tell me, anyway. It's not like I couldn't guess. You get lost, sometimes. I see it in your face. You go a little blank."

Horrified, mortified, Maura shook her head. "Oh. Wow. I'm sorry!"

"I figure you're missing him. I just wait until it passes. I know how it feels," Daniel said. "It's not a problem, Maura. Really."

"It's so rude. So insufferably rude. And useless. And horrible." She drew a hitching breath.

He nuzzled her again. "Shh. I'm sorry I brought it up."

They were quite again for a while, until she

started to drift again. Something seemed important to tell him though, something she wanted to say before she went back into dreams. "I'm glad I have you in my life, Daniel."

"Ditto, kiddo."

It made her laugh. A second later though, she gasped when his hand slid under the waistband of her PJ bottoms. "Daniel —"

"Shhh," he said again. "You need this."

Oh, yes. She did. Dreams aside, she hadn't had an orgasm in weeks. Sexual pleasure was as much a necessity as brushing her teeth or drinking coffee in the mornings. Normally, she didn't let more than a couple days pass without a climax, even if she had to go solo. But she hadn't felt up to it.

Still, she murmured his name like a protest, stopping when he nipped at her shoulder, bared a little by her neckline. The pain flipped her switch. When he slid his fingers lower, across her clit, she lost all words. Her thighs parted as she arched, one hand going behind her to cup the back of his neck. Daniel dipped his fingers inside her, bringing them up again to circle her clit. That little bit of pressure inside, so fleeting yet delicious, eased a moan out of her.

"Oh, you like that?"

"Yes."

"This?" Again, his fingers pressed inside her. Then deeper. In. Out. Up to circle her clit, then inside again.

In a minute, her hips were rocking. Cunt clenching. Her clit throbbed and when he rubbed it, and sparks of ecstasy made her shudder.

There was no fighting it. No resisting. Pleasure filled her, and Maura let it take her. She cried out at the end of it and put her hand over his to stop him from moving. When the tremors had eased, she rolled to face him.

She kissed him, and he kissed her back, but when she nudged a knee between his legs, it was clear he wasn't hard. She put her hand there, touched him. He didn't tell her to stop, but he did put his hand over hers.

"It's not you," he whispered into her mouth a moment later when she broke the kiss but hadn't yet pulled away. A few seconds later, he rolled onto his other side, away from her. The soft sounds of his breathing told her he'd fallen asleep a half-minute after that.

It wasn't her, and yet…of course it was. Maura stared into the dark for a little while before she slipped out of bed, grabbing her phone from its dock. Without turning on any lights, she padded through the cold night air to the living room, where she curled up on her couch under an afghan someone else, at least, had managed to finish.

Many late nights like this she'd spent with her phone in her fist, messaging with Ian. Sometimes talking to him, but most often, at least in the beginning, she'd had to type everything she wanted to say. It had made it easier, sometimes, to reveal herself to him. Something about the anonymity of that distance between them, the comfort offered by reading and writing instead of having to say it out loud. It had been harder, too, because when you were writing and not talking, there was never any excuse for sentiment to simply slip out.

If you said something, you had to mean it.

She had deleted, unfriended and removed him. But that didn't mean she couldn't find him. With cold fingers, Maura downloaded the instant message app she'd deleted.

"Idiot," she murmured.

It took a few seconds for the app to finish downloading, and only a few more after that to log in with her account information. She held her breath. Hoping. No, more than that. Praying to any god or goddess who would listen that even though he hadn't texted or called her, that he'd sent her a message. She watched the small spinning gear with her heart in her throat.

Connecting. Connecting. Connecting.

Her profile picture appeared. Her list of contact names. Her hands shook. She couldn't look. Maura closed her eyes, forcing herself to count to ten. Then another ten, giving the app plenty of time to populate itself with messages, should there be any to list. At last, she opened her eyes.

"Please, Ian. Oh, please, please, please."

But even in the "blocked messages" list, there was nothing.

***

"Someone had a good lunch." Madge beamed from her cubicle as Maura passed.

Maura paused. "Hey, you."

"I was going to stop by with these, but here." Madge handed over a manila file folder bulging with the office's collection of kids' fundraising and home party catalogs. "Get it out of here before I buy more garlic bread and cookie dough I don't need!"

Maura tucked the folder under her arm. "No kidding. How've you been? I haven't seen much of you lately."

"That's because you've been going out to lunch every day." Madge leaned an ample hip against her cubby wall and gave Maura a significant look. "Anything you want to tell your dear friend Madge?"

"He's just a friend."

Madge raised both brows. "Uh huh. Just a friend who comes to pick you up every day for lunch and brings you back looking like you just spent the hour winning the lottery."

"It's not every day," Maura demurred.

"Every day this week," Madge said with a grin. "And a few last week, too."

Had it been that often? Maura would have had to do a quick count to be sure, but if Madge said so, she was willing to believe it. "He's going to be leaving soon for work overseas."

"Make hay while the sun shines. That's what George says." Made leaned a little closer, conspiratorial. "Me, I like to say eat steak while you still have teeth."

"Good advice." Maura shifted the folder to her other hand and leaned on the cubby wall across from Madge. "I like him. That's all. It's not permanent, so…"

"So why not have lunch with him every day? Dinner, too." Madge chuckled. "It's good to see you smiling, that's all."

"It feels good to smile." That was the truth. Maura held up the folder. "I'll pass this along, if you're finished with it."

Madge waved a hand. "Definitely. Stop me before I buy again."

Laughing, Maura headed toward her cubicle. There wasn't anything in any of the brochures that she wanted to buy, though she would probably order a few things anyway. Daniel liked garlic bread, and she could pick up one or two of those pizza kits….

She stopped herself. By the time the stuff was delivered, Daniel would probably be gone, and what would she do with all that food for herself? Her easy mood vanished as quickly as cotton candy in a rainstorm. Dissolved. Washed away. Destroyed.

Sitting at her desk, slick catalogs spread out in front of her, Maura choked back her sudden sorrow. Not because Daniel would be going away — that she'd known since their first date. This renewed relationship, this twist of friendship that was a little more but not quite enough, had not been meant to last. No, her grief was not for that.

It was for how easily she'd let him make her happy.

How quickly she'd begun to move away from Ian. It had been a month since the last time she'd talked to him. A month without a call, text, instant message. This hadn't been what she wanted, but it was what she'd asked for, and now she had to live with it.

She had done this, she reminded herself as she piled the brochures and catalogs back into the folder and took them to the next cubicle over. Cindy wasn't at her desk, but Maura left it there for her. Back at her desk, she forced herself to put her phone in her purse so she wouldn't be tempted to download the messaging app again, or to stalk him on Connex. No good could come of that. What would she see, anyway? What would she do if she found he'd been tagged in pictures with another woman the way she'd been tagged in Daniel's recent photos? Just because she'd unfriended him didn't mean she couldn't find him if she tried.

She had to give up trying.

Fourteen

It's not always about sex. Sure, that's a big part of it. All I have to do is look at him, and I start to shake inside. When he touches me, I swear it's like everything I ever read about in those books Shelly and I used to sneak from her mom's bookcase. All those old romance novels full of heaving bosoms and ripped bodices.

But there's more to it than that. Ian listens to me. I mean, really listens. You know how I can tell? Because he pays attention, he remembers. If I tell him I like mint chocolate chip ice cream, that's what he has waiting for me when we find time to meet up some random summer afternoon in a park far away from any place either of us normally ever goes. He knows my favorite color and how my hands get cold so easily, and he brings me a pair of funky gloves knitted from purple yarn. He pays attention, that's all.

Ian knows me.

Do you know how delightful it is to be…known? To be understood? It's what we all search for in relationships, that person who discovers every part of you and not only finds each filthy, embarrassing secret acceptable, but wants you because of your flaws and not just despite them.

It's Ian with whom I share my fears. My struggles. Those long nights when our conversations roam from topic to topic without hesitation, I tell him everything there is to know about me. I open to him like a flower…

I am Ian's flower.

"Water me," I whisper into the phone. "I need you to water me, Ian, or I'll die."

He knows what I mean. I need to talk to him. To see him. I need to touch him. Ian is my water; without him, my roots will wither. My petals fall away. Without Ian, all I'll have left is my thorns.

"What do you want?" He asks. "Tell me."

"I want you to kiss me."

"I'll kiss you."

I close my eyes. The weight of my phone in my hand, the pressure of it against my ear, is no substitute for him. But it's all I have tonight, all I'll have for the next week or so until the next time we can be together.

"Will you touch me?"

Ian laughs softly. "Yes. I'll touch you."

"Where?"

"Anywhere you want."

"I miss you, Ian."

"I miss you, too." His voice scratches the inside of my ear, low and hoarse, yet buttery. Delicious.

I shiver. "Tell me about your day."

"Why do you want to hear about that? Boring."

I want to hear him talk, that's all. If I can't fall asleep with his arms around me, I want to enter dreams on the sound of Ian's voice. "What did you have for lunch?"

I love it when I make him laugh. He describes his lunch to me. Turkey sandwich. It's always a turkey sandwich. I don't care. It doesn't matter what he's saying, so long as he's talking to me.

"I wish you were with me right now," he says abruptly.

"Me too."

Someday, I think. Already I've set the plans in motion, though that's my secret and I haven't told him. I'm afraid if Ian knows I've started the process of leaving my husband, he will freak out. He's already told me, more than once, he doesn't want me to do anything rash. He doesn't understand this has been a long time coming, it's something I have to do for myself. Ian is just the bonus.

"I want to sleep with you," he says. "I mean sleep. Not…well, the other stuff too. But I'd like to sleep with you."

So far, we've only ever made love. I don't remember sleeping much. But yes, I've thought about what it would be like to snuggle into the covers with Ian next to me, to fall asleep to the sound of his breathing. To wake up next to him.

I wonder what it would be like to share my life with him.

"That would be nice." It's not everything I feel, but it's all I can really say.

"Hey, how's that project coming along at work? The one you told me about?"

I'm touched he remembers my complaint of a week or so ago about a tough project. More moved he bothered to ask me about it. The man who's supposed to love and cherish me hasn't bothered. In fact, when I tried to talk to him about it, I had to replay the entire conversation we'd already had about it, and even then he didn't remember anything about I'd already said.

Ian and I talk until the sun starts to come up. Only then does he ask me, "doesn't he notice when you're on the phone all night?"

"I sleep on the couch most nights. He snores."

"Oh," Ian says quietly. "How long have you been doing that?"

I chew the inside of my cheek, exhausted and still not ready to disconnect from him even though I'll be a zombie at work in a few hours. It won't help me with that pain in the ass project. I don't care.

"About six months."

"Oh," Ian says again.

I wait for him to ask me something, anything, about the state of my marriage. Most of the time this relationship is a boat floating on a deep black lake, and our fingertips only occasionally trail the surface, making ripples as we row. We don't pretend I'm not married, but we hardly ever talk about it. I don't complain to him about my husband. It would feel like a worse betrayal than anything else we've done.

"That can't be good for your back," Ian says when I'm silent.

I laugh, low, pulling the cover to my chin and letting my eyes sink closed. "No. Not really."

But it's good for my state of mind. Things have been getting worse, and yes, I'm sure it's my fault. I've stopped wanting to try. I stopped before I met Ian, though I know he doesn't believe it, and anything I say to convince him will only sound contrived.

"I need to see you," I say. "I thought I could

wait, but I can't."

"Hold on." The wonder of smart phones — Ian can take a picture and text it to me without ending the call.

The photo is of his face, a little blurry. He looks sleep rumpled, though we haven't slept, and I want to eat him alive. My fingertip traces the curve of his jaw. His mouth. I put the phone back to my ear.

"It's not enough."

He laughs, and I imagine his expression. Self conscious, but pleased. Sometimes I think Ian has no idea what to do with me. The other women he's dated have been sedate, coy. They've played the game of push and pull that I don't see the point of.

"Okay. Hold on."

Another minute passes. I hear shuffling. The sound of his breathing. My anticipation heightens, growing as I wait to see what he will send me. I know better than to expect something explicit — he can talk dirty but is still sometimes surprisingly shy.

The next photo pings through. It's a shadowy and off-center photo of his hip, part of his thigh, a hint of his belly. I laugh as my heart seizes, because I know he wasn't trying to be artistic, even though this picture is.

"I love it," I whisper. "It makes me want you."

"Well," Ian says, "I have to keep my flower watered. And put up a screen, to keep away the drafts and wild animals."

I curl my fingers into claws. "I have my four thorns to protect me."

We've both read The Little Prince. Ian even

read it in the original French. It was one of the first things we discovered about each other. He claims not to like the story, but he humors me.

"It's almost time to get up," Ian says. "It's almost time to get up. We need to go."

I know he's right, but that doesn't make me want to leave him. "Yes."

"Goodnight, my flower," he says, then, "Good morning, too."

"Goodnight, Ian. Have a great day." I love you rises to my lips, but I keep it locked behind my teeth, bittersweet on my tongue. I haven't told him yet. I'm not sure I ever will.

I love you, Ian.

***

"I've never been a flower for anyone else." Maura looked up at Daniel. She'd been resting her head on his lap while they watched a movie, but it was one they'd both seen before, and they'd fallen into conversation instead of paying attention.

"I'd never think of you as a flower. You're pretty enough." Daniel poked her side to make her wiggle. "But you're stronger than a flower."

Maura sat up and turned on the couch to pull her knees to her chest. She tucked her cold toes beneath his thigh to warm them. "First of all, flowers can be super strong. They grow through asphalt. Concrete. Anything. But also, I'm not strong, not at all."

"Yes, you are."

She studied him, not wanting to fish for a compliment but genuinely curious about what he thought about her. "Why do you say that?"

"Because I know your heart's breaking, and you don't show it." Daniel shrugged, his gaze going distant for a moment.

At that, Maura got up on her knees to lean toward him. She took his collar and kissed him, slow and sweet. "You know something, Mr. Petruzzi? You are pretty fucking awesome."

He laughed and pulled her onto his lap. "You think so, huh?"

"I do." She nodded, settling close to him. "Just thought you should know."

"The feeling's mutual. And everyone should get to hear they're awesome once in a while. Flowers do need water. You're right."

Maura frowned a little before she could stop herself. "No. You're right. I'm not a flower. I guess maybe I never was."

"Sorry," he said after a moment. "I shouldn't have said that. I know you wouldn't want me to call you the same thing he did."

"I don't compare you," she told him. "I want you to know that."

"Of course you do. How could you help it?" He pulled her closer, tucking an arm around her so she could press her face to his chest.

Maura sighed. "I don't compare you unfavorably. How about that? I mean, if anyone is compared unfavorably it's him, not you. You're —"

"Awesome. I get it."

She looked up at his tone. The frown. He didn't

look mad, but the conversation had taken a sudden dip.

"Daniel..."

He stared past her at the TV, mouth a grim line. Maura got off his lap to sit next to him, their easy affection now strained. Together they watched in silence until finally, he said in a low voice without looking at her, "Pretty fucking close to perfect, right? Except for the fact I can't get it up. And don't...don't say it doesn't matter, Maura. Because we both know it does."

"I wasn't going to say it doesn't matter."

He looked at her then, and it made her sad to see his pain. "Good."

"I like being with you," she told him. "I always did, even back then."

"When we fucked like rabbits."

She laughed, not embarrassed. "Yes. But I liked hanging out with you then, too. And I still do. I have fun with you, Daniel."

"I have fun with you, too."

She inched closer to rest her head on his shoulder. She took his hand, lacing their fingers together. He was silent, listening, while she tried to find the best words to say. Truth that wouldn't sting or hurt his pride.

"In some ways, it's better this way. For now. For me, I mean. Less pressure, I guess."

Daniel snorted soft laughter. "Uh huh."

Maura poked him. "Just listen to me, okay? I'm in no place to be getting involved with someone seriously right now. All those dates I went on were a ridiculous effort. Wasted. I'm sure at least a few of them were nice guys, maybe even compatible with me, but I wasn't interested in them. It wasn't fair to them, what I was doing. Trying to prove a stupid point."

"It wasn't stupid." He paused. "The spreadsheet might've been a little excessive."

She poked him again, harder this time. "I'm organized."

"You're in love with Ian," Daniel said without accusation in his voice. He looked down at her. "But I won't lie, I'm kind of glad he was a dumbass who didn't grab you tight when he had the chance."

"Thanks."

"I mean it." He leaned to kiss her, taking his time. He pulled her onto his lap again.

The kissing went on long enough to sent a flicker of heat through her, and Maura broke the kiss with a small sigh. She pressed her forehead to his. "Why do you keep seeing me? Knowing I'm not over Ian?"

He scritch-scratched her back in the way that made her want to purr. "Well, first of all, because you keep wanting to see me."

They laughed.

"Because I like you, duh." He shifted her weight on him. "You're smart and funny and not bad to look at. You're sexy as hell. You've got your shit together, mostly."

Maura made a face. "I thought you knew me."

"I do know you. And I know what it's like to miss someone and want to be with them when you can't. And I'm leaving soon." He ran a fingertip over her collarbone then up her throat to her chin, tickling her to come closer. "I could've spent all this time alone, but that would've been boring as shit. Better to hang out with a cool chick like you who doesn't expect more than I can give."

It was a little bit of an echo of what Ian had said, and it didn't sit well with her even though she'd said much the same thing herself a few minutes before. She frowned anyway. "Yeah."

"I didn't mean it like that," he told her hastily. "Just that...well, if I started seeing anyone seriously, they'd want to move it toward the bedroom. Hell, even if it wasn't that serious. And it's tough, Mo. Telling a woman I can't make love to her. I've had to do it three times now, and you're the first one who didn't act like I told her I had something contagious."

She toyed with the buttons on his shirt. "Have you...umm, I don't know, seen a doctor?"

"It's not physical." He said this too shortly, a little too harsh, but she didn't take it personally.

"Any kind of doctor?"

"You mean a shrink." She thought he might pull away from her when she nodded, but Daniel only shrugged. "No. You're not the first person to suggest it, though."

"It might help you."

"To talk about my loss? The grieving process?" He sounded so scornful she didn't want to push it, but then he looked at her, and his expression softened. "Sorry. I'm being a little bit of an asshole."

She'd never actually been with a man who said he was sorry for that, right up front, and she told him so.

Daniel laughed. "My wife told me once that any man who could admit he was being an asshole would always get extra bonus points for doing it. The trick was, she said, was not just admitting being a jerk, but then stopping whatever it was you were doing that was making you an asshole in the first place."

"Sounds like good advice."

"She had a lot of good advice." His voice cracked, and he put a hand over his eyes. "Fuck, fuck, fuck. I miss her so fucking much."

Maura put her arms around him, pulling his head to her. She stroked his hair while his shoulders heaved. She wasn't used to men's tears. Silent, unsure of what to offer but the comfort of her embrace, she waited until he'd stopped shaking. She kissed the top of his head and squeezed him closer.

"Shit. I'm sorry." He sat up and rubbed at his face, clearly embarrassed.

"Don't be sorry. Friends take care of each other. That's what we do," she told him sternly. "Don't be sorry for that."

He shifted her weight on his lap. "If I tell you something, as a friend, I hope you won't take it the wrong way."

Maura's brows lifted. "What?"

"My leg fell asleep. You're killing me." Daniel grimaced.

They both started laughing, and it cycled up and up while she climbed off the couch and he stood, hopping on one leg to get the other back to life. Then they laughed some more until the hilarity softened and faded and they both flopped back onto the couch to wipe away tears that could've been grief or joy, it was too hard to tell the difference. And maybe, she thought as she snuggled up against him to finish watching the movie, it didn't really matter.

Fifteen

The shadow of pain brings with it a certain satisfaction. I breathe through this pain now, the burning sting of the needle as it presses the ink into my flesh. Focusing on this pain distracts me from any other.

My husband does not like tattoos. He told me he thought only sluts and addicts get themselves inked, and he was totally serious when he said it. This from a man who met me when I already had two small tattoos — the shooting star on my left hip and the celtic knotwork around it. Together they made one design, though I'd had the work at two separate times.

"I never knew you felt like that," I had said to him this morning in our kitchen, where I drank coffee that had been brewed to bitterness and watched him eat toast over the counter without use of a plate. He would walk away and leave the crumbs, and I would have to decide if I were going to refuse to clean them.

He'd shrugged. "I don't see the point in them."

"Guess you'd better never get one, then." I hate the coffee. I hate the crumbs. I hate his face.

He'd shrugged again. "I'm just saying."

I had put the mug in the dishwasher and said without looking at him, "I'm getting another one."

"You're going to do whatever you want to anyway," he'd said then, and left for work without kissing me goodbye.

I had waited until he was gone before I cleaned

the counters. And the sink. The table. I even made time to clean out the fridge, tossing containers of leftover Chinese food and hard, crusted slabs of cheese with mold growing on them. I was almost late to work because of all the cleaning, and none of it made me feel any better.

Now I lay face down on the chair, my face pillowed on my left hand. The other rests at my side, because I need to keep the skin on my right shoulder smooth. That's where the tattoo is going.

I've chosen a Victorian octopus, ornately detailed, inked in shades of red, orange and gold. I couldn't tell you why an octopus, other than I've always loved them. They're smart and adaptable, and lots of people fear them needlessly. The other thing about octopuses that most people don't know is that they mate only once and die shortly afterwards.

I don't think this is romantic. It's biology. Yet there is something appealing about the idea that there is only one person for you out there, the one worth spending your life on. I don't believe it. I think we are programmed for monogamy because it's easier in today's society. It's more romantic to hold onto this notion that somehow when you find that special person you love enough to shackle yourself to financially and emotionally, every other love you've ever had is somehow supposed to fade in comparison, or to no longer matter as much. I don't believe that, and yet something about octopuses appeal to me enough that I want one permanently embedded in my skin.

I haven't made the choice lightly. I've thought

a lot about the design and colors, the location. It will be more visible than the others, which is something to think about. Outing myself to the world as someone with art indelibly inscribed on my skin. How many people will think I am a slut or an addict, I wonder as the woman leaning over my lifts the needle to give me a rest for a second. The swipe of the cloth she uses to wipe away the stencil is briefly soothing.

"Ready to go again?" She murmurs.

"I'm fine."

The sting begins again. Getting deeper this time. I breathe with and not against it — sort of the way Shelly told me she had to do during childbirth, though at this point in my life I have to accept I will probably never know that sort of pain. Just when I think I won't be able to take it any more, the artist gives me another pause.

"You doing okay?"

"I'm good." My voice is thick. Not muffled, but a little slurred. Endorphins, maybe.

"Your skin just soaks up the ink," she says. "Fucking awesome. This is going to look amazing."

I laugh. I sound drunk. "Good. Good."

More pain. It doesn't really cease, even when she lifts the needle, because my skin is on fire. Every so often the burning gets a little stronger, but I don't wince or pull away. I let the pain caress and cover me. I give up to it. I float in the haze of growing agony that builds and builds the longer she works. Eventually the pauses become a different sort of pain, the few seconds of relief worse in a way than the constant pressure of the needle biting into me.

It hurts worse when the pain stops.

***

"I left him about a week after that." Maura looked over her shoulder, bared by the straps of her bra. She wore only the bra and leggings, and Daniel had stopped her just before she pulled her sweater over her head. He traced the outline with his finger until she shivered. "Not because he hated this tattoo. I mean, he truly hated it," she told him, turning. "But it was sort of the impetus. We had a big fight about it. He accused me of wanting to live my own life without him in it, and…well. I told him the truth. That I did."

Daniel stepped back to lean in the doorway to her bathroom. "Tattoos are sexy. On the right people."

"Uh huh." Maura laughed and reached for her sweater. She craned her neck to look at her shoulder in the mirror. "I didn't get it to be sexy. And, even though my ex thought so, I didn't get it to piss him off, either. I got it for myself."

"That should probably be the only reason to get one."

She pulled her sweater over her head, which made a mess of her hair. Finger combing it while she opened her makeup case, she gave him a sideways glance. "Yes. Absolutely."

He watched her line her eyes, her mouth, and

dust her face with powder. She paused before putting her mascara on, thinking about this intimacy she'd never even shared with Ian. She looked at Daniel.

"You don't have to stand there."

"I like watching you." He shrugged. "There's something intensely sexy about watching a woman put on her face."

"That sounds kind of like a creepy serial killer thing to say." Maura stroked the wand through her lashes and put it back in the tube, then made a scary face. "Like next thing I know, you'll be making a coat out of me."

He laughed. "Goofball."

She waved the mascara at him. "It places the lotion in the basket, or it gets the hose again!"

He gave her a curious look. Ian would've — but no. She gave herself a mental shake. She wasn't going to keep doing that. Thinking about how Ian would've understood the joke, probably made it before she did.

"Silence of the Lambs," she explained.

"Never saw it."

Maura shook her head. "Dude, that's kind of like a crime against society or something."

"I guess it came out while I was working overseas or something. Hey, hey, wait." He moved forward to release the edge of her sweater, which had snagged on one of the drawer knobs when she turned. "You're going to put a hole in it."

"I'm so comfortable with you." She hadn't meant to say it, not really. The words just slipped out. She looked up at him, tipping her face for a kiss he gladly gave her. Then a hug, which lingered. She closed her eyes for a minute, breathing in the scent of soap and his cologne. "You always smell good, too."

Daniel squeezed her gently before they pulled apart. "Thank ya, ma'am. I think you smell right purty yourself."

Giggling, she waved him away. "Get out, I have to finish getting ready."

"I don't mind —"

"I have to pee," she said bluntly. "And I prefer to do that in private. We haven't quite reached the bodily functions portion of our relationship, yet."

He held up his hands, backing out of the bathroom as she followed to close the door behind him. "Fine, fine…"

She finished up what she had to do and took a little extra time to add some shimmery shadow to her eyelids along with a little extra liner and a bit darker shade of lipstick. She hadn't been planning on going all out with the makeup tonight, not just to go to dinner and the movies. But that was the thought of a woman not terribly invested in the date, and though she and Daniel certainly had surpassed the need to impress each other, that was no excuse not to make an effort.

She changed out of the sweater and into a clinging shirt that dipped low enough in the front to show off a dangling pendant made from a slice of polished, glittery rock. She pulled her hair on top of her head, leaving a few tendrils to curl around her face. The style emphasized her bare neck and collar bones, and the pendant drew attention to her cleavage. The leggings hugged her ass like a drunken ex-boyfriend, and she gave herself a wink and a grin in the mirror before spraying herself lightly with perfume. Her efforts were worth it for the look on Daniel's face when she came down the stairs.

"Whoa," he said from the couch, where he'd been flicking through the TV channels. He put the remote down and stood to look her over. "I mean…whoa."

Pleased, her cheeks hot, Maura bit back a smile before giving in and beaming. She twirled and gave him a little hip shake. "You like?"

"You look smoking fucking hot." He came to her, those big hands settling on her hips.

She pushed upon her toes to brush a kiss on his mouth. She meant it to be light and quick, but his hand came up to capture the back of her neck. When he dug his fingers into her hair, Maura sighed into the deepening kiss.

"We're going to be late," she breathed after a moment when he showed no signs of stopping.

"How hungry are you?"

She nibbled at his lower lip. "Starving."

He kissed her harder, fingers winding in her hair and tugging her head back so he could move from her mouth to her throat. The moan slipped out of her, unbidden. She hadn't noticed his hand sliding from her hip upward until he cupped her breast, brushing a thumb across it.

Maura broke the kiss abruptly, breathing hard. She licked her lips, watching Daniel's eyes as he followed the motion of her tongue before looking into hers. "Daniel…"

She wasn't sure what she meant to say, but he stopped her words with another kiss. It was shorter this time. Softer, sweeter. He let her go.

"You're right. We should get going. You ready?"

Sexual tension was a fist curled in her stomach, but she nodded and found her coat. He was chatty in the car, talking about music and movies and his upcoming job. Maura kept up her end of the conversation, but it there was an almost manic undertone to everything he said that concerned her. He kept it up in the restaurant, too, ordering them both a bottle of wine without asking her what she wanted, then looking faintly surprised at himself.

"Sorry. I should've asked."

"It's ok. I'll try it." She didn't usually care for red wine, but she could try it. Maura reached across the table to cover his hand with hers. "Hey. You okay?"

Daniel put his on top and turned the one beneath upward so he was grasping hers. "Yeah. Just thinking how close this is to being over."

She curled her fingers into his for a squeeze. "Hey. None of that. We'll keep in touch…."

His laugh was caustic. "Uh huh. I've heard that before."

"That's not how I meant it." Gently, she extricated her hand. "I just meant that it's not like we're going to…break up. I mean, you'll go off to your new assignment the way you'd planned, and you'll email me or check in on Connex. Or something. Won't you?"

For a moment, alarmed, she was sure he was going to say no. Then he shook his head. "I won't have much internet access. Very little cell service. I'll be able to send you old-fashioned letters."

"That could be fun." She smiled at him, leaning back as the waiter brought the wine and poured it. "Letter writing is a lost art."

"It won't be the same."

"No. I guess it won't." She didn't lose her smile, but it faltered a bit. She drank some wine, though the flavor wrinkled her nose.

Daniel drank too. "I guess we should just enjoy the time we have left, huh?"

"Yes. Of course. Always." She lifted her glass and clinked it to his. "To good friends."

"To friends." He gave her a steady look. "Actually, Maura, I was hoping to talk to you about something tonight…"

She flashed back to high school, standing by her locker, waiting for Shelly to be done in the guidance office. Stan Slever tapping her on the shoulder, staring at her with those huge eyes behind the thick glasses, his perpetually wet mouth open as he started to ask her to the prom. He'd opened with that same phrase. Maura, I was hoping to talk to you about something…Whatever he wanted to ask her, it was bigger than the prom, and all she could do was sit there and listen with the same slack expression she was sure she'd had the day with Stan.

"I was hoping, maybe…you'd consider taking this a little further." Daniel looked nervous, then drank some wine, sloshing it. He swallowed hard but gave her a hard smile.

"Further?" How much further could they go? Oh, God, he wasn't asking her to move with him, was he? To Malaysia?

He must've seen her confusion and dismay, because he coughed into his hand. "Maybe further isn't the right word. Um...I mean, I was hoping maybe you'd consider taking this relationship a little...beyond friends."

She chewed the inside of her cheek at that. "I thought we were beyond friends. I mean, I don't sleep with my friends. I don't kiss or fool around with my friends."

"Shit. I'm making this a mess."

"A little," she said. "But it's okay."

"I like you. I'm comfortable with you. We get along great. We have a history together." Daniel paused.

Maura breathed out, unsure of how she felt about this. "Yes. All of that. I like you, too, Daniel."

"So maybe we could consider ourselves dating?"

Again, she was confused. "What have we been doing all this time, if not dating?"

"Oh. I thought we were just hanging out."

She thought about drinking more wine, but hadn't liked the first sip and was pretty sure she wouldn't like the next. Something in this conversation wasn't sitting right with her, though she couldn't have said exactly what it was. "Hanging...out."

"Well. Yeah. I mean, with all the talk about me leaving and it not lasting. And Ian," Daniel added.

Maura frowned. "But now you...what? Want to make me your girlfriend?"

"Yes." Daniel straightened. Squared his shoulders.

"A week before you go to the other side of the world?" Maura sat back in her chair, hands in her lap, bunching her napkin. "You want something permanent, with a name, now?"

"I wasn't thinking of it like that, but...yes. I would like you to be my girlfriend. For real. Official and all that." He gave her a hesitant grin. "Feels weird, huh?"

"I wasn't ever your girlfriend, really, even way back in the olden days. Yes. It feels weird." More than that. It felt like doublethink. Wrong and right at the same time, and she could easily believe both.

"Will you think about it?"

She nodded after a moment's hesitation, not ready to contemplate all the complications of it but unwilling to turn him down outright. "I'll think about it. I'm not sure how it will work, but sure. I'll think about it."

He reached for her hand again. Palm to palm — the kiss of holy fools, she thought, butchering Shakespeare. She couldn't pull away, though she didn't want Daniel to feel the shaking of her fingers and misinterpret it.

"Good," he said. "That's all I ask. That you think about it."

And after that, the conversation turned to other topics. A little strained, but not too bad. Maura tried not to think too much about what he'd asked her, even though she'd promised. She concentrated on her dinner, which she now found she could barely eat.

Girlfriend. Daniel's girlfriend. What was there to fear about that, other than the distance? Other than the physical issues, which she was ashamed to admit hadn't bothered her as much when she thought he'd be leaving in a couple months but now, faced with the possibility of trying to make a romantic long-distance and also chaste relationship out of what she'd thought had been a lovely, if unconventional friendship…

"Dessert?"

Startled out of her thoughts, Maura looked up at the waiter. "Oh. No. I don't think so. I'm stuffed."

"Would you like a box for that?" The waiter asked, making her sound like a liar because it was clear she'd barely eaten more than a few bites of her dinner.

She declined the box. And, quiet for the rest of the meal, thinking hard about what she wanted not only from Daniel, but also from life, Maura forced herself to focus on not only him, but everything around them. There were couples holding hands across the table and those who were clearly at odds, avoiding eye contact. There were girlfriends giggling over the hot waiter and, far in the back, a bunch of men being rowdy. Bachelor party, maybe. Relationships all around her. Some that worked, some that didn't.

"You okay?" Daniel asked her after he'd paid the check and helped her on with her coat. "You're very quiet."

She gave him a smile. "Fine. Just thinking."

"Ah." He didn't ask again.

She appreciated that. Paid attention to his consideration. She paid attention to the way he held the door for her, offered to pay for the movie, asked her if she wanted butter on her popcorn. It wasn't the money, but the way he was trying to make this night fun for her. It was how he looked at her, too, with a smile that reached his eyes. It was also the way he didn't look at her.

The movie was something full of explosions and aliens, with some kissing at the end. He held her hand through the whole thing, their fingers linked and resting on his thigh. And it was nice. More than nice. It was lovely, she thought when the credits rolled and the lights came up, and blinking, he turned to her and said, "What's next?"

"I have an idea," Maura said.

***

Getting a tattoo is never something you should do on a whim, but Maura had been thinking about it for a long time. The place she'd gone to get her octopus had closed some time ago, but the girl who'd done her work had sent out postcards announcing that she was working at a new place. It was open, and it took walk-ins, and it was right around the corner from the movie theater.

"You don't mind?" Maura asked Daniel.

He looked up from the binder of photographs he'd been flipping through. "No. Of course not. I can go back with you and watch, right?"

"Yep." She leaned over his shoulder to point out a particularly stunning pin-up girl on some anonymous calf. "You sure you don't want something like that?"

He laughed. "Um, no. Maybe another time."

"Ha." Maura studied the different licenses on the walls. The framed dollar bill. She liked the poster that said "No, it didn't hurt. My tattoo was licked on by a couple of kittens."

In another minute, Gretel, the tattoo artist, was calling her back. Maura got settled in the barber chair and held out her right wrist. It was going to be something very simple. One word.

Enough.

Daniel hadn't asked her what she was getting, or why, but Gretel did. She wet the stencil and pressed it to the inside of Maura's wrist. "Take a look at that. Why 'enough'?"

Maura didn't look at Daniel, who'd taken a seat on the stool beside her. "It's a reminder."

"Cool." Gretel didn't press for more information. She settled herself on her stool and held up the gun. "Ready?"

"Yes."

"It won't take very long," she promised, and Maura knew that was true.

It would take long enough.

The sweet sting began, and something like a moan slipped out of her. Gretel laughed softly. Maura wasn't embarrassed. She was sure Gretel had heard everything from screams to whimpers. A semi-sex noise couldn't possibly faze her.

Maura glanced at Daniel, though, and his eyes were gleaming. He leaned forward, looking from his wrist to her face. "It hurts, huh?"

"The skin's thin here." Gretel sat up for a second to wipe away some of the excess ink. "The top of the feet hurts worse."

"It hurts," Maura said. "Enough."

Daniel met her gaze and gave a small nod, like he understood. Maybe he did. But after that, Maura closed her eyes and let the pain warm her.

It didn't take long for Gretel to finish, since it was that single word in a plain script, done in black. "Check it out."

Maura looked at it. As always, it was trippy knowing that she had marked herself permanently, that she would never again be able to look at that spot without seeing this new piece of her. And, like the other times she'd had work done, the euphoria left her a little woozy. She stood, reaching for Daniel to steady her.

"I want one," he said.

Gretel looked up at him. "Yeah? Right now? I have time, depending on what you want to do."

Daniel looked thoughtful. "You know the infinity symbol?"

"Sure."

Maura knew it, too. "Where do you want it?"

He tapped the spot over his chest thoughtfully. "Here?"

"That would be cool." Gretel nodded, and Maura wondered if everything seemed cool, or if she'd ever given someone advice against a design or location.

Twenty minutes later, Daniel stared in the mirror at the new addition to his formerly flawless skin. He turned a little to the left and right. Then he nodded a little at his own reflection.

"You like it?" Maura asked in the car.

"It's too late now if I don't, isn't it?"

She wanted to ask him why the infinity symbol, but something stopped her. He hadn't asked her about hers. Maybe that would come later, or maybe they'd never ask each other.

"It does hurt," Daniel said and tapped himself just above the tattoo. "More than I expected."

Maura flexed her wrist, feeling the ache there. "Yes. Sometimes it does."

***

Daniel was good looking. Generous. Kind hearted. He was handy, too. He built a fire in her fireplace without any effort at all and looked at her over his shoulder, his face lit by a grin that could make a woman fall in love.

If she could.

Maura had put on some music, something light and chosen at random from the online radio station she'd programmed to play. She had a bottle of wine. It was cold outside and warm in. She had a handsome man who wanted to try to make something work with her, and this was her chance to figure out if she wanted that, too.

"Dance with me," she said impulsively as he

stood, brushing off his hands. She held out hers, and he took them.

Daniel looked down at her with a faint smile. "Yeah?"

"Yep." She snuggled close to him, her head on his chest. The sound of his heart was comforting, and so was his warmth. The weight of his hand on the small of her back was so familiar, though, so full of memory and association with Ian that she could not quite relax into this embrace.

Daniel didn't ask her to. He didn't say anything about being his girlfriend. All he did was dance with her. Slowly, slowly, their feet shuffling on the rough shag of her carpet. The songs blended, one to the other, and still they danced.

Sometimes there was so much to think about that it was better to think of nothing at all. Maura looked up at him, studying his face, remembering how it had looked so many years ago. She'd fallen a little in love with him back then, in some way. Maybe…maybe she could, again.

"If we're going to try this," Maura said, "we need to lay it all out, what it means. I'm not jumping into this randomly. I want to put the expectations on the table. Negotiations. I want everything to be upfront and totally clear between us. No surprises."

He nodded, solemn. "Okay."

"Does that sound too business-like?" She chewed the inside of her cheek for a second.

"It's not very romantic, that's for sure."

"Sorry."

He laughed and pulled her close again. "It's

okay. I want you to know what you're getting into. I mean, I think that's good for both of us."

"This is definitely the weirdest way I've ever started a relationship," she said, then added, "though on second thought, it's already been started, I guess. And that wasn't weird. Just this part is weird."

Then they both started laughing again, until he cut it off with a kiss that got deeper and deeper until she had to break away for a breath. He tasted good. He smelled good. He felt good against her.

It wasn't love, not even close. But it was something, wasn't it? And maybe that would also be enough.

Sixteen

There's a certain comfort in being with someone you can be in your PJ's with. Face scrubbed, hair in a bun on top of my head to keep it from getting tangled while I sleep, I get into bed beside Daniel in my favorite flannel jammies. They're not sexy, but they are warm.

He's propped up on the pillows, reading something on his phone. I lean to kiss his bare shoulder before tucking myself into my own pillows. I'm tired, a little tipsy from the wine and this new decision to make what we had something more official. I'm thinking of nothing but sleep when he turns out the light and rolls over to spoon me. I mean…there's nothing more to expect, really. I already know there won't be any sex.

Except he kisses the back of my neck, his breath hot. His hand moves up to cup my breast. Thumb my nipple erect. I don't mean to react so quickly, but I guess I'm wired for touch. Should I feel bad about this? Because I don't.

My hand goes behind his neck as I turn my face for his kiss. I roll to face him, my knee nudging between his thighs. I press myself against him. Mouths open. Tongues stroke. We kiss for long minutes. When he slides a hand between us, I gasp a little.

"You like that." It's not a question.

"Yes," I say.

"Good." He rubs gently on the outside of the flannel.

I want him to push his hands inside. Touch my bare skin beneath. But that's selfish of me; even if he has already on a few occasions made me come without any hope of reciprocity, that doesn't mean I should take advantage of it. Still, I shudder a little at the pressure of his fingers on my clit through the soft fabric.

"Too many clothes," he murmurs. "Take these off."

I hesitate. "Are you sure?"

Even if he seems to have at least mostly accepted his inability to get an erection, I don't want to pressure him. I don't want to be unfair, or teasing. But Daniel nods and gives me a grin I can see in the light from the window outside. He tugs at the waistband of my pajamas.

"Off."

Together, we work me free of the confines of my pajamas. Naked, I lay on my back and put my hands over my head to grip the spindles of my headboard as he moves his hand over my body. Daniel covers me with caresses. Hands, followed by mouth. He draws a line of kisses along my collarbones, over my breasts until he takes my nipple in his mouth and tugs gently at it.

"Oh, yes." It feels so good. I arch into the touch. He sucks a little harder. Then to the next one while his fingers keep up the delicious pressure on the first, still wet from his mouth.

His breathing becomes ragged as he moves back and forth between them. He pushes my breasts together so he can get his mouth on both more easily. Lying between my legs, he pushes his belly against my cunt and I rock my hips upward without a second thought. My clit on his bare skin makes me want to moan, but my breath is so caught in my throat all I can do is let out a long, shuddering sigh.

"So fucking sexy," he says against my skin.

Daniel's mouth moves lower. Over my ribs. Along the inside of my arm. He pauses at my elbow to mouth me there; it tickles and I squirm. A little lower. He holds my hand, turning my wrist upward so he can see the word inked there.

"Enough," he whispers, but doesn't kiss my still-wounded flesh.

"Yes." I sit up, and so does he. I touch the skin close to his new tattoo. "I chose enough. You chose forever."

"Could mean the same thing," Daniel says.

I don't think so, but I don't say it. I find his mouth with mine and let the kiss speak, instead. My body will tell him what I can't convince my words to say.

He pushes me back against the pillows again. Kneeling in front of me, he pushes his pants over his hips, his thighs, then off. I don't want to stare, so I keep my eyes on his face. Daniel covers me with his body as we kiss.

He moves down it again, marking every spot with his mouth and hands. The residue of pain euphoria from the tattoo faded hours ago, replaced by a less pleasant stinging ache, but his kisses ease that to the back of my mind. I let myself relax into the caresses.

Daniel's mouth moves over my hip, nibbling at the tattoos there. My thigh. My knee, which makes me giggle and squirm. He cuffs my ankle to hold my leg still as he works his way down, making sure to kiss the tops of my feet. Gretel said that's the place tattoos hurt the worst, and I understand why — I don't think anyone's ever kissed me there, and the sensation is tingly and prickly and utterly delicious. His strong hands work at my arch, easing aches I didn't know I had. When he kisses my instep, my foot jerks involuntarily.

"I'm not going to suck your toes," he promises with a laugh. "Unless you're into that sort of thing."

"I don't think so."

He moves up my leg. Inner thigh. His breath caresses my pussy, and I hold my breath, waiting for his kiss. The slickness of his tongue. His fingers inside me.

He makes me wait.

When at last I feel the pressure of his mouth on me, I arch and sigh. Eyes closed, my hands again find the headboard, gripping tight. I want him to take control of this. Do whatever he wants. It feels important to me, somehow, like I'm giving him something he wouldn't think to ask for.

His moan resonates inside me, and for a moment I tense. I don't look at him. I rock my hips against his mouth, but just a little. His tongue flickers on my clit. He pushes my thighs wider apart, hands going under my ass to hold me to his lips and tongue. When he sucks gently on my clit, I cry out.

Daniel moans again. He moves me against him, and the synchronicity of mouth and hands has me edging closer and closer. The headboard creaks from the tightness of my grip.

"You are so good at this." My voice is low and rough, rasping. My back arches a little more, pressing my head onto the pillow. I turn it from side to side, slowly, as my hips rock.

"You taste so good. You feel so good. Fuck, Maura. You are so…" He trails off, his attention back on my clit.

I'm riding this wave of pleasure, getting closer, when he stops so abruptly I have to look at him. Daniel's kneeling between my legs, his mouth wet and open. Eyes hungry. His fist grips his cock, stroking…and he's hard. Getting harder as I watch.

I don't know what to do, what to say. He knows I see it, but if I say something, will it ruin it for him? Will he lose his erection? Should I touch him?

"Just…stay right there," he says. "Can you touch yourself for me, Maura? While I watch?"

My hand moves between my legs without hesitation. I'm already so close that the tweak of my fingers on my clit is enough to make my cunt clench. I push two deep inside me, finding heat and wetness. My thumb strokes my clit while I move my fingers in and out, mimicking the pace he's set with his fist.

Daniel's head goes back. The muscles in his arms stand out. The infinity symbol over his heart is very, very black against his skin. It jumps with the beat of his heart. He pumps his cock slowly, then faster. We're working together though neither of us is touching each other.

"I'm going to come." I say it quietly, each word

almost a stutter. So close. Feels so good. I know how to bring myself pleasure faster than anyone else ever has, but it's different when I do it myself. I'm teasing, letting myself get closer to the edge without going over. I'm waiting for him.

Praying for him, actually, though I'm sure God has better things to do than worry about a guy losing a hard-on. Still, I know this is embarrassing for Daniel. Something hard to live with. If I can do anything at all to help him come, I'll pray.

"Oh. Fuck." He grits his teeth, fist pumping faster. Sweat has beaded on his brow and lip. His face is flushed. "Oh, yeah…"

I take a chance, offer him the encouragement of my voice. My fingers circle faster. I groan. I sigh. "Come for me, Daniel. I want to see you come."

He looks at me, really at me. Focusing. "I'm going to come."

"Yes," I breathe, tipping over with him. "Come for me."

The first shot hits the bed next to my head like a bullet, so hard I actually hear it thump the pillow. He jets, shuddering, cock throbbing. It spills over his fist, over his belly. All over mine. My orgasm hits me in slow ripples — it feels good, but I'm pretty sure it's not even close to what he's feeling.

He comes forever. Shaking. When at last his hand stops stroking, his shoulders hunch. He lets out a long, low sigh. When he looks at me, finally, I can only imagine what he must see — he's covered me with the evidence of his pleasure.

He crawls up my body to kiss me. "Thank you."

"You're…welcome." It feels silly to say, but it's the only thing I can think of.

Without asking, Daniel pads naked into my bathroom and comes back with a warm, wet cloth that he uses to clean me and the bed and anything else that needs it. Then, still naked, he crawls into bed beside me and falls asleep.

I am sexually sated. I am more than a little humbled and flattered. I potentially have a boyfriend, now, and yes, it looks as though we might eventually, actually fuck.

But I can't sleep.

I get up from the bed and slip on my pajamas. I go to the kitchen to make myself a cup of tea. I think about what it means, this new thing. If I want to do it with Daniel. Or at all. If I even can. And while I'm thinking, I go to my laptop and scroll the blogs I read, my Connex wall. It's late and I'm tired, and I'm not…unhappy.

But if this boyfriend thing is going to work, I'm sure the negotiations will include no dating, so though I haven't even logged into my Luvfinder account in over a month, I figure I might as well delete it now while the world of dreams dances out of reach. I log in. Scroll through my profile, to my account. I try to find the place where I can delete my account, unsurprised to discover they don't make it easy. I find what I need, and in one last moment of casual curiosity, I check my nudges.

And that's when everything falls apart.

That's when my world breaks, shatters. Because when I click on the long list of requests, there is only one name that stands out to me in all of them.

Ian.

***

Her decision shouldn't have been as easy as it was, but Daniel hadn't heard more than Ian's name before he turned on his heel and left the kitchen without waiting for Maura to finish her sentence. She watched him go, her stomach in knots, but didn't go after him. Not right away. Not soon enough.

That, she guessed was her answer about what she really wanted, anyway.

Still, when she heard the front door open, she forced herself to move fast enough to catch him before he could get to his car. "Daniel. Wait."

He'd paused on her porch to put his shoes on, and he turned. "What."

"You didn't even let me finish."

"Was there more?" He shoved his foot into his shoe and stood, shaking the leg of his jeans to straighten it.

Maura didn't blame him for being upset, but at the same time, his instant assumption that she was going to dump him for Ian set her stubborn function in motion. "All you let me say was that Ian asked me for a date on my Luvfinder account."

"I think that's enough to know, isn't it?"

"I didn't say I was going to go."

"What were you doing on there, anyway?"

Daniel moved closer, his eyes bright. Cheeks flushed. "After we...shit, Maura. I thought we were..."

"I was going on it to delete my account!"

"At two in the morning?"

Maura's shoulders straightened. Her jaw set. "I told you, I couldn't sleep."

"Yeah. Whatever. I'm out of here." Daniel made a pushing away gesture. "See you around."

"Don't go like that."

At least he stopped again, though this time he wouldn't turn to look at her. "Just...forget it. Okay? I was stupid to think this would work. I'm going off to Malaysia. You've got Ian, and I know you're in love with him. He's just going to fuck with your head again, you know that, right? But I guess it doesn't matter."

"I didn't say I was going to go out with him!"

Daniel shook his head. "But you want to. Don't you?"

She didn't have a ready answer for that. Her first response had been vindication. Ian wanted her. Ian was apologizing. Ian was, finally, the one doing the chasing. But vindication isn't satisfaction, and despite her reservations about committing to a relationship with Daniel, she had agreed to it, and she hadn't been willing to back out simply because Ian had finally seemed to get his shit together.

"Never mind," Daniel said without waiting for her to answer. "Just forget it. I should've known better."

"Daniel. Wait." But once she'd asked him to wait, Maura didn't know what she wanted him to wait for. Hesitantly, she reached for him, but he didn't reach back. She let her hand fall back to her side. "I'm sorry. Please don't go like this."

"I'm not sure what you expect me to do or say, not after that little story you just told me."

"Stay for breakfast, anyway. I can make eggs and toast…"

Bitter laughter barked out of him. "Oh, sure. Break it off with me, then make me breakfast. Real classy, Maura. Thanks. But no, I think I'll pass."

"I didn't break it off with you! If you'd just listen —"

Daniel waved a dismissive hand in response.

"You know what?" She snapped, crossing her arms, "Go, then. I could've told you nothing, but I wanted to be up front with you. He contacted me. Would you rather have had me say nothing?"

"I'd rather have you just turn him down!"

Maura rubbed the tip of her tongue along the back of her teeth as each word of her response seemed to form itself letter by single letter.

"You can't say you don't want to see him."

"No," she said. "I guess I can't say that and be telling the truth. But that doesn't mean I was going to dump you. Especially not after…"

At the look on his face, she stopped herself from saying more. Daniel drew himself up as carefully as a man who'd been kicked in the junk. In a way, maybe he felt like he had. He took the first step off the porch, then looked back at her.

"Good luck. He's going to fuck you over again, because that's why guys like him do. And you're going to let him, because that's what women like you do. Can't see what you have right in front of your face. Fuck you, I'm over it."

Maura recoiled at his vehemence. "Wow. You know what? If that's how you're going to be about it, yes. Go. I'm over it, too."

Daniel stayed put, glaring at her. Maura glared back. She didn't blame him for being irritated or uncertain — but his attitude? That could get fucked with something hard and sandpapery.

"You couldn't even give me the rest of the week?" He bit out the question. "I'm going out of the country, for God's sakes. You couldn't just fucking give me a week?"

"And then what, we could've started some kind of fucked up, long-distance relationship?"

"Maybe...we could've..." Daniel glared at her. "You could've broken it off a helluva lot better than this, anyway."

She goggled, mouth open wide before she shut it with a click of her teeth. "I was trying to be honest with you! I guess maybe I should've lied to you. That would've been better?"

"Then I could've hated you," Daniel said, "instead of just thinking you're stupid."

She blinked. Then again. Then carefully, slowly and deliberately, she backed over her threshold, maintaining eye contact the whole time. Then she firmly shut the door without saying another word to him.

Seventeen

I used to be incapable of imagining any way Ian could ever disappoint me; that's how hard I'd fallen. Everything he did was perfect and alluring and delightful. My head knew that the realities of things like sharing space and debts and chores would surely wear that all away. That's what happens in relationships. You get used to each other, and the habits and mannerisms that once you found so charming become the grain of sand in an oyster. If you love each other enough, you make a pearl around the things that make you crazy. If you don't…well. Lots of people don't. My head knew that, but my stupid heart refused to pay attention.

Still, I did find it hard to believe Ian could ever make me go white-hot with rage. There were none of those niggling, back-of-the-mind excuses about behavior I'd made for other lovers. And with so little time, all of it stolen, there was no place for silly arguments.

And that's the issue. Time. I don't have enough of it, and Ian doesn't seem to understand that whatever time there was, it needs to be cherished. Not wasted.

"Lunch," I say to his tiny, precious face in my phone's screen. I should've known better than to let him video call me. It always makes it harder to resist him, but who am I kidding. I can never resist Ian. "An hour?"

Ian's nose wrinkles, and he shakes his head. "I'd have to leave the office, fight traffic…plus I already brought my lunch."

"So you're saying you'd choose a dry turkey sandwich at your desk over lunch with me?" I keep my voice light, almost teasing. I don't want him to know how desperate I am to see him. It's been over two weeks, and the last chance we had was only for an hour or so. If that's all I can get, I'll take it, but it's not enough. It's never enough.

"What time would you want to meet? And where?"

"How about Ambrosia. It's that new place about twenty minutes from your office. At eleven? So it's not crowded, we'll avoid traffic…" I trail off, already seeing the 'no' in his face. I won't beg. I won't chase.

"Nah. That's quite a hike. Just can't make it work. Another time, maybe. Sorry." He doesn't sound sorry at all.

We make another few minutes of small talk, but my answers are curt and I can't really look at him any more. I cut the call short and sit with my phone in my hands, staring at the screen, which seems blanker without his face decorating it. I eat my own lunch at my desk, and though my phone pings with a message from him, I don't even look at it until it's time to go home.

It's not the only time Ian passes up a chance for us to get together. For days he'll message me constantly throughout the day, sending photos, jokes, flirty emoticons. Sometimes, he makes wistful comments like "really wish I could see you."

But when I give him the chance to really see me, not in a photo or a video call but my real face, my real hands, my real mouth…he can't manage to make it happen. It makes me desperate, hating myself for being the stereotypical, clinging girlfriend who can't let her man out of her sight long enough to have a life to go out with friends or even time alone.

Except that I'm not Ian's girlfriend, and we don't have much time as it is. There are vast, long stretches when seeing him is impossible, so when I am able to make the space in my complicated and increasingly stressful life, is it so wrong for me to expect him to find a way to see me?

Apparently Ian thinks so, and that's when I discover I can be disappointed in him, after all.

It is our first fight, and it's a doozy. Predictably, it happens when we actually are together, which makes me feel all the more irrational for complaining — and I fucking hate feeling irrational and out of control with the fire of a hundred thousand supernova suns. I've managed to convince Ian to meet me for an hour or two in one of those cheesy roadside motels that feature little cabins instead of a long row of rooms. Our cabin is number six, and I paid forty-nine dollars cash for the night, even though we won't be staying much past eight o'clock.

The double bed doesn't look particularly comfortable, but the comforter is a whimsical quilt and the artwork is framed photographs that look as though an actual person took them, not pictures in frames bought in bulk. I study one — a covered bridge. It's a common theme around here, but this black and white shot has managed to capture something almost creepy about the traditional composition of bridge and stream and road.

"Cry Baby Bridge," I say with a snap of my fingers. "That's what it reminds me of!"

Ian has turned on the television. Without a remote, he has to flip through the channels by hand. The first flicker of annoyance sidesteps its way through me. We're here to fuck, not watch The Price is Right.

"Ever heard of it?"

He looks at me. "Huh?"

"Cry Baby Bridge. It's supposed to be about an hour from here. It's one of those urban legend things." I watch his face for any signs of recognition, but of course that sort of stuff is my purview, not Ian's. He'll dismiss it as silliness, I'm sure. "Some young unwed mother in 1880 or something like that was supposed to have jumped to her death there. You're supposed to be able to hear the baby crying."

Ian shrugs without much interest. "Creepy."

"We should go." I say it impulsively. I cross to him, pull him by the collar toward me for a kiss. "You wanna?"

"Now?"

"No." I think for a moment, calculating ahead, putting pieces together that hadn't, until just now, fit. "Sunday."

Chad will be out of town with his fishing buddies from sometime before dawn until probably late at night. Ian and I could have the whole day together. A nice drive. A creepy bridge. Lunch. And, if the timing's right, I'm sure we could find another of these roadside cabins and get naked, but really...

"I want to spend the day with you. I just want some time." I find his mouth for a kiss. I pull him closer, breathing him in. Already my breath is quickening, my pulse leaping. Heat in my throat and chest and between my legs.

"You're spending time with me right now." His hands roam along my back, my ass, anchor on my hips. His mouth finds my throat and I want to tip my head back to take advantage of this embrace, but something in his tone stops me.

"Well...yeah. But does that mean we can't spend the day together on Sunday, too? It would be fun."

Ian looks shifty. Not guilty — if I didn't know better, I might think he has someone else to spend his Sunday with, and I know that's not true. At least, I used to know it. Now I'm not so sure.

I step out of his embrace. "Ian."

"Let's just enjoy the time we have right now." He tries to pull me closer, but I'm not having it.

Ian often makes my hands shake, but from desire. Now another heated emotion is twitching my fingers so I have to curl them into fists and tuck them into my armpits, my crossed arms a shield. "You don't want to spend the day with me?"

Ian sighs and scrubs at his mouth with the back of his hand for a moment. "Look, we're here together, now. It's Wednesday. You're talking about Sunday already. Spend the day together? And before you know it, we'll be sneaking off for nooners three times a week…"

"And?" I shoot back at him. Shit, my voice is shaking as much as my hands. "What's your point? You don't want to see me three times a week? Or is it just that you don't want to see me unless you're fucking me? We can fuck on Sunday, if you really want to, I'm sure we can find someplace to go."

I've never seen Ian angry. Maybe, like me, he never thought I could make him. He's pissed off now, though. His entire expression goes hard-edged and fierce.

"Stop it, Maura."

I should stop it. I should not pick a fight now, wasting the precious minutes we have. The only ones, apparently, I'm going to get until who knows when. But I am tired of being put off. Tired of excuses.

"Spend the day with me on Sunday. The whole day."

"I can't make it work," Ian says, voice flat and final. "Sorry."

"Why not?"

"Because first you want to meet me for lunch, then you want to meet me here, then you want to spend the day with me. It's too much. We need to put the brakes on this."

Medusa has nothing on the look I give him. "Are you fucking kidding me?"

Ian hasn't turned to stone. He reaches for me, but I duck away from his grasp. "C'mon. Maura. Don't be like that."

"Like what?" Eyes narrowed, voice harsh, I'm daring him. To call me a bitch, maybe a crazy bitch. Maybe he'll throw 'needy' in there, too.

"Just don't."

"I'm asking you for too much? Is that what you're trying to tell me?" Fighting tears, I search for my purse. Thank God we aren't naked. Thank God I can get out of here before I burst into hysterical, wrenching sobs.

"It's going too fast!" Ian shouts.

I stop. Turn. We've known each other for almost two years. We talk several times a week, several times a day— when Ian wants to. Less often but still frequently when he does not. It's only been a few months since we started fucking, but we do that when he wants, too.

This is an imperfect thing, what we have, but it's all there is for us right now. And after all that, he's telling me it's too much. We're going too fast.

"Snails could outrace us at this point, Ian." I shrug my purse over my shoulder and head for the door.

Ian manages to snag my sleeve enough to turn me. "Don't go."

"Why? You want to get your dick sucked before I do? Is that it? That's not too fucking fast for you is it? I promise you," I say with a smile that has nothing to do with joy, "I can make it slow."

I can see the struggle in his eyes and the shape of his mouth as he works to form words he's smart enough not to say. Even so, what he does say is bad enough. "It's just crossing a line."

"What is?"

"Spending the day with you. It would be too much." Ian shakes his head and backs up a step. "That's all."

"But fucking me, that's okay? Texting me pictures of your hard cock, that's not crossing a line?" My voice is getting louder, raking at my throat. I'm sure I am wild-eyed, and I don't care. "Telling me you love me, Ian, that's not crossing a fucking line?"

I'm screaming by the time I get to the end of my sentence. I don't care who hears me. I don't even care if he thinks I am a raging harridan. I throw my purse on the ground hard enough to spill everything out of it. I hear the crack of something breaking. I don't care about that, either.

"Maybe you didn't mean it," I shout, "but I sure as fuck believed you. You know how I feel about you, and I ask you for next to fucking nothing, Ian, because I'm so goddamned tired of being told no, and every time you turn me down, I tell myself it is the last fucking time. Because this is not working. Because I have shit I need to deal with in my life, and it's tearing me apart and breaking me down, but I am fucking doing it, Ian, I am ripping my life apart at the seams, and I am not doing it for you. I'm doing it because I can not fucking live another moment the way I have been, and because…" I falter, voice raw, breath harsh in my throat, tears blinding me. "Goddammit, Ian. I love you. And maybe you don't love me back, but you just keep letting me. So tell me again why spending some time with me is crossing a line. Please. Tell me how that works, because I just don't understand."

"What the hell do you want from me? What do you think this is, exactly? A relationship?"

I hate him in that moment, for making me into everything I despise. Weak and clinging and needy. Desperate. But I will be damned if I let him see me that way.

"I hate to break the news to you, sweetheart," I tell him in a cold, faraway voice, "but like it or not, yes. That's exactly what this is."

Ian says nothing.

I bend to gather the contents of my purse, shoving everything in haphazardly, not caring that I spill coins and tampons and lipsticks all over. I find my keys, but when I try to stand, I can't. I can not stand. All I can do is crumple to my hands and knees on that shitty motel room carpet and begin to cry.

I want to fight his hands on me, but I can't do that either. Ian helps me up. Leads me to the bed. I turn my face away from his kiss. Fight him when he tries to hold me. I make my body stiff and unyielding. I make myself refuse him.

Ian pins my wrists with one hand. Locks his fingers in my hair. He's stronger than I am, holding me when I struggle, but I want to make him hurt me. I want the bruises. They'll be proof of my pain he won't be able to ignore. I fight him, but Ian won't let go.

"I'm sorry," he says, over and over. "I'm so sorry."

He kisses me, and I let him.

"Don't cry, Maura. Please don't cry."

He touches me, and I let him.

"I never wanted to hurt you."

He undresses me, and I let him.

Ian pushes me back onto the bed. Works at my clothes. His fingers and tongue find my bare skin. His mouth slides along my inner thigh. He finds my clit. Fingers inside me, tongue working, Ian murmurs a long list of everything he plans on doing to me.

He makes love to me with his mouth, and I let him.

When it's over, and I am spent, panting on the bed with him kissing my mouth, Ian says to me, "you are my flower, Maura. My flower in the desert. I'm sorry. I'm so sorry. Please forgive me."

Ian apologizes to me, but I can't forgive him.

***

"I saw him only once after that. Chad and I had a fight, and I ran out of the house. Literally ran to Ian's house, which was really far away. We fucked that night, and I was going to tell him I was leaving Chad, but I didn't. I guess I wanted to get all my ducks in a row before I told him, so that he'd have no excuses. That he'd know it wasn't…that he didn't have to feel guilty…" Maura swallowed hard. "Guess that didn't turn out the way I'd hoped."

Shelly poured more wine into Maura's glass and pushed the plate of bruschetta toward her. "This is good. Eat this."

Maura sipped wine and took one of the squares

of toast heaped high with Shelly's homemade bruschetta. So far she'd been able to avoid the platters of cookies and cheeses, but she couldn't hold out for much longer. The food at Shelly's parties was legendary, and she'd gone all out for this one. It was her daughter Melody's eighteenth birthday and she'd just been accepted to Princeton. The celebration was on.

"It was the only real fight we ever had, at least the kind with shouting. It was the worst one, anyway. I was so angry with him for the things he said. But I let him go down on me." Maura shook her head, blushing at the memory.

"It's a little thing I like to call ragefucking." Shelly laughed.

"Well, if Daniel had tried to so much as blow me a kiss, I'm pretty sure I'd have kneed him in the nuts."

Shelly gave Maura a knowing look. "Were you in love with Daniel?"

"Nope. But I liked him. I thought maybe we could try to make something. I didn't mean to hurt him." The wine couldn't quite erase the bitterness of the memory. "But if that's the way he was going to react to things, better I found out first, I guess."

"Ragefucking only works if you're crazy mad in love with someone." Shelly offered this bit of advice as she scooped a carrot through a bowl of hummus. "Something to do with hormones."

Maura rolled her eyes. "Uh huh."

"So what did you tell Daniel when he called you?"

"I said that I understood why he was angry, and

I apologized, but I told him I was not going to be his long distance girlfriend and that honestly, I thought he needed to get his shit under control." Maura paused with a grimace, remembering. "He got kind of cold and distant after that, but he didn't yell at me again."

"He's a shit show," Shelly said flatly.

Maura laughed. "Well. Yeah. But like I'm not?"

"You should just tell Ian you miss him. Call him up, tell him you're going crazy without him, and that you need to talk to him," Shelly said.

Maura shook her head. "Can't. Won't. Can't. It doesn't matter. I'm not going to tell him that."

"Why the hell not?"

"Because," Maura said carefully, "then he'll know."

"And that's a problem because…?"

She sighed, loving that she had a friend good enough to understand, hating that the friend was good enough to also call her on her bullshit. "It's been over a month. What if he doesn't miss me? What if he's not waiting around for me to call him? What if he's actually happy and relieved and fine with not hearing from me, ever, at all?"

"Girl, I never knew you to be scared of stupid stuff like that." Shelly gave her head a woeful shake. "Damn. What the hell has this dude done to your self confidence?"

"He ate it," Maura said. "And now it's all gone."

"Bullshit."

It was, maybe, bullshit. Maybe not. Maura

sipped her wine, then shrugged.

"So. Ian sends you a date request through Luvfinder. What, he can't just call you up? Send you a personal email? What's his deal? Is he trying to be cute, or what?"

"I don't know. I haven't answered it yet."

Shelly groaned and stabbed the air with her carrot stick. "Maura! What the actual fuck are you doing?"

"If he thinks he can just send me a date request and that I'll jump on it, well, he's wrong."

"It's been like, forever since he sent that message. That's not jumping on anything. Besides, he's not wrong. What are you doing? You should at least call him and ask him what he's up to." Shelly paused to point again with the remnants of her carrot before crunching it loudly. "I can't believe you."

Maura could barely believe it herself. "I don't know. It's like…have you ever been really, really sick?"

"I had a hundred and four degree fever the last time I got the flu. That was pretty sick."

"Yeah. Something like that. So you're feverish and sick and kind of out of your mind, but eventually the fever breaks and you start to feel better? And you wake up and realize you're finally going to be okay?"

Shelly nodded, but looked wary. "…Yeah?"

"That's kind of how I felt after breaking it off with Ian that last time. This weight lifted off me, I felt this…relief. Like I wouldn't have to try any more, you know? It was all over, and I was the one who'd finally chosen it. I mean, I didn't want it. But I chose it. Which seemed important at the time." She hesitated, putting into words things she'd only thought about before. "Like it was some kind of game, and I won."

"But you didn't, sweetie. Did you?"

"No."

Shelly smiled. "He came back to you. That has to count for something, right?"

"He always came back to me. Always. I tried to break it off with him a bunch of times, and he was the one who always came back. It's why he made me so mad when he tried to tell me how it was just me pushing us forward. Like it was all my fault. I hated that, him not owning his shit."

"So he's not perfect."

Maura laughed ruefully. "Wow. No. Definitely not."

"Nobody is. Except Keanu Reeves." Shelly gave a happy sigh. "He's perfect."

They laughed together at that. There wasn't much time to talk about it after that, because Melody came into the kitchen to give her mother a hug and kiss and tell her that people had started to arrive. Shelly went into perfect hostess mode, and Maura found her way from the kitchen into the living room to mingle with the other guests.

Maura's phone weighed heavy in her pocket. She could remember a time when being constantly connected to the world had seemed like a burden. Repulsive. She'd resisted getting a cell phone for a long time because of that. But once she had a smartphone with all its access to the internet, it had become her Precious. Like Gollum's ring. She was never without it, and even when she wasn't using it, there was a comfort in knowing that it was there to help her answer random trivia, find her way when she was lost, buy stuff, listen to music.

Keep in touch.

Luvfinder had a special app. She'd never bothered to use it, but it was easy enough to download. In a minute she had the small red square with its happy heart logo staring at her from her phone's screen. Tapping it, she entered her information into the login screen and pulled up her messages. She had almost a dozen other date requests, with one or two repeats but the rest all new. She hadn't updated her profile or posted anywhere on the site, but that didn't matter. She was female, and for a lot of these guys, that seemed to be enough.

Cupping the phone in her hands, she scrolled through, deleting the messages one by one until she came to Ian's. Luvfinder had a set of five generic message templates. He'd chosen the plainest one. Black and white, nothing cutesy about it. Simple, elegant, straightforward. All the templates had spots for contact information, along with places for the sender to choose what sort of date they were offering. Movie, coffee, dinner, sporting event. The list was long and comprehensive, and still left a place at the bottom for the sender to fill in anything that hadn't been listed.

Ian had checked every single option.

Skydiving. Horseback riding. Scuba diving. Go cart racing. Mini golf. Was he crazy?

She could ignore the situation totally. Or, she could hit 'accept' on the date request and see what happened from there. Everything with Ian had always been like standing on the edge of a cliff, and Maura had always leaped.

Before she could stop herself, she hit 'accept.'

Eighteen

The phone pinged, predictably, at two in the morning. The light from the screen woke her more than the sound, and Maura reached for it at once. Apparently Ian didn't like the Luvfinder app any more than she did, because the message had come through on text.

I'm glad you said yes.

She dialed his number. "I am not skydiving with you."

"Okay." His low laughter sent a frisson tingling down her spine. His voice, oh, that voice. "We can scratch that. How are you?"

Maura started to cry.

She tried to hold it back, not wanting him to hear her. Not wanting to ruin their first conversation in so, so long. Still too proud to let him know how much she hurt.

Ian was silent for a moment. "How's my girl?"

More tears boiled out of her, and she turned her face into the pillow to stifle them.

"I thought you'd say no," Ian said after a few sniffle filled moments passed without her being able to speak. "I wouldn't blame you, if you did. But I had to try."

Maura got herself under control enough to speak. "I'm not going go kart racing, either."

"Hot air balloon ride?"

"Is that really what you planned?" She grabbed for a tissue and wiped her face, settling into the covers.

Ian laughed again. "If that's what you want. Is it?"

"I've never been in a hot air balloon."

"I can make that work, if you want. Really."

She laughed through the tears still leaking down her cheeks. "Isn't it sort of cold for a balloon ride?"

"I don't know. I've never been on one either." Ian paused, voice lowering. "You okay?"

Her voice betrayed her, cracking. "Fine. Great. Perfect. Never better."

"Switch to video?"

"Ian...it's two in the morning...I look terrible."

"You never look terrible," he told her.

Three minutes later, there he was. She searched his face in the tiny screen for any changes — it had been months, but it felt like an eternity since last she'd seen him. She rubbed her thumb over the screen, tracing line of his jaw and his brows, remembering the feeling of his skin.

"There's my girl," Ian said.

Maura lost it again.

"Hey, hey," he said soothingly, and also infuriatingly amused. "Shh. No crying."

She swiped at her face, then buried it again in the pillow to keep him from looking at her, even though it meant she wouldn't be able to see him, either. Shoulders shaking, she tried to breath through this sudden combination of joy and grief. "Fucking emotions!"

Ian was silent while she got herself under control. Eyes still streaming, but at least with the ability to speak, she held the phone up in front of her face again. She wiped everything with a soggy tissue and cleared her throat to keep her voice steady, at tactic that didn't really work.

"This is it, Ian."

"What's it?"

"This is the last time." She'd probably said it before, or something like it, but Daniel's parting words rang in her head. "If you fuck me over, so help me, God…"

"I'm not going to fuck you over."

"I mean it. The last time. I don't expect you to promise me happy ever after," she said and went on before he could reply, "but goddammit, Ian, I surely expect you to fucking try."

"Don't you tell me not to go for that happy ever after. I'm aiming right for it."

She laughed, despite herself, because he could always make her laugh. "Stop. I don't want you to make promises you can't keep. We don't know what could happen. I don't need that from you, I just want to know that you're going to at least see what happens."

"Hey, I asked you to go skydiving with me. If that's not an indication of how serious I am about this…"

"Stop," she whispered. "Ian. I meant it."

"I'm going to try. I promise. Okay?"

She nodded. "That's all I'm asking for."

Silently they stared at each other. When he smiled, everything inside her melted. She smiled, too.

"There's my girl," Ian said again.

This time, she didn't start to cry.

***

Ian and I are going dancing tonight.

Really, I'm going dancing with Shelly and a group of her friends, for her birthday. But Ian will meet us there. It's our anniversary, after all. We met a year ago, tonight.

In the past few weeks, we've been talking every day. Sometimes multiple times. I should feel guilty about this, except that for the past year, all we've done is talk. Yes, sometimes the talk has slipped into flirting, but where's the harm in that?

In the shower, I smooth shaving cream over my legs. The razor strokes my skin, leaving it smooth. I scrub and exfoliate, wash and condition. Then, with one hand on the wall and my head bent beneath the almost-scalding spray, I run my hand over my body.

I imagine my touch as his.

Shuddering, I pinch my nipples to tightness. There's an answering pull of sensation in my cunt, but I don't touch myself there. Not yet.

There'd been a time when I was sure I would never feel this way again. Needle prickles of arousal all over me. When the mere sight of a notification on my phone could make my heart leap, my breath catch, and the sound of his voice, that low and somehow secret laughter, could make me want to writhe.

The truth is, I have never felt this way before

about anyone. Lust, yes. Love, too. But never this powerful pull, this instant reaction of my body to the simplest of stimuli. Everything about Ian turns me inside out. Makes me needy.

I open my mouth to the water and imagine the taste of him. The stroke of his tongue on mine. I want Ian to kiss me so much it's all I've been able to think about for the past few weeks, ever since I'd casually dropped into one of our instant message conversations that I'd be going out with Shelly to the same club where he and I had met.

"Yeah? What night?" Ian had asked. "Maybe I'll see if some friends of mine want to go out, too."

"Sure, that would be fun." Oh, fun. Oh, foolishness. The right response would be to tell him that isn't a good idea, but who am I to say he can't go to a public place? "Maybe we'll see you there."

I will see him there, tonight. Will he ask me to dance again? Will he pull me close, nudge a knee between my legs? Will he put his hands on my hips and nuzzle at my neck?

This time, will I let Ian kiss me?

Oh. Yes. I will. And if he doesn't try, I think I will push him into some dark corner and take that kiss even if he doesn't offer it, because I can not get the thought of his mouth out of my mind.

The water is so hot my skin has turned red and the shower is thick with fog, but still I shiver. The water has washed away wall remnants of soap, but between my legs I am slick. My fingertips slide against my clit. The fingers on my other hand curl, nails scratching on the tiles.

I am no stranger in how to bring myself

pleasure. I discovered the joys of orgasm in my early teens and there aren't many days in a row that pass without me making myself come. Climax is as important to me as clean hair and shaved legs, and there've been days when I substituted a ball cap and knee-high socks for those, but still spent a few minutes getting myself off. But most of the time, it's fast and easy. Self-maintenance, not indulgence.

This, on the other hand, is pure indulgence.

Slow, slow, I rub my clit in small circles. Every so often, I slide my fingers lower to push inside. I tease myself until my legs shake and I have to fall onto my hands and knees.

Head down, ass up. If Ian were here right now, he could fuck me from behind. All we did was dance once a year ago and talk for hours since, and yet here I am, imagining the length and width of his cock filling me. Shelly is fond of saying that you can tell how a man will fuck by how well he dances…and Ian is a really good dancer.

I could've come already, and in fact the water will soon run cold. I'm going to make myself late to meeting Shelly, late to seeing Ian for real, if I don't finish up soon. I think about edging myself close to the brink and stopping so that when I do see him, it will be with my pussy already wet, my clit already swollen.

"Wow," I mutter, voice thick and masked by the pounding of the water. "Filthy, Maura. So fucking dirty."

I've climaxed with the water pounding down on my clit before, but I've teased myself too long. The water is lukewarm now, not conducive to passion. On weak legs I turn off the water, towel myself dry. Run a comb through my hair. I rub my skin with scented lotion, all over, and add a matching body spray. Layering the scent so it lasts. I put my wrists to my nose and draw in a deep breath, loving the smell. It makes me think of sex, but then lately, so has everything.

Naked, I stand in front of the mirror and assess. I cup my breasts, lifting them. I have pretty lingerie to wear, a bra that will push my tits up and out, but even if I didn't, I'm not unhappy with my breasts. I flick the nipples again until they stand upright. The dress I've picked out for tonight is casual enough to look like I'm not trying too hard, made of t-shirt material. My nipples would show clearly through it…if I was so bold as to go without a bra. The thought excites me even as I curl my lip. I'm not in the habit of going without a bra. I'd think that was trashy on someone else. Yet knowing Ian could see that I'm aroused…

Fuck, I'm so wet, so fucking on edge. I pull lacy panties from my drawer, along with the matching bra, but I don't put them on. I pace a little, wondering what madness is this, that has made me incapable of making the simple decision about what to do next — get dressed, dry my hair, put on my makeup. My mind's a jumble of images culled from porn and movies and my imagination and real life experiences, all cobbled together in an erotic collage that pushes me, finally, to my bed.

Most of the time when I make myself come, I use my hand. But I do have toys I sometimes like to use. I won't need the extra stimulation of my vibrator, but there's something else tucked away in bedside table. I haven't used it in months, maybe close to a year. I'm not a huge fan of internal stimulation when I play with myself; not sure why, just that usually I'm fine with getting off from clitoral stimulation.

Tonight, though, with Ian on my mind, I am open and aching with the need to be filled.

The piece I pull from the drawer is weighty. Made of medical grade steel, about eight inches long, and curved. One end is rounded, the other pointed with a series of ridges. That end is made to go in your ass, but I've never used it that way. You could probably kill someone with it, it's that heavy, and the sharp end could easily crack a skull. It looks like a weapon, not something made for pleasure, and that might be why I hardly use it, though tonight it seems perfect.

The metal's cold when I push the rounded end inside me. A low, breathy moan escapes me as the curved metal presses upward on my G-spot. It warms quickly from the heat of my body as I slide it in and out. I'm so wet there's no need for lube. It's longer than any cock I've ever had inside me, so long it presses my cervix when I push it in all the way.

In, then slowly out. Smooth, smooth, the metal unyielding, not at all like flesh. Maybe that's what excites me. Or maybe it's the flash I have of last year, dancing with Ian to something mournful and sexually tense by Kings of Leon. How he pulled me close, right up against him, how he smelled, how his hands felt on me, how his knee had pressed so briefly, so quickly against my crotch…

Then, oh, fuck, oh yes, that's it. I'm coming. Hard and strong, my hips pumping. I haven't touched my clit since the shower, but nevertheless, my entire cunt clenches down on the metal toy still pushing in and out of me. Pleasure bursts through me, leaving me weak and panting and trembling, but not even close to sated.

I get up. I put on my pretty bra and panties and the blue dress I picked out especially to please Ian. I do my hair and paint my face. I slip on shoes comfortable enough to dance in but sexy enough to show off my legs. And on the dance floor this time, when he pulls me close, I don't pull away. I melt into him. I put my arms around him.

This year, when Ian leans to kiss me, I let him.

Nineteen

Madge rapped on Maura's cubicle and popped her head in. "Hey, you! Just wanted to see if you were going to be around for dinner. I need to put in the catering order before noon."

The office was having a day-long, intensive corporate training session, and to treat everyone, management was ordering in dinner. That most people would stay for it on a Friday night instead of booking it out of there to get home said a lot about her coworkers, and even a week or so ago, she'd have been one of them. But not tonight.

"Got a date," she said with small smile, bracing herself for Madge's response.

It was, typically, over the top. Beaming, Madge whirled into Maura's cubicle and plopped herself into the chair. "Tell me all about it."

"It's not a big deal —"

"Not a big deal? I don't believe it for a second. Look at you, it's all over your face!"

Maura laughed, self conscious about the heat flushing her cheeks. She put a hand to cool them. "It's just...a date."

"With someone special. Your first date, yes?"

It would be their first official "date." She'd been trying not to think of it that way. Too much pressure. But now she giggled, giddy, and ducked her head. "Yes."

"Good for you!" Madge slapped a hand against her thigh and rocked forward. "Is he your George?"

Maura wasn't quite ready to say yes,

superstitious she might jinx it. "I hope so."

"Me too." Madge grinned. Then her smile softened. "Sometimes, you have to be ready to take a jump even when you have no idea what's at the bottom of the pit, you know?"

"I know. Scary." Maura gave an exaggerated grimace.

Madge stood. "Well, I'll go put in the catering order, minus one. I hope you have a great time tonight."

"Me too. Thanks." Maura waited until Madge had left before she checked her phone for any messages.

There was one. A photo text from him, a picture of a black limousine. Ian hadn't told her what the date would be, only that she was going to be surprised, every step of the way. Considering that they'd never gone on a date, she had no trouble believing him.

An hour later in the middle of the training session, her phone vibrated again. Another message from Ian, another photo. This time, it was of the front of a flower shop on the other side of town. Her heart leaped, and she grinned so wide it hurt her cheeks. Was he going to bring her flowers?

Corporate training had to be the most boring thing ever to sit through. Add to that her distraction over seeing Ian later, and the hours passed so slowly Maura thought she might go out of her mind. She was supposed to be paying attention to new policies and procedures, but all she could do was wait for the next message from Ian.

Another hour passed, and the next message

came during the break. Management had provided doughnuts and coffee, and though Maura's stomach had started twisting so that even a thickly glazed treat couldn't tempt her, she grabbed at the coffee like it was a lifeline. She burned her tongue, wincing, and swiped at the screen on her phone.

This picture was a little blurred, off-center, and a bit harder to figure out. A green circle in Ian's palm. It looked sort of like the kind of air freshener you hang from the rearview mirror. That didn't make any sense at all. She peered closer, trying to read the text.

"Oh," she said under her breath with a small, surprised laugh. "Oh, that."

"Oh what?" Madge asked from beside her. A doughnut in one hand, coffee in the other, Madge looked as happy as a woman could be.

"He's taking me to that Brazilian steakhouse."

Madge ooohed. "George took me there once. It was delicious!"

Maura paused. "He knows I like steak."

"Sounds like he's really making an effort." Madge peeked at Maura's phone. "How much longer?"

Maura looked at the clock. "He's picking me up at six-thirty at my house."

That would give her enough time to get ready, provided she left the office promptly at five — and woe to whoever tried to make the training run even a minute longer.

Madge winked. "Good luck!"

The afternoon session was interminable. The man they'd brought in to conduct the training was so enthusiastic he made Maura's teeth ache. He'd obviously had a lot of experience in motivational speaking, but frankly, policies and procedures relating to new corporate policies were never going to be interesting no matter how many stress-balls and t-shirts you air-cannoned into the audience.

The four-o'clock picture was of a movie poster.

This date, she thought, is going to be out of control.

At quarter to five, Ian sent another picture. This time, a puzzling one, of the sign for a veterinary hospital. With a sense of foreboding, Maura snuck her phone onto her lap so she could reply.

What's going on?

Rowdy ate some electrical wires and a bunch of other stuff. Had to take him to the dog ER.

How shitty would it be for her to ask him if this was going to change their plans? Pretty shitty, she decided, and tried to focus on what the team manager was saying in the front of the room. Her phone hummed with another message a few minutes later.

We're going for an x-ray. Shouldn't make me late, but can we push it back until 7, to be safe?

Sure, she typed quickly. No problem. Hope Rowdy's ok.

Nothing came through after that, and though the training did run a few minutes later than five, Maura no longer worried as much. She gathered her things and headed for her cubicle to get her coat and purse. Her boss, Angela, stopped her.

"Staying for dinner?"

"No. I have other plans."

Angela frowned. "Oh? The team thought dinner together would be a great way for us to talk over some last-minute questions about the training."

"I didn't sign up for the dinner," Maura pointed out calmly, knowing it didn't matter. Angela had obviously gotten a stick up her behind about the dinner for some reason.

"Oh. Well. You know the rest of us are going to be in the break room. Everyone else is staying."

Maura knew for a fact at least two others from the team weren't going to stay — Jeff had to get home to his wife and toddler, and Mary needed to get home in time to take her kids to some school activity. But if she pointed that out, it would not only sound like whining, but Angela would be likely to say smugly that Jeff and Mary had excuses because they had families. Instead, Maura smiled blandly.

"Is there something in particular I need to go over with you, Angela?"

"No. I mean, unless you had any specific questions about the training?" Angela paused, then delivered the cut. "You were pretty busy on your phone today."

The problem with Angela, was that she was a bully. Or tried to be. Maura wasn't about to give her the satisfaction, but, on cue, her phone buzzed. Angela stared at her as though daring her to answer it.

Maura smiled. "I'm going to head out now. Have a great weekend."

But when she checked her phone, her stomach sank.

Still waiting for the x-ray. Doc's concerned about some other things. Still aiming for 7, but I called the restaurant to change our reservation to 7:30 in case.

She typed off a quick reply and finished packing up her stuff. On the bright side, now she'd have time for a luxurious soak in the tub rather than a quick shower. On the downside, her stomach was already rumbling. Waiting an extra hour was going to be tough.

At home, she ran the water and filled the tub with scented oil, then lowered herself into it. She kept her phone by the tub's edge in case Ian texted her again, but nothing came through. She took her time with pampering herself, even painting her toenails a pretty shade of red. Walking around her bedroom on the balls of her feet with cotton balls between her toes, heavy hot rollers in her hair, Maura felt like every stereotype ever made about a woman getting ready for a date.

At six-thirty, Ian texted. No surgery. Got meds. Will have to bring him back for a followup if it doesn't get taken care of on its own.

Gross, she thought.

Heading home, Ian typed. Need to drop off Rowdy and make sure he's ok, and jump in the shower. I'll be there at 7:30.

No worries, she typed.

She concentrated on getting herself ready, though by now her stomach was eating itself and no matter how much pampering she tried to give herself, it only took her so long to get ready. The extra coat of mascara only took thirty freaking seconds.

Ready with everything but her dress, which she'd put on last minute to keep it from stains and wrinkles, Maura found a package of peanut butter crackers in her pantry. She was only going to eat one, but as soon as she did, every hungry cell in her body gaped open, demanding food. She hadn't eaten since breakfast.

She was just slipping into her stockings when her phone buzzed. She didn't even want to look at it, but the message was simple. Call me.

"I'm driving," Ian said. "Stuck in traffic on the bridge. Some car flipped over. I won't be able to get there by seven-thirty, I'm sorry."

Maura sagged onto the nearby chair and put her face in her hand. "Are you kidding me?"

"I wish. I'm sorry. As soon as I get past this part of the roadblock, it looks like traffic is getting better. And from there it's only fifteen minutes until I get home. I'll shower real fast. I promise. And still be there to pick you up. I changed our reservation to eight-thirty."

She'd expire of hunger before eight-thirty. Already, even with the crackers, she felt a little woozy from low blood sugar. "Maybe we should just…"

"No," Ian said firmly. "We are not canceling. I had this whole great night planned out, and we're going to do it. I won't be too much later, I promise. We can make dinner by eight-thirty and see the ten-forty movie instead of the nine. It'll be great, Maura. Don't…don't give up on me yet."

"I'm not giving up on you, Ian."

"Good."

An hour later, when her phone buzzed again, Maura almost did.

"You're never going to believe this," Ian said.

Maura, who'd changed into sweatpants and a t-shirt and had been nibbling on pita chips to stave off her meltdown, snorted softly. "Let me guess. You're going to be late."

"The limo company didn't get my message about changing the time. They gave away our ride to a bunch of bachelorettes going to Philly." Ian paused. "I can come get you in a Hummer, a '78 Caddy convertible, or a refurbished armored truck."

"Oh, Ian."

"It has a disco ball and a full bar inside," Ian said. "It'll just take me about twenty minutes for them to get here, and we can head over to pick you up."

"I don't need any of that. Just get here. You. Get. Here."

He laughed. "But I wanted this to be the best date ever…"

"It's already almost nine o'clock," she told him. "I don't care about the limo. Or what you're wearing. Or flowers. Or —"

"Shit," Ian said. "Oh, shit. The flowers."

"Forget the flowers!" Maura cried. "Just get here, Ian!"

"I'll be there in half an hour," he promised, and disconnected.

Half an hour? She'd spent hours already on her hair and makeup, and now that he'd be here in half an hour, she felt rushed. Maura flossed and brushed her teeth, freshened her makeup and perfume. Her hair needed a little more work. The curls she'd so painstakingly set were now limp, but she saved them by pulling her hair back from her face and leaving the rest to hang down in an artful tangle. Her clothes were a little easier, since she hadn't been fully dressed.

The hook on the bra she'd picked out had been mangled in the drier, and the bra wouldn't close. "Shit!"

Maura dug through her underwear drawer, looking for another bra that matched the lacy panties she'd already picked out — no go. Which meant she had to change her panties, too. With a nervous look at the clock, she pulled out every piece of lingerie she owned, tossing everything onto the bed. Mix and match. How could she have only one set of matching scanties? She'd have to go without the garter belt, she decided. Find a pair of elastic-topped stockings, because there was no way she'd put on pantyhose for this date. With her luck, he'd want to strip her naked in the backseat of that armored car or whatever he arrived in, and she'd have cock-blocked herself with nylon.

She had three pairs of sheer black stay-up stockings. The first pair she tried on had no life left in the elastic, and sagged. She tossed them into the trash. The second pair snagged as she slipped her shoes on, sending a jagged runner up the back of her leg. Since she wasn't going for the punk rock look, she tossed those, too. Three was a charm and she smoothed them over her legs.

Finally dressed, Maura paced in her living

room. Every single nerve in her entire body felt stretched and tense. Every sense, heightened. Colors, brighter. Light-headed with hunger, yet also somewhat nauseous, she sipped at a can of cola even though she knew it would only make her need to go to the bathroom.

Ten minutes passed. Twenty. Thirty interminable minutes dragged by while she wore a hole in her carpet. Her palms sweated and, disgusted and distraught that her deodorant was going to fail her, she opened a window to stand in front of the frigid December air.

On my way, Ian's text said.

Get here, Maura replied.

Ten minutes later, another ping. Hitting every red light.

She laughed because she wanted to cry. The universe had given her Ian when she couldn't have him, and then when she could, she'd been convinced she'd lost him. Now, when everything seemed as though they might finally, finally have a chance, here went the universe again, throwing every obstacle in their path.

Just forget it, she started to type. We can meet up another time.

But she didn't hit send. Five more minutes, she thought. Maybe ten. But no more than that. I won't wait longer than that.

Ten minutes later, one more message from Ian came through.

I have an idea.

Unless it's you knocking on my door, she typed back, I think you should just forget it.

Open the door, came the reply.

And there he was.

"Ian," she said. "Hi."

She'd imagined herself launching into his arms, covering his face with kisses. She'd pictured them tumbling to her floor in a tangle of arms and legs, clothes flying off, making love with barely a hello passed between them. She'd even thought about slamming the door in his face and telling him to get lost, she wasn't interested — but that had been only in a moment of pique, never true.

Now they stared at each other awkwardly across her threshold before she stepped aside to let him in. Ian had never been in her house and suddenly, all Maura could see were the flaws. She loved this tiny bungalow, which had fallen into her post-divorce budget and also satisfied her desire for things like built-in bookcases and window seats. But Ian lived in one of those mini-mansions in a new neighborhood with a homeowner's association and rules about keeping your garage door closed. Now all she could see was the cracked plaster, the lack of furniture she'd left behind and hadn't yet replaced.

"Hi," Ian said.

Then he did the perfect thing. He kissed her. Softly, more than a peck but not a lingering, passionate embrace. Just enough to take the edge off their mutual awkwardness. A perfect, first-date kiss.

"I'm starving," he said.

Maura laughed. "I had to eat a snack so I didn't pass out. But…yeah."

"The steak place closes at ten. We'll never make it."

"I don't care where we go," she told him. "Really."

The forecast had been calling for snow, but what had started was icy rain. Ian grabbed her elbow to keep her from faceplanting on the icy driveway, but by the time she got in the car, Maura's hair was a mess. Her dress, soaked from the rain that had trickled in the back of her dress coat, because she'd forgotten to grab a scarf.

"Cold?" Ian asked as he fiddled with controls. "I have heated seats."

He backed carefully out of the drive, and the car's wheels spun. There was little traffic on her neighborhood's streets, which was good because he skidded at the stop sign and stopped only halfway through the intersection. Maura gripped the door handle in automatic reaction, and Ian glanced at her.

"What are you hungry for? We could stop for a quick snack before the movie, then get something more after?"

She wasn't sure what would be open by that time, especially if they were still aiming for the ten-forty movie, but by now she'd have eaten just about anything to keep herself from passing out. "Sure. There's that coffee shop just ahead to the left, they're open late. We could grab a muffin or something."

"And dinner after." Ian kept his eyes on the road, but shot her a grin. "Okay?"

The coffee shop sign said open when they pulled up, but as it turned out, they only had what was in the case for sale. And what was in the case was an oozing cheese danish and a crumbly scone. Neither selection looked appealing.

"Umm...popcorn at the movie?" Ian asked. "I'll even buy you nachos."

Maura laughed. "Okay."

"And dinner, after," Ian promised.

They got to the theater just in time to miss the last seats for the very popular movie he'd intended to take her to see. There was another movie that had started a few minutes earlier — they'd miss the previews, but should be able to make it in time for the movie, itself.

"You go on ahead," Ian said, "get us some seats. I'll get the popcorn and drinks."

The problem with entering a theater already gone dark, Maura realized, was that finding a seat was difficult. In a packed theater on "date night," it was even harder to find two seats together. The choices seemed to be in the very front row, which would give her neck a strain and probably motion sickness, considering the movie was a sci-fi shoot-em-up. Or, they could take two seats in separate aisles. Opting for the front row, Maura snagged the last two seats and sent Ian a quick text to let him know where to find her.

He made it just as the lights went all the way down. He handed her an enormous bucket of popcorn and a drink big enough to swim in. Maura put the bucket on her lap and the drink in her cup holder, trying to get organized enough so that she could lean back in the chair at the right angle to see the movie without killing herself. She was annoying the woman beside her, and shot an apologetic look, but before she could get fully settled, Ian reached for her hand.

Surprised and pleased, Maura stopped fussing with the food and looked down at their linked fingers. She and Ian had held hands a few times, but not like this. Not casually dating. Palm to palm, fingers entwined, their hands rested on his thigh. Heat flooded her, anticipatory but not quite sexual. They shared a look, grinning.

The movie began, and as she'd expected, the fast-paced action and special effects made it hard to follow while sitting so close. She already had a headache only a real meal would fix, and the movie was making it worse. Ian's hand in hers made it worthwhile, even as the steady throbbing behind her eyes made it impossible to enjoy the movie itself.

Twenty minutes in, the entire theater went dark. Screams rang out. The emergency exit lights flickered on, but nothing else did.

"Power went out." Ian leaned to murmur in her ear, sending a shiver through her. "Must be from all the ice."

Maura would gladly have sat, holding Ian's hand in the dark, for hours, but theater staff showed up with flashlights and started waving people toward the exits. The power had gone out and the backup generators weren't kicking in with enough juice to power all ten screens. The uproar was instant and furious — Ian tugged her gently toward the exit without even trying to fight their way to the ticket booth for a refund.

Outside, the icy rain had started to come down

at an angle, spanging against the slick ground and off the cars in the parking lot. Ian kept his hand on her the entire time, which was good because just as they reached his car, Maura completely wiped out. She was saved by falling on her face only because she landed on her hands and knees, scraping both and shredding that last pair of stockings. Ian went down too, on one knee, his hand grabbing the door handle, but his pants tore.

He was quiet when they got in the car, waiting for the fogged windows to clear. Then he looked at her. "This is the worst date I've ever been on."

She'd been thinking the same thing herself, and not even the ache and sting of her scrapes could stop her from bursting into tear-edged guffaws. It must've concerned him, because he turned to her and gingerly took her hands in his. He kissed her freezing, aching fingers.

"I'm sorry, Maura, I wanted this to be the best, and I totally messed it up."

"No, honey, it's all fine," she assured him, though with tears sliding down her cheeks and her inability to catch her breath properly, she was sure he didn't believe her.

"I'm sorry," he said again, miserably.

Maura stretched across the center console to kiss him, though the fact her teeth had started chattering made that difficult. "Ian, I'm freezing, I have an almost blinding headache, and if I don't get something to eat I'm going to start chewing these leather seats."

"I promised you dinner. I'm going to make sure you're fed," Ian said, determination glinting in his eyes.

The power outage had not only affected the theater, but also the entire chain of stores surrounding it. They drove a block, then another, and even the all-night diner was dark. The roads were horrible, too. When Ian's car skidded again, Maura turned to him.

"Take me home. I have plenty of food there, and if the power's out, I can build a fire."

Stopped at an intersection, Ian looked at her. "Are you sure?"

"I'm sure," she said. "Take me home."

***

The power had gone out in her part of town, too, but as she'd said, Maura built a fire. One of the reasons she'd bought this bungalow was for the working fireplace, and though it could be a pain and a mess, she loved the smell of a real wood burning fire. With marshmallow, chocolate and graham crackers, they could even make s'mores. She'd also pulled out a can of chicken noodle soup and heated it over the fire — along with some French bread, it satisfied her gnawing hunger as well as any gourmet meal, and she told him so.

"Best laid plans," Ian said, though not as dejectedly as he had before. With a glass of wine in him and bundled in a pair of her overlarge fleecy sweatpants to replace his wet and torn khakis, his mood had lifted.

Maura had spread out a large sleeping bag for them to sit on, with the thick quilt from her bed to wrap around them because even with the fire going, the old house was full of drafts. Now she scooted closer to him. "You know what? Just the fact you had all of this planned, this whole night, all of it…that's what means the most to me. Even though none of it worked out the way you wanted it, the fact you went through all the effort of trying to make this night special means more to me than anything."

She kissed him softly, waiting for his mouth to open under hers. When it did, she slid onto his lap and cupped his face with her hands. She'd changed into yoga pants and a long-sleeved t-shirt, and she could clearly feel his growing erection through the thin material. Stroking his tongue with hers, Maura rocked slowly forward against him. She let her breasts rub against his chest. The t-shirt she'd lent him was oversized on her, but fit Ian like a second skin. She could feel the points of his nipples through it, and she shuddered.

"Ian, I want you."

His arms went around her. Fingers pressed the trigger points on her back, the pleasure-pain making her squirm on his lap. She broke the kiss with a gasp, still holding him close. Ian's hands moved down to settle on her hips. Between them, barely restrained by the sweatpants, his cock was even harder.

"I want you, too, but it's only the first date —"

"Shut up," she said into his mouth. "Don't you dare."

Ian's fingers tightened on the bare skin of her hips between the hem of her shirt and the waistband of her pants. "Yes, ma'am."

She kissed him again, savoring his mouth. Soft, sweet kisses, interspersed with harder ones. Their breaths mingled, and she drew him into her slowly. Other than the subtle rock of her hips and her mouth on his, she didn't move.

Ian groaned, at last, and Maura couldn't hold back a secret smile. She ground herself against him, loving the way he reacted. His kiss stuttered for a moment before he broke it to look into her eyes.

"I've thought about this," he said. "Dreamed about it, even."

It seemed impossible that she should be able to press herself closer to him, but somehow Maura managed. She stroked her thumbs over his eyebrows, then over his mouth to tug it open for her kiss again. Pressing her cheek to his, she whispered, "me, too."

He held her close for a minute or so in silence broken only by the throb of her heartbeat in her ears and the crackle of the fire, now burning low. They breathed in unison. In. Out. His hand stroked down her back; hers cupped the back of his neck.

"There were nights when I couldn't sleep because all I could do was think about you," Ian said. "I'd think about the feeling of your hair against my face. The way you taste and smell. I'd imagine the sound of your laughter, and it would kill me, Maura. Slaughter me."

"And then you'd text me."

He laughed. "Yes. Sometimes. When I couldn't

stand it any more. But there were lots of nights when I couldn't make myself do it."

"Those were the nights I was bargaining with God," she told him. "Please, please let Ian text me."

They both laughed at that.

"I was stupid," Ian said.

Maura kissed him again. "Yes. You were. Touch me, Ian."

"Where?" His sly grin told her he already knew.

Maura guided his mouth to her throat. "Here."

Ian groaned again, teeth pressing her flesh. When he bit down harder, Maura gasped. When his hands slid up to cup her breasts, thumbing the nipples erect through the thin material of her shirt, she cried his name. Already aching with need for him, she ground herself against the thickness of his cock.

The tent they'd made of the quilt had warmed them, and now when Ian threw it off them the air seemed extra cold even in front of the fireplace. Maura shivered, her skin humping into gooseflesh from the chill but also from the scrape his teeth against her. She let her head fall back. Ian's mouth skimmed lower to nibble at the hollow of her throat. He put his mouth to her breasts, hot, damp breath pressing through the fabric. She cried out again when he took a nipple in his mouth, the sensation blunted enough to tease, but still delicious.

"Take this off." Ian eased her shirt up over her head, and gave a happy, muffled sigh at the sight of her bra. "So hot."

She cupped herself, pushing her tits together.

"You like?"

"I want to bury my face in there."

"Go ahead," she said with a laugh. "Maybe later you can put something else in there, too."

Ian gave a choked laugh. "Are you trying to kill me?"

"No. Just get you hard." She reached between them to stroke him. "Oh, Ian, Ian, you feel so good. I want to taste you."

Fuck, she loved the look on his face when she said things like that. His eyes went wide, pupils dilated, mouth a little slack and wet from her kisses. She loved knowing that just her words could turn him on so much.

"Will you let me, Ian?" She drew out the syllables of his name, knowing it was a trigger for him. Also her expression, wide-eyed, bordering on innocent. She ran a finger across his chin, then tapped his lips. "Will you let me taste you?"

"Oh…shit, yes. Please."

Maura smiled and got off his lap, standing so she could hook her thumbs in her waistband and push her yoga pants over her hips. She stepped out of them and stood in front of him in the bra and panties she'd so agonized over. She did a little wiggle, meaning to tantalize him.

She wasn't expecting Ian to reach for her, or to go to his knees in front of her. Maura coughed in surprised when he kissed her, his hands gripping her ass to hold her in place. Ian looked up at her as he reached over his shoulder to pull off his t-shirt. Then, still kneeling but proving his agility, he wriggled out of the sweatpants without getting to his feet.

"Wow," she breathed.

"I'm nimble."

Then his face was between her legs again, and Maura couldn't find her voice for more than a long, shivery moan. He licked her already swollen clit through the lace. His hot breath urged her hips forward. She needed his touch, his tongue, his fingers inside her, but Ian didn't pull her panties off. He licked and nibbled at the inside of her thighs before going back to her cunt, but he was teasing her on purpose. Her legs were starting to shake when he looked up at her again.

His eyes gleamed. Cheeks flushed. His mouth was wetter than it had been before, and he swiped his tongue across it. "Let me taste you."

Without waiting for an answer, he tugged her panties down and buried his face between her legs. Maura's hand went automatically to the top of Ian's head, her fingers digging into his thick, dark hair. He flickered his tongue along her clit until she whimpered.

"Sit," he said, and snaked an arm to pull the rocking chair close enough for her to obey.

She fucking loved it when he took charge like that. Maura sat, the curved wood cold on her bare ass. Ian pulled her hips to bring her to the very edge of the seat.

"Hold the arms."

She did. When he pushed her legs apart, she arched her back, giving into whatever he wanted to do to her. Ian's mouth on her was magic; everything about him had always been magic.

"You taste so sweet. You're so wet already. For me?"

"Yes, Ian, for you. Always for you."

She caught sight of a very pleased look on his face before he bent back to rub his mouth along the seam of her pussy. He parted her with his tongue, then focused again on her clit. Maura's grip tightened on the arms of the chair, but she didn't let go. She let her ass slide a little closer to the edge of the chair.

Still kneeling, Ian covered her clit with his mouth and began to rock the chair. A little bit, just enough to move her body back and forth beneath him while he stayed still. The sensation was so new, so different, and pleasure arced through her like crackling sparks. The muscles of her belly and inner thighs leaped. She had a hard time staying still.

"You like this?" He murmured muffled, and the motion of his mouth forming words sent another coil of desire spiraling through her.

"Yes."

"You want me inside you?"

She wanted that more than anything at that moment. Ian teased her, though. Instead of pushing inside her with his delicious cock, he slipped a finger inside her. Then another. Fucking slowly back and forth, he timed his strokes to the back-and-forth motion of the chair and the sliding of his tongue.

Her body contracted around him, and Ian groaned. "Fuck, that's so hot. I can feel you getting tight around me. I want to feel you come, Maura."

She was close, but not quite there. All she

could manage was a shaky, "mmmm." When he fucked deeper into her with his fingers, curling them upward to get at her G-spot, she shook so hard the chair's rockers squeaked on the hardwood floor.

"Easy girl," he whispered against her. "Let it go. Come for me."

It was too much, almost. This pleasure. So fierce it took her breath away, so concentrated, so targeted. Ian curled his fingers again.

"Oh. Oh, my God," Maura said. "Oh, Ian, that's..."

"This?" Ian said, still suckling at her clit while he rocked her against his curling fingers.

Maura was lost. Tipping over. Pleasure overtook her, sweeping her into a whirlwind of ecstasy. Her vision focused to a narrow pinhole, and all she could hear was the sound of her own voice, begging him to let her come. And still he teased her, holding off, while the sensation built and built in her clit, her cunt, everything contracting until she could stand it no longer.

Her orgasm ripped through her with blunted edges, the pleasure of it edged with the pain of how strong it was. She cried his name. Her hips bucked. The wooden rocking chair creaked and protested, but it didn't matter because everything felt so good, she thought she might die.

A minute or so passed while her breathing slowed and she could focus again. Ian had laid his head on her thigh to look up at her, and Maura uncurled her stiff and aching fingers from the grip she'd had on the chairs arms. Most of her body ached from the somewhat awkward position, but the heat and gloriousness of her orgasm made every odd pain insignificant.

"I want you," she told him. "Inside me. Your cock, not your fingers —"

"I thought you liked that," Ian interrupted, and she swatted at him. He stood, pulling her to her feet, before turning to take her place in the seat. "Get on my lap."

At first she wasn't sure how to do it, but then she put her legs through the openings under the chairs arms. She could get her feet flat on the floor that way. Her hands on Ian's shoulders, Maura lowered herself onto him, slowly, inch by inch. He groaned when she'd seated herself completely.

"You feel so good inside me."

"I'm not sure how long I can last," Ian admitted. "You're so fucking wet, Maura, I'm about to go out of my mind."

"Shhhh," she told him. "Easy."

They laughed, and it was pure pleasure. Maura pushed off the floor with her feet, setting the chair to rocking. It moved him inside her. Back and forth, they rocked, while she kissed his mouth. Adding a little roll of her hips brought her clit to rub his belly, and that felt good. She'd come so hard, she was sure there wasn't another one left in her, but that didn't mean she wasn't going to try.

This position meant neither of them had to do a lot of gymnastics to keep moving, and they rocked that way for a long time. Every time Ian started to shake, Maura eased the pace. Kissing him, she lost herself in every sensation. His hair on her face when she nibbled his neck, the points of his nipples beneath her palms, the jut of his hipbones pressing into her thighs when she squeezed him with her legs. She'd thought she knew everything about Ian's body, but there was always something new to explore. Some new way to make him sigh.

Tucking herself against him, her face against his neck, Maura rocked the chair. Ian's breathing grew raspy. Under her palm, his heart beat harder, faster. Knowing how close he was turned her on, and she reached a hand between them to give her clit just enough extra pressure…

"Oh, God," she breathed. "That feels…"

"So good," Ian said. "I'm gonna…"

"Me too."

"Come with me," Ian said. "I want to feel you clench around my dick."

It could've sounded crude, but it was what finally tipped her over the edge again. Maura rode him, the chair creaking its protests for the second time. She came in slow, shaking waves. Ian cried out, fucking upward so hard it lifted her feet off the floor. He bit at her throat until she cried out again. He finished within seconds of her, and the chair slowed, slowed…stopped.

"I love you," Ian said against her skin. "I'm sorry it took me so long to figure it out."

She wasn't going to cry, not even happy tears. Swallowing the tightness in her throat, Maura looked at him, cupping his face. "All that matters is that you did. And you're here. And we can try."

"It's all anyone can do, right?"

"Yes, Ian."

He smiled, and she fell in love with him all

over again. "You sure you want this? I'm cranky, especially when I'm not sure things are going to work out, and I can be hard to deal with —"

"Shut up, Ian." She stopped his words with a kiss. "This is it. You don't get to back out now."

He paused to look at her, his smile going solemn. "No. I don't want that. Not at all."

"I love you." Maura ran her fingers through his hair. "And no, it's not supposed to work with us. I know it's taking a chance. I know it's being reckless…"

"Perfectly," Ian interrupted, and after that, there was more kissing.

Lots of it.

About the Author

I was born and then I lived awhile. Then I did some stuff and other things. Now, I mostly write books. Some of them use a lot of bad words, but most of the other words are okay.

I can't live without music, the internet, or the ocean, but I have kicked the Coke Zero habit. I can't stand the feeling of corduroy or velvet, and modern art leaves me cold. I write a little bit of everything from horror to romance, and I don't answer to the name "Meg."

MeganHart.com
Twitter.com/megan_Hart
Facebook.com/megan.hart

Made in the USA
Middletown, DE
28 February 2017